THE GRASSHOPPER KING

FOR WAN CHING

Duncan 4.27.09

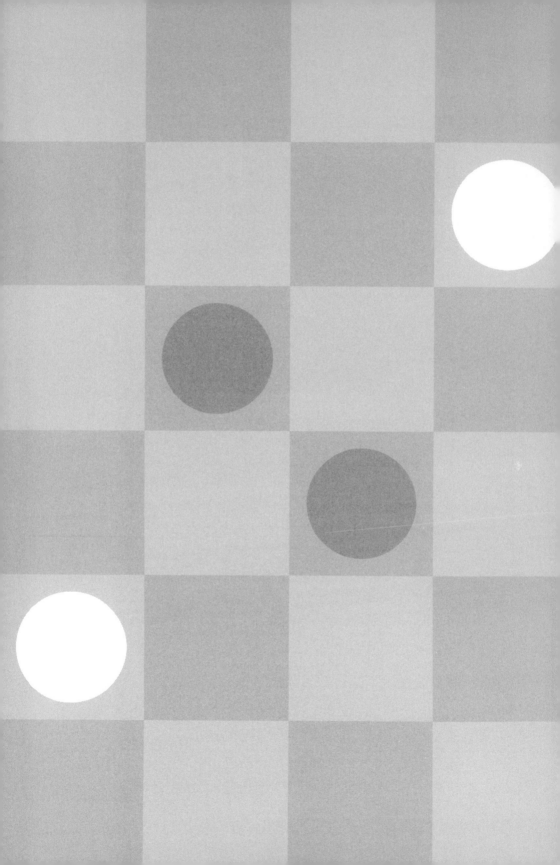

THE
GRASSHOPPER
KING

by Jordan Ellenberg

COFFEE HOUSE PRESS 2003

COPYRIGHT © 2003 by Jordan Ellenberg
COVER + BOOK DESIGN by Linda S. Koutsky
COVER ILLUSTRATION by Marcia McEachron
AUTHOR PHOTOGRAPH © Pryde Brown

Coffee House Press books are available to the trade through our primary distributor, Consortium Book Sales & Distribution, 1045 Westgate Drive, Saint Paul, MN 55114. For personal orders, catalogs, or other information, write to: Coffee House Press, 27 North Fourth Street, Suite 400, Minneapolis, MN 55401.

Coffee House Press is a nonprofit literary publishing house. Support from private foundations, corporate giving programs, government programs, and generous individuals help make the publication of our books possible. We gratefully acknowledge their support in detail on the last page of this book.

To you and our many readers across the country,
we send our thanks for your continuing support.

LIBRARY OF CONGRESS CIP INFORMATION

Ellenberg, Jordan, 1971–
The grasshopper king / by Jordan Ellenberg. — 1st ed.
p. cm
ISBN 1-56689-139-6 (alk. paper)
1. Europe—Study and teaching (Higher)—Fiction. 2. Poetry—Study and teaching (Higher)—Fiction. 3. College teachers—Fiction. I. Title.

PS3605.L435G73 2003
813'.6—DC21

2003041236

FIRST EDITION, FIRST PRINTING
1 3 5 7 9 10 8 6 4 2

PRINTED IN CANADA

ACKNOWLEDGMENTS

First and most, I thank my teachers:

Harold White, Adrienne Marek, and Peggy Pfeiffer.

Thanks, too, to Stephen Burt, Malinda McCollum, and Tanya Schlam;

Michael Martone and Jill McCorkle; the Writing Seminars at Johns Hopkins;

Jay Mandel, Rosalie Siegel, and everyone at Coffee House Press.

for my parents

THE GRASSHOPPER KING

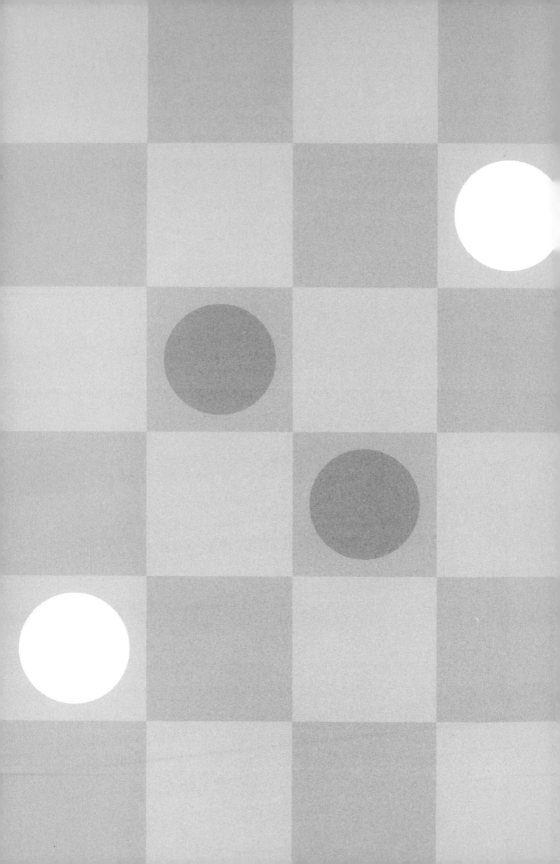

PART ONE

"TITHONUS: *a member of the royal family of Troy, who married Eos, the goddess of dawn, and subsequently suffered an unusual fate. Eos loved Tithonus desperately, and could not bear the fact that, as a mortal, he was doomed to leave her when his time for death had come. So she petitioned the gods to grant Tithonus immortality; and her heartfelt request was granted. But Eos had forgotten to ask also for eternal youth. So Tithonus grew older and older, unable to die. His mind became deranged and he lost the power of speech. Eos kept him in a baby's crib in a locked room. Some versions of the story have it that, out of mercy, Eos eventually transformed poor Tithonus into the chirping grasshopper.*"

—HEINRICH DUBLER,
Enzyklopädie der griechischen Mythologie

ATHENAE OCCIDENTALIS AMERICAE

I think it's best that I begin with a legend—a mostly true one.

It goes like this: in 1871, a luckless prospector and aesthete named Tip Chandler, lost in the desert, his mules weakening and his canteen two days empty, came to the edge of a tremendous mesa. Seeing that he could travel no farther, and knowing that no salvation lay behind him, he fell to his knees and resigned himself to death. But at that moment, a spring of fresh water gushed out from the desiccated ground. Chandler threw himself down, pressed his lips to the earth, and drank; and when, at last, bloated and drenched, he allowed himself to lift his head and breathe, he was overtaken by a vision. He saw, he wrote later, "a splendid City, replete with and dedicated to the sundry pursuits of Knowledge, Art, and Faith; truly a second Athens, through whose avenues progressed Architects, Mathematicians, Clergymen, Poets, and Scientists of all sorts; and having in it a great College, which stood upon the Cliffside, a Testament to the Power of Reason whose Beacon shined forth unto the savage and uncomprehending Plain!"

Hallucinations were hallucinations, and Chandler had seen his share; but the next morning, fortified by the springwater and the roasted flanks of his mules, the old prospector, for the first time in his dismal career, struck gold. As was customary, he interpreted his good fortune as a supernatural directive. He devoted the remainder of his life, and the balance of his riches, to realizing the learned city of his vision.

But the architects and the poets, for the most part, stayed East, and the ones who did not stay passed over Chandler's city for the more agreeable frontier of California. The museums and zoos were never built; the electric railway, half-completed at the time of Chandler's death, was left to sink, slat by slat, into the clay. The streets—laid out in golden rectangles, each named for a hero of the antique world—filled up with roughnecks, unsupervised children, and shopkeepers. The Temple of Reason stood empty for years. Finally it found use as a municipal convention center. By the time Stanley Higgs arrived, in 1950—thirty-five years before I met him, thirteen before I was born—the only reminder of the prospector's vision was Chandler State University, Higgs's new employer, which sat moodily on the mesa's edge. The rest of Chandler City stretched out to the west, hanging back from the cliff.

Then, as now, Chandler State was known primarily for doling out a four-year diet of Western Civilization to whatever men and women of our state came forward to be educated, and for fielding a basketball team that could be relied upon each year to make a more or less brief appearance in the national collegiate playoffs. None of our academic departments were much thought of in their fields. The worst of them—the "hoops houses"—survived almost entirely on their reputations as dependable sources of credits for the basketball players. So the arrival of Higgs, a scholar of much-heralded promise, was an occasion of rare optimism; some, caught up in the excitement, went so far as to call it hope.

Higgs's subject was the literature of the Gravine, a tiny valley-nation in the Soviet Carpathians. He had made his reputation on a thoroughly forgotten Gravinian poet of the thirties, a child of British expatriates named Henderson. Two years before, Higgs—gung ho back then for comp lit, combing Düsseldorf for certain letters of

Hölderlin and his circle, to be digested into his dissertation thereon—had come across Henderson's *Poems Against the Enemies Both Surrounding and Pervading Us* in a trashbin. He could tell from the first poem (untitled: "The wanton whores of Germany gum up my sight . . .") that Henderson was not a great poet, or even a good one. Nonetheless, walking zig-zags through the blasted streets, holding the sour, mottled book in one hand, his gaze flickering from book to traffic to beggar to sky, Higgs was smitten. Smitten! He had not in general been given to discontinuity of feeling. But now—the awful, shriveled poems of Henderson firm in his memory, after a single reading—he saw that his life had been shunted to a new course, instantly and by accident, as in the ten-cent novels he suffered himself to read on the train. Henderson, in his hatred for the reader, for the female sex, for his adopted Germany—really, for everyone—had arrived at a sort of perfection of which ordinary and good poets could not be capable. His work was cleansed entirely of affect, wit, and sense. And so, as he read, was Higgs. He had to lean on a wall; he was shell-shocked; he could smell the evening's fog coming in, and the fish. It was like a glimpse of a world where all laws were suspended: not just human laws but natural selection, the relation of energy to mass, gravity.

Higgs thought of his half-written thesis, its measured conclusions, its cadences, heaped on his dim desk at the rooming house, and was struck with a deep disconsolation, tinged with nausea. The thesis seemed a foolish waste of his energy and youth, and furthermore it seemed to him that he had known this for some time, months perhaps, the knowledge helpless until now to break through the sea wall of his consciousness. Again he looked down at his rescued volume. Absently, he flicked a daub of mayonnaise from its battered spine. He began to decide.

(This is a kind of legend too. The facts are checkable; I've checked them. But for Higgs's thoughts I have had to rely on the testimony of his wife. Less than ideal, I admit—but the best I can do, under the circumstances, the unusual circumstances, which are perhaps, even at this early stage, gathering themselves above him, us . . .)

Four weeks later, back at Columbia, Higgs strode into his advisor's office in an attitude of silent challenge, shut the door behind him, and dropped a stack of one hundred eighty-five typed pages on the desk. The pages were the first draft of his new dissertation, the paper that would earn him his degree a year early and make both him and Henderson household names—where by household, of course, I mean department of Gravinic literature. We have modest expectations, here in the business of learning. And even Higgs's small celebrity was enough to arouse long-dormant ambitions in the sardonic, wizened hearts of our senior faculty. He was young and appropriately humble; his references were effusive; best of all, he had grown up in Chandler City and graduated from Chandler State itself. (Not a few professors spoke quietly of having remarked, even then, his promise—though he'd made B's, though he'd been admitted to Columbia in the first place only because our state was "underrepresented," their courteous way of saying "unrepresented.") There was no question that Higgs could have had his pick from dozens of preferable institutions. But he had fixed on his alma mater. His fierce affection for his native terrain, he wrote our dean, had only been reinforced by his time East.

"Is he joking?" Dean Moresby thought, peering out at what terrain he could see from his office window: the campus lawn, gamely struggling to cover the unnourishing red clay, and the blacktop paths that crisscrossed the lawn, and the students progressing along the paths, themselves gamely struggling through the April heat, their curls drooping. Beyond the row of cloned Parthenons (the philosophy building, history, math) was the skyline: a few smokestacks, half obscured by a low, off-red awning of haze. "He's joking." But Higgs was serious. He made it clear that his intention was to stay on at Chandler State as long as he was welcome. By all indications it would be a long time.

The dean, accompanied by his wife and younger daughter, met Higgs at the train station. Above them, on the pediment, Hephaestos wrestled sullenly with an ingot. And at the appointed time came Higgs, doing little better with his luggage.

Dean Moresby moved forward: "I'll get it."

Higgs shook his head, withheld his valises.

"But it's perfectly all right," the Dean maintained, without conviction: then, as they turned toward the exit, "Let me introduce my wife, Mary, and my daughter, Pamela."

"Our oldest attends Vassar," Mrs. Moresby said.

"All right," Higgs said. They proceeded in silence to the car, looking, Dean Moresby thought, like a family retrieving their son from school back East—Higgs could have passed for twenty. Clean living? More good news, if so. But then again, Higgs was silent on the drive back, which could betoken secret thoughts; and, more worrying, for the length of the trip, despite all Moresby's collegiality, his exclamations on the unexclaimable scenery, even an arm thrown genially, and at some risk to all involved, about the new man's shoulders, Higgs—like a coward, like a banker, like a sneak—refused to meet his eyes.

But it turned out Higgs was always like that. His eyes, turned down at the corners like a sheepdog's, were never still. Otherwise he was handsome. His face was boyish and broad, his skin clear; his hair sprigged out above his ears in an agreeably academic fashion. In photos from those days he comes off as one inclined to good cheer, committee membership, uncontroversial politics. He seems the picture of easy charm; but in fact he was not charming. It was those eyes. And then, too, there was the way he talked. Higgs never said a word that was off the point, and it was unknown for him to commit an error of fact. His sentences hewed tightly to every standard of grammar and usage, so that he gave the impression of reciting from memory. But his speech was marked by judicious pauses, tiny and ever-present, and during these pauses, it was understood, he must have been composing his remarks. He was polite—everyone agreed on that. But even his politeness was eerily precise; as if he'd had to learn about politeness in books, had skimmed through all the formulas of courtesy and rehearsed the ones he thought he'd need.

So not charming, no, but still . . . it was Higgs's uncanny eloquence, more than his prestigious degree, more than the brilliance and influence of his dissertation, that kindled in his new colleagues the hope that the university might come in their lifetimes to resemble the motto that Tip Chandler, in the giddy aftermath of groundbreaking, had affixed to the college seal: *Athenae Occidentalis Americae.* But: no Athens without Pericles, no Algonquin without Dorothy Parker, no Metropolis (if I may) without Superman. Now there was Higgs. And among the professors there was a sense of bare possibility, a sense that things might be about to change for the better, sharply and finally, as if by a sudden tectonic shift.

Higgs seemed completely unaware of the commotion his arrival had occasioned. He was installed in a private office with an air conditioner and a cliffside view; he seldom left it. Toward the affairs of the university outside that one room he maintained a perfect indifference. Once that fall, at the regents' dinner, in the thirtieth minute of an address on the patriotism of the American farmer, Dean Moresby leaned across a feathered matron and said "Stan." (The dean hated calling Higgs "Stan." He wanted badly to call him "Professor Higgs," like everyone else. But there was something wrong with that from a dean.) "Stan," he said fiercely—the matron drawing back ungracefully from the boggish smell of steak and bottom-shelf scotch—"Please let me thank you again for coming here."

"It's my pleasure," Higgs said. "The steak is perfectly prepared."

"Here to Chandler State," Dean Moresby, dogged, went on. "Not here tonight. You can't possibly imagine what it means to us—to the university. To the *community.*"

At this Higgs clicked into a thoughtful aspect.

"No," he said, "I suppose I can't."

The state senator at the podium apostrophized an agricultural virtue whose very mention drew a swell of applause.

"Keep up the good work," said the dean. Then both men joined the general clapping.

Higgs's work, for now, consisted of assembling a chronology of Henderson. It would necessarily be fragmentary; Henderson had avoided notice not only as a poet, but in every other facet of life. His lone impingements on the public record were a Gravinian birth certificate dated December 16, 1900 ("the nineteenth century produced me and promptly expired in horror," Henderson wrote in a rejected letter to the *Frankfurter Zeitung*) and a 1936 littering citation from the Berlin Department of Works. He rated occasional mentions, none long, few charitable, in the memoirs of his contemporaries. (In a never-performed verse play *à clef* by Hannah Höch, the character of "Heinrich the vile Pole" was believed by some to represent him.) Where he might be now, or even whether he was still alive, was unknown.

That first year, Higgs published papers on Henderson's political stance (apathetic, occasionally reactionary), his education (cut off at sixteen by the Revolution), his tuberculosis (chronic), his influences (Greek mythology, the Kaiser). He wrote letters: to policemen who had served in Henderson's neighborhood in Berlin, to the operators of local restaurants, to madams, druggists, launderers, to the building workers in his apartment house and to the crew who had fixed the road by his window, to his landlord and his landlord's partners at cards, to every newspaper, large and small, within a hundred miles of the city. To the post office in Henderson's part of town he sent two hundred posters and fifty dollars for the trouble of nailing them up. Each bore the same message: Anyone having knowledge or reminiscence of a certain man—a thin overtall man with a wet cough, perhaps carrying a notebook or other writing platform, poor command of German, mostly seen alone—is urged to address correspondence to Stanley Higgs, *bitte;* there follows the university's address. There were few responses, and most of those that did come back were useless: obvious misidentifications, intimations of sightings joined to requests for advance payment, letters suggesting blackly that Higgs was somebody or other's agent, and offering, again for a price, not to tell. Perhaps one letter in a hundred came back a success. A newspaper salesman recalled overhearing Henderson curse a photo of King George v. He was said to have worn a coat sewn together from rags. A bricklayer reported that Henderson wore a gold crown on one of his teeth. (Higgs sent letters to every dentist in Berlin.)

With each of Higgs's papers the Henderson scholars grew in number and influence. A Henderson Society formed up, whose presidency Higgs courteously, and curtly, declined. Graduate applications began arriving in Chandler City from Harvard, Princeton, Oxford, even Moscow, each one breathlessly setting forth the extreme desirability— no, the *necessity*—of its author being chosen to work side by side with the great man, Higgs. It was unprecedented. And when Dean Moresby, trampling all protocol, offered Higgs tenure at the end of the year, there were few grumbles from the faculty. For the first time in decades they were united in a higher purpose than their meager individual advancements.

Whatever naysayers remained were silenced when Higgs was invited to address the plenary session of an international literary conference at Trieste. The conference was at the height of its fashionability that year, and Higgs's speech was a tremendous success. A profile in the *New York Times* ensued, along with a spray of prizes, recognitions, various memberships in learned societies. The last faculty member invited to speak overseas had been an elderly astronomer who, misaligning the lens of the campus telescope, had inadvertently photographed a new satellite of Jupiter. That had been 1920.

The Gravinics department was a hoops house—one of the worst. The chairman, Professor Rosso, had been a Princeton cager, and was willing, even eager, to invent passing grades for members of the squad. Under the circumstances, Dean Moresby told Higgs, it was perhaps the best thing to waive the ordinary teaching requirement, and it would be no trouble. But Higgs insisted. He would be happy to teach, he told the dean; he did not want to be perceived as commanding special favors, and, moreover, he was confident that the athletes, presented with an enthusiastic and thorough account of the material, would become inclined to learn.

And against all reason, Higgs was right. Something in Henderson's crabbed, defiled poems struck a resonant spot in the minds of the basketball players. His persecution was somehow their own. In his commingled affection and condescension toward the Kaiser ("my blundering, beloved uncle with the spiked derby") and the German war machine, they saw mirrored their own ambivalence toward the nonstop routine of competition; his dismissals of religion, rule of law, and the rights of women were topical and thrilling; his scarlet hatred of the intellectual and all his accoutrements was not unfamiliar to them. Soon Higgs's course was joined by players from the other hoops houses: from physical education they came, from Spanish and journalism, from agricultural studies and the rest. By the end of the semester the whole team was in his class. There were no absences or late papers, and no end-of-term visits to Rosso. Higgs had made students of them. Quite a few quit basketball altogether to devote themselves more fully to Henderson; though among these there was only one starter, and he'd broken his wrist.

And the rest of the team: in practice they were sullen and insubordinate, slogging through drills as if each layup, each free throw were a personal and spiteful imposition. But at game time they played with a fierceness such as Coach Mahemeny had never seen. It made him uneasy (he told me) but he knew that he was an older man and it was his time to become uneasy with the new ways of doing things. And it worked, whatever it was. His unsmiling players had developed a ghostly way of slipping out from their coverage, then, alone, flicking in a jumper, not even watching to see the shot drop in—was it a kind of contempt he saw in their eyes? But it worked. They were humiliating the opposition.

In 1956 the Prospectors won the national championship in Syracuse. To celebrate the players' return the university organized a gigantic reception at the convention center downtown. Some five hundred of Chandler City's notables filed between the chipped, stolid columns of the former Temple of Reason, into the great open ballroom, lined floor to ceiling with empty marble shelves. It was to have been the library.

Higgs drifted among the celebrants, bearing an untouched scotch and water. Arnold Meadows, the mayor, was calling the players to the podium one by one. The P.A. lifted their names to the marble ceiling, where they shattered and echoed down into the crowd, incomprehensible. The mayor was fresh from his own national triumph. He had convinced the previous session of Congress to attach to an uncontroversial appropriations bill a provision to study the feasibility of tapping the mysterious source of Tip Chandler's spring for geothermal energy. The first group of federal geologists, and the first installment of the concomitant federal funds, had arrived in town the month before.

At the party too was Ellen Moresby, the dean's daughter, home from Vassar on spring break. Her father had made her come. She made a point, whenever she could, of avoiding university functions, which she found provincial, and which were always well-attended by old men in ridiculous mustaches who wouldn't stop looking down her dress. She was halfway through her second gin and tonic and she knew she would soon have to find something to do but drink. Otherwise she would start laughing at people and it would be bad for her father.

When she saw the slight young man standing in the corner, bearing an expression of such perfect peace and detachment that he seemed to believe himself alone in the cavernous ballroom, she thought: ah, there's someone. She supposed he was a teaching fellow—he'd wrestled the starting point guard through Math I, or something, and this was his reward, this hallful of cold cuts and deviled eggs and awful bores.

Presumably he was a bore as well. But he was almost certain not to tell her what a fine young lady she'd grown up to be.

"I hate these things," Ellen said, joining him.

Higgs leaned back thoughtfully, resting his hands on the shelf behind him as if testing its ability to hold his weight.

"I'm sorry to hear it," Higgs said.

His politeness made Ellen's face hot. "I mean it," she said.

"'Hate' is a strong word," he said. "Do you really mean it? It suggests malice. Are you willing to say you want this party"—he gestured upward and outward—"destroyed? If you could, would you end it now and ensure that it was never repeated?"

"Don't joke. It's asinine."

"I'm not joking. I'm only making sure I understand what you mean."

"Well, I don't hate it, then, not the way you take it. I *dislike* it—is that all right?"

"It's all right with me."

"And I dislike basketball too, if you want to know. It's moronic. It makes me sick the way they go on about it as if they'd cured polio or something. I dislike that. The absolute honest truth is that there isn't anything about this stupid place I *don't* dislike. What do you think of that, mister?"

She was too drunk already. The sickening realization silenced her. She had embarrassed herself in front of a stranger, her father would have to leave early to drive her home, he'd be furious; and wouldn't he be right?

But Higgs didn't denounce her; didn't stalk away, didn't summon her father. He just stood there, head cocked, at a loss for words. If Ellen had known who he was, or had heard anything of his reputation, she would have known just how extraordinary this was; but she didn't know. She thought he was giving her another chance.

"I'm sorry," she said. "That was inappropriate. I'm a little drunk."

"It was perfectly appropriate. As long as you meant it."

"I did mean it." She was confused now as to what they were discussing.

But she liked the stranger's weird forthrightness. It emanated from him like a soothing light. It inspired her to forwardness.

"Do you like it here?" she said.

"Yes," he told her. His eyes were fixed on her face—and this great anomaly, too, she was unequipped to recognize. "I like it here a great deal."

"You must be nuts."

"Do I look like nuts?" Higgs said.

"Excuse me?"

Higgs cocked a finger at her. A joke. Suddenly it seemed the funniest thing she'd ever heard. She knew it was the alcohol, or relief at not being in trouble; but she couldn't stop laughing.

"Acorns," she said, when she could breathe. "Almonds. You look like a big pile of pistachios."

"If I'm nuts," Higgs said, "who are you?"

"I'm Ellen Moresby," she said. "My father is the dean."

There it was: the admission that had gotten her chucked from a dozen fraternity parties in her teenage years—"See you at school," her friends said from the front porch, beaming, each with a brother's thickset arms around her lucky waist. . . . She studied Higgs's face. If he blanched—or, still worse, if opportunism clinked to life in his eyes—the conversation was over. She could walk home from here.

Higgs just nodded. He offered his hand.

"I'm Stanley Higgs," he said. "It's a pleasure to meet you."

And this last conventionality was uttered with an expression of such concentration that it seemed not a conventionality at all; it seemed like something that had never before been said. It seemed, that is, as if Higgs meant it.

The party went on around them: hundreds of hands lifting pigs-in-blankets to equally many champing mouths, feet shuffling, arms pumping, the echoing din of men punctuated by shouts of recognition—"Rogers!" "Old man!"—the drink-reddened cheeks of the triumphant crowd . . . Three hours passed. The Prospectors departed, the floodlights were shut off, the drunkest guests sat morosely alone, faces cupped against the half-light. And by the time Dean Moresby arrived, query-eyed, to take his daughter home, she and Higgs were lovers—more or less.

Ellen went back to Vassar, and the two exchanged long letters for the remainder of the term. In July they were married in a businesslike ceremony at the university chapel; Dean Moresby, relinquishing his daughter, could not help reflecting glumly that now he would always have to call Higgs "Stan." Ellen transferred to Chandler State, which she had come to dislike much less, for her final year. The couple moved into a gabled two-story house on the edge of campus—that is, on the edge of the cliff—from which the anthropology department had been summarily ushered out. Ellen, who had never been handy, surprised herself by taking great pleasure in the house's workings, in checking the caulking and the soundness of the joists, the bolts of the thick mahogany door. Might one suppose she felt some premonition of the day, still nearly two decades in the future, when she would set that bolt in vain against the men from the university with their wires and tape recorders; or even speculate further that Ellen's habit of leaving the radio on all day, turned so loud she could hear it in every room, was a remedy in advance for the silence that was on its way? One might. But what would be the use?

An unlabelled, water-damaged reel tape, fifty minutes long, in the university library's repository downtown, is the only recording still in existence of a lecture by Higgs. Click the tape into the apparatus, lean firmly on PLAY (the button sticks) and listen: an aggregate of youthful voices, the beseeching scrape of desks. Professor Higgs has not yet arrived. There's about a minute of this; a soft voice behind the microphone saying, "Check. Check. Check"— and then Higgs enters, or so we infer from the sudden settling of conversation. Mentally we grant him ten or fifteen seconds to mount the dais. But the pause is longer; it stretches; we wait thirty seconds, a minute, and still there is no sound but the anxious coughing of the undergraduates. What is he waiting for? We strain to hear the rustling of notes on the podium; but Higgs, we remember, never used notes. He lectured from memory, or, for all we know, impromptu. Someone close to the microphone says to his neighbor, "That's what she actually said, can you believe it?" The neighbor: "I can't believe it." The first boy: "And you know what I said?"

But we never find out, because just then Higgs begins to speak.

"Henderson between the wars," Higgs says, "was a figure of solitude, and an object, when his solitude was interrupted, of derision and contempt. He was an expatriate in Berlin held fast by perfectly balanced hatreds for Germany and his homeland. His linguistic skills were negligible and his philosophic viewpoint was juvenile. For all these reasons, and for other reasons which I will put forth to you during the term, Henderson's body of work constitutes one of the most important poetic moments of the century. In this class—"

But here the aged tape gives way to the inflictions of moist years. The lecture dissolves into a high angry screech, ten minutes long, like a superhuman trumpet blast, and when the sound comes back Higgs is reading from *Poems Against the Enemies Both Surrounding and Pervading Us.*

He reads: ". . . the hectoring of the vendors of spoiled fish/ is equal in offensiveness to/ the/ hideous coughing of my mother/ Berlin is dying/ of syphilis and I/ am its rotting nose."

And from the lecture hall there is silence, a perfect and unnatural silence, unbroken by the clearing of a throat, the scratching of a pen, or the shifting of a single chair. The students are transfixed. Before five minutes have passed the tape goes silent too, all the way to the end, and that is all that remains of the voice of Professor Higgs—all, that is, except one word. But here, again, I'm getting ahead of the story.

So: years passed, uneventfully enough. Higgs had gained a measure of fame among the undergraduates, not so much for his scholarly standing as for his habit, when warm weather came around, of playing checkers with students on the outdoor tables in the quad. He was very good. He was known to play one man down, or blindfolded, with an onlooker calling out his opponent's moves. When the whim struck him he would play three blind games at once, striding between the tables with his arms waving madly in front of him. Girls crowded the tables to watch him; in concentration he was fascinating, his fickle gaze hidden behind the gingham blindfold, his arm's motion, as he reached for a checker, as smooth and quiet as a submarine.

After a particularly commanding victory, or trio of victories, the bravest of the coeds might press forward to ask Higgs a question: what was his secret?

Higgs seemed embarrassed by this attention. He lifted the blindfold from his face and let it dangle off one finger as he surveyed his opponents' hopeless positions—as if he didn't know exactly what he'd see. He demurred: "It's simply a matter of thoroughness. One has to consider every possible move and eliminate those that lead to defeat. That's all."

Out in the world there were the missiles in Cuba and all the nagging worry that followed—red-starred boots tromp-tromping on Fifth Avenue and all that. The university, miles from anyplace that could even generously be called strategic, went about its sober business. The basketball team continued winning many more games than it lost; the children of the state kept marching through the terms, en route to the slots awaiting them in the middle levels of hardware stores and banks; and Higgs went on publishing.

His project now was a survey of Henderson's influence on his contemporaries. Henderson ought to have—was previously thought to have—influenced exactly nobody. His books were underprinted and unreviewed; worse, they were in a hinterland language that no one of any importance bothered to understand, and whose grammatical complexities had frustrated even those few who had attempted to so bother. Before Higgs, only *Poems Against the Enemies* had even been translated, and that so amateurishly that the German edition appeared as *Verses for the Foreigner Who Lives Inside My Body*. But Henderson's work, despite all, had made its way to the literary heroes of Europe. A German girlfriend had given Sartre *Poems Against the Enemies* as a joke. Brecht, like Higgs, had found it in the trash—so had Böll. Paul Celan, caught in a downpour on the Kurfürstendamm, had ducked arbitrarily into Café Maeterlinck, where Henderson was giving a rare reading in his execrable German. And so it went. Higgs exposed these links, and dozens more like them; not satisfied, he probed the writers' works, line by line, teasing out the traces of Henderson's thoughts, the echoes of his maladroit phrasings, his psychic fingerprints—unmistakable once pointed to—blotting their clean white pages. Henderson had infiltrated the world's literature through the low cunning of coincidence; now Higgs had found him out.

In the midst of this, in March of 1965, Higgs received a letter from Dr. Georg Knabel, Henderson's dentist. Higgs had located the man years before, in connection with the matter of the gold crown. The dentist had responded to Higgs's inquiries with one uninspiring sentence: "I recall Henderson only as a particularly contrary patient."

But now Dr. Knabel had come through. He had gone to London for a three-day conference on cosmetic prosthodontics, and on the last night, careening drunkenly down Fleet Street with his fellow whiteners and unsnagglers, he had seen Henderson in a window. Was he sure? Higgs wrote back. Absolutely sure. He had recognized the upper left canine, his handiwork.

Armed with the dentist's description and a business map of London, Higgs was able to narrow the list of possible addresses to a few dozen. To each of these addresses he sent a letter, respectful but not obsequious, in perfect Gravinic, stating the author's admiration for Henderson's work, summarizing his research thus far, and gently inquiring as to Henderson's possible interest in a mutually beneficial correspondence.

Twenty of the letters returned unopened in the first two weeks, stamped "NO SUCH OCCUPANT." More trickled in over the days that followed, each bearing the same gray message. Before long there was only one letter left extant. Months went by. Higgs's colleagues did their best to encourage him. Surely, they said, Henderson was lingering over his response. No doubt he was tossing draft after draft out into the beery, ancient street.

But when the letter came back it was Higgs's own, sealed in a new envelope; under Higgs's signature, a single Gravinic word was scrawled in red. The closest translation of Henderson's response is "bastard"—but the English word fails to capture the specific connotation of a son who, not content with dishonoring his mother by his illegitimacy, rapes her upon achieving manhood and abandons her to the poverty of soiled women. In Gravinic there was no firmer way to say no. Higgs must have been disappointed; but he could not have been surprised.

Soon afterwards, Coach Mahemeny retired. His replacement, a marginal ex-Piston named LaBart, found his players' dedication to Gravinic more troublesome than Mahemeny had.

"You can't paddle a ship with two oars," he told Dean Moresby significantly. "You can't have two captains in the middle of the stream."

"You're making sense," Dean Moresby said.

LaBart recruited players from his home territory: the flat, sun-blasted counties around Los Angeles. The new boys, shivering and dull-eyed, had no interest in Higgs's class, or any class. LaBart enrolled them all in the brand-new mass communications department, to graduate from which they had only to perform mock sportscasts once a week and pass a multiple-choice test at the end of senior year.

So Higgs's course was cut in half, and subsequently it continued to dwindle. The ideological savor of those years had reached even to Chandler City, and it was becoming increasingly clear that Henderson was not—as they called it then—relevant. His views on women and racial minorities were retrograde, and his attachment to patriarchal

33

militarism, in the person of Kaiser Wilhelm, was no longer endearing. The feeling was not restricted to our university. On the contrary, because of Higgs's presence it was weaker there than elsewhere. Gravinicists worldwide were turning away from Henderson in favor of other, more palatable artists. A particular favorite was a poet from Henderson's own hometown, a woman who for thirty years had worked loyally on the line at the provincial collective bread factory, tucking a revolutionary stanza into the crease of each loaf as it rolled by. The remaining Henderson scholars became defensive and mistrustful, exchanging beleaguered late-night calls from their home phones. There were further failed attempts to track down Henderson in London; he'd moved, or had convinced the post office to bounce his mail. This surprised no one. Their journal diminished to a dittoed newsletter, then gave out. Their field had settled into the status of a shared peculiarity; like it or not, they were in with the matchbook collectors now, the cat fanciers, and the Esperantists.

For the few students who remained, there was still the matter of Higgs's deteriorating teaching. Often he would stop during a class and cock his head as if he'd heard an untoward noise; it would be a while before he started speaking again, and when he did, he sounded distracted and empty of conviction. The tiny pauses in his elocution grew to seconds, then to minutes, so that in an hour-long lecture there might be only fifteen minutes of actual speech. And more often than not, he let his class out at half-past. What he did say consisted mostly of difficult allusions which he left unexplained; he met all questions with a pained expression and an interval of weary silence. No one could explain Higgs's behavior. There was speculation, among those who knew about it, that the rejection from Henderson was to blame; but the change in Higgs had started before Dr. Knabel's news, and had if anything eased a bit with the arrival of Henderson's letter. He seemed healthy. He expressed no bitter dissatisfactions. But the pauses kept growing longer; and the students kept growing fewer. They moved him from the auditorium in Gunnery Hall, now embarrassingly empty, to a seminar room at the department. Soon after that, his class was canceled altogether. No one had enrolled.

Dean Moresby, worried, visited his daughter for lunch.

"You've made a nice little place here," he told Ellen. His daughter stood at the stove, grilling him a ham and cheese sandwich, humming along with the radio in the sitting room. She looked barely older than a teenager; though there was no trace left of the bracing, willful girl she'd been.

She stopped humming. "If you say so, Daddy. It's not as though we've redecorated. The basement's a mess."

"I don't exactly mean the decorations."

Ellen waited silently at the stove.

"I mean—you can always tell the house of a happy married couple. It's not so much a matter of what it looks like. There's a certain sense of permanence. Your mother and I—"

The two of them were quiet for a while as the smell of frying ham, greasy and reassuring, filled up the kitchen.

"Are you trying to ask me something?" Ellen said. "I'd like it if you'd just ask."

"I don't want to intrude."

"So it's about Stanley."

He swallowed glumly. "Well, he hasn't seemed to be himself, has he? And we just thought you might know if there was anything he needed, or wanted—we could certainly see to it, if it were something of that sort."

"Thank you for asking," she said, "but no. You've been very generous already."

"And as your father," he went on, "naturally I've been concerned . . ."

"Oh," she said. "That we're on the outs."

There, now, was the willful girl.

"If you think it's necessary to put it that way."

"Well, you were right the first time," Ellen said. "We're perfectly happy." She lifted the sandwich off the pan and set it on a plate before him; her frown smoothed out. The battle was over before he'd had a chance to take a swing: "If you think it's necessary . . ." Pathetic! Resignedly he wished his wife were there. She had a finger on Ellen's switch; with a single word she could have turned this into a screaming all-afternoon affair, just like in the old days.

Ellen produced a scotch and water in a tall, heavy glass and set it on the table. The dean took down a third of the drink in one forceful, medicinal swallow. Sprightly drums pounded in the sitting room.

"Your mother asked me to ask you something," he said.

"I guess I know what."

"It's already nine years."

"Stanley believes in sharing the work of raising children equally," Ellen told him. "And he's very busy right now."

The dean adopted his warmest and most fatherly aspect; he was Santa, he was a Norman Rockwell cop on an ice cream stool. "It would be a big change," he said. "Your mother and I would help you in any way we could."

"But we don't need to change," Ellen said. And Dean Moresby realized—as he sent his final hot slosh of scotch down the hatch—that he believed her.

Whatever it was got worse. Higgs arrived at the department at dawn and left in mid-afternoon; he kept his office door locked when he was inside. He met all disturbances politely, but with such obvious forbearance that no one could stay for long; it was choking. Each visitor felt he'd flouted an article of some unforgiving etiquette of which only Higgs was aware. And there were steadily fewer visitors. Higgs spoke with hardly anyone; and when he did speak, each word seemed to have swum up from a deep and secret grotto, which at any moment could snap shut. He quit playing checkers. He published nothing.

In December of 1971, Professor Rosso organized a conference to mark the 40th anniversary of Henderson's first book, *God of Bile*. Higgs, to everyone's surprise, agreed to deliver the opening address. His title was "Henderson and the Meaning of Grubs."

Despite Henderson's decline from fashion, the turnout at the conference was substantial. News of Higgs's turn inward had spread quickly through the erstwhile strongholds of Henderson scholarship, and his name, in those constricted circles, had acquired a connotation of intrigue. People who hadn't deigned to write on Henderson in years had come, just to see what Higgs might say. Why not? The Henderson Society, flush with cash, had flown everyone in. There was a new donor, a transistor heir from Tokyo named Koiichi Kosugi, who'd found a Henderson pamphlet in his dead father's army chest, and within a month had redug the channels of his family fortune. Opera and cancer wards were out; now the money flowed our way, toward Henderson and Henderson's servants.

The campus was overrun with Gravinicists, perched on every flat surface, spilling over with disagreement but eerily alike. They were men, they were not too old, their glasses were somewhat dirty and they favored greasy food; though none were fat. They talked in spurts. Not a few lisped. Their hair, what there was of it, was for the most part dark, and they had a shared habit, in concentration, of hooking their fingers into it and tugging; so that a group of them together, bent over plates of corned beef hash, of fat-flecked chili mac, resembled a troop of macaques at their grooming, waging their fervent, hopeless battle against the ecosystem of their own too-hospitable heads.

When the time came for Higgs's address, every seat in the auditorium was full, and there were scholars huddled in the aisle.

Higgs climbed to the stage; the audience, as one, craned forward. Higgs looked around. As always, he had no notes. His eyes flicked from one curious face to another, betraying nothing; to the ceiling lights, trained on him; to the fire exits on each side; back down to the podium. He cleared his throat. The audience waited: a minute, then two, then five. Something in Higgs's carriage, the determined set of his mouth and the angle of his jut over the podium, made him seem continuously on the verge of beginning. It was impossible to leave.

It was forty minutes before Higgs—his audience still intact—said a word.

"The 'feasting grubs' in the 1939 folio should be construed as referring to the banquet of maggots in the original Book III of *God of Bile,* rather than to the fall of the Basque provinces to the nationalists, as has been conventionally understood."

Interesting, came the murmurs from the crowd, yes, I see that, interesting! Now things were moving along! And they waited, pens cocked, free hands tangled in hair, to see how Higgs would continue.

But Higgs was done. He had nothing to gather up; he walked off the left side of the stage and out the door.

There was a pause. "This is sad," one scholar said. "I saw him at Trieste," said another. "Didn't I meet you at Trieste?" Someone had a copy of the relevant folio and a crowd formed around him, bending to the pages, the folly of the heretofore prevailing viewpoint already becoming clear.

Dean Moresby had hurried from the auditorium when he saw Higgs leave. He caught up with him on the low rise that immediately preceded his son-in-law's house. Below him he could see the house, the cliff, and, off to his left, the gray, morose water of the reservoir. Breathing hard, he put a hand on Higgs's shoulder.

"Stan," he said (wincing), "what's going on? What kind of an idea is that speech? What is your idea in making everybody wait for an hour and then, and then saying just the one thing and walking off?"

"What else did you want me to say?" Higgs asked. And Dean Moresby didn't have an answer.

Less than a month later—to be precise, on the tenth of January, 1972, sometime between 8:30 and 9:00 P.M.—Higgs entered Happy Clappy's, the undergraduate cafeteria, through the north door, and proceeded approximately ninety feet to the à la carte counter, where he ordered a cheeseburger, medium rare, with lettuce and mayonnaise. The student on grill duty was Cheryl Hister, a junior.

She recognized Higgs. After the one-sentence address the school paper had run a photograph.

"That comes with fries or baked potato, Professor Higgs," Cheryl said. "Which would you like?" Higgs thought for a good long time.

"Potato," he said.

"Potato?" Rosso asked. Around him sat the members of the emergency faculty committee, nursing stale coffee. "You're sure that's what he said? Potato?"

"I *told* you," Cheryl said tearfully. "I asked him which he wanted and he said 'Potato.'" She dragged one frilly sleeve across her nose. They'd made her wear her Happy Clappy's uniform for the reenactment.

"You're doing fine," Rosso told her. "Nobody's saying otherwise."

He directed a gathering-in gesture at the row of wan faces flanking him, soliciting consensus. Oh no, came the murmur. Nobody's saying that.

"But I want you to think back very carefully now, one more time, and tell me if Professor Higgs might have said anything *besides* 'Potato.'"

"Potato," Cheryl said. "That is absolutely the last thing and then I gave him his cheeseburger. Which he ate and then left. Can't I go home?"

The rest of the committee was growing restless. It had been two hours and they'd learned nothing. Dean Moresby leaned forward. "I think we ought to end this," he told Rosso.

"All right," Rosso said, reluctantly, "the meeting is adjourned. Thank you, Cheryl." Still crying, clutching her starched sides, the girl fled.

What had happened? In brief: the word "potato" was the last one Higgs had spoken. After eating his cheeseburger he'd gone back to his office and begun writing letters: a note authorizing Ellen to make financial arrangements in his name, references for his few persisting graduate students, a petition for sabbatical, effective at once and continuing until such time as Higgs saw fit to end it. Since then he had not spoken to anyone, nor had he communicated in writing. The professors and the Dean had tried every flavor of cajolement and threat; all in vain.

Only Ellen seemed unperturbed. "I suppose he'll talk again," she said, "when he has something to talk about." After she'd gone, the committee members buzzed at her equanimity. Rosso wondered aloud how long she'd keep it up. Rosso, Dean Moresby reflected, hadn't known the girl when she was twelve.

Months went by; Higgs remained speechless. His story went out as human interest on the AP wire. In April, Harry Reasoner arrived on campus to film a piece on Higgs for *60 Minutes*. The segment, when it aired, implied strongly that the whole enterprise was a veiled act of protest against the war. A movement, Reasoner hinted darkly, might be on its way. In those days it was possible to imagine such a thing; silent professors on every corner, accusing and significant, our home-grown variety of torched monk. But it didn't catch on.

Higgs retreated to his house on the cliff. Every so often the student paper ran an article: "PROFESSOR STILL IN SECLUSION" or some such, on the back page, under the comics. That was all.

One afternoon in September, Ellen responded to a knock on the door to find her father on the stoop, accompanied by two professors she didn't know, a nervous-looking graduate student, and a pair of technicians laden with tape recorders, microphones, and yards of wire.

She stepped into the doorway and crossed her arms. "What's this all about, Daddy?"

Eyes fixed on the lintel, he explained: the Henderson scholars had formed a plan. Recalling that Higgs's shorter pauses had invariably concluded with some concentrated insight, they had reasoned that the current silence promised a breakthrough on a previously unimagined scale, a Grand Unified Theory of Henderson. They were terrified of missing it, when it came. They had no reason to be confident that Higgs would publish, or even repeat himself for their benefit. So the Henderson Society had arranged a substantial fund to assure that Higgs's next words would not go unwitnessed. The nervous graduate student would sit all day with Higgs; the tape recorders would run all night. In this way an exhaustive record could be kept.

"Absolutely not," Ellen said. "There will not be strangers in this house bothering my husband." She shut the door and barred it.

"Honey, be reasonable," Dean Moresby said through the door. "You'll get used to it."

"Out of the question."

He took a deep breath. "I don't like to have to remind you that your house is owned by the university."

"Then don't."

"Think how terrible it will be if the police have to come."

After a meaningful interval Ellen pulled back the bar, allowed the intruders to file shamefacedly past. Higgs was sitting in the kitchen, eating corn chips one by one from an ancient-looking wooden bowl. Ellen stepped behind his chair and laced her fingers together; and in this conjugal tableau, silent and stubborn, they remained, as the workers installed the recorders and the mikes. But when the technicians started upstairs to the bedroom she balked.

"But in case he should talk in his sleep . . ." her father explained.

"He does not," she said icily. And Dean Moresby ordered the men back downstairs. He didn't want it to be any harder for his daughter than was necessary. And this *was* necessary: that, he believed. He was as convinced as he had been two decades before that in Higgs, somehow, lay the university's salvation. With his decline the rest of the faculty had slunk back to its traditional malaise. The torrent of graduate applications was a dripping tap again. And LaBart's boys had never really adjusted to the climate; the taller and more playful Eastern teams were drumming them off the court. A word from Higgs, he thought, the *right* word, could change everything back. Whenever he imagined letting go of that certainty he felt sick and confused. He did not expect Ellen to forgive him.

And indeed, she never did. She made some inquiries about a suit; but the Henderson Society was wealthy, who knew how, and conversant with strange byways of influence, and it was clear before long that the scholars could mire any litigation perhaps indefinitely—certainly beyond her ability to pay a lawyer on Higgs's salary. She had no money of her own with which to move out, and, under the circumstances, she couldn't ask her father. So Ellen made do with a more personal defiance. Whenever the nervous graduate student, or one of the successors to his position, was with Higgs, she made a point of banging pots, vacuuming, knocking over chairs, running the blender empty. The radio was always on, as loud as it would go. She didn't speak to her father. And Higgs didn't speak to anyone.

Thirteen years later, I, Samuel Grapearbor, graduated from Chandler State University—penniless, dissatisfied, experienced at nothing, in need of a job.

PART
TWO

"*The importance of the opening moves in a game of checkers cannot be overestimated. The first few moves determine the type of formation into which the mid-game will develop, and it is in the complicated mid-game that the student, if he is on unfamiliar ground, is apt to be forced into a position so inherently weak that it defies all efforts to successfully defend it.*"

—Arthur Reisman,
How To Win At Checkers

CHAPTER 2

A LITTLE ABOUT MYSELF

Now that my younger self is about to enter the story, I find myself a little reluctant to get on with it. So let me pause for a moment and explain how I came to be involved with Henderson, and thus with Higgs—a story, in its own way, as unlikely as the professor's own.

I was born in 1963 on the outskirts of Chandler City, in a three-room apartment above my parents' business, the Grape Arbor Café and Grill. Eight months before, my parents had moved from New York, where they had operated a restaurant by the same name which enjoyed much traffic in the dignitaries of the nascent counterculture. Look it up: you can find my mother in any number of poems, minor, uncollected ones, from that brief and in its own way exalted period when people *wrote* poems in restaurants, on the backs of checks, or rather when anything written in a restaurant, on the back of a check, was a poem, simply by virtue of its staggering and implausible success at existing in the world. But those times were coming to a close. Our reputation had become great enough that thrill-seekers flooded the café after the plays let out, hoping for an overheard snatch of cool, or at the very least a whiff of reefer. And the poets, in their fickle way, were tiring of the spontaneity of unmediated experience; the most advanced ones were rhyming again. Many were going back to school. "It's time to go," my mother told my father; and when she read the story of Tip Chandler in a magazine, she knew where.

My father, a mild man, dedicated to prudent consistency, demurred. But my mother kept at it. They would be close to the wilderness, she pointed out, and far from the draining pretentiousness of city life. And artists were bastards, who left insulting tips, if any. The disappointed thrill-seekers were no better. It wasn't long before he came around.

There was one more reason to move, which she didn't bring up, because my father didn't know about it yet: there was me. I think she had some idea that, born in the West, I would grow up steely, level-voiced, inclined to swift action. My mother is a woman of passionate opinion, and has been wrong about many things; but never, I believe, more wrong than in this.

The Grape Arbor's vegetarian leanings failed to catch on with the miners, drillers, and mountain men, and we were too far from downtown to attract the university crowd. Before long my parents had to learn to grill cheeseburgers to survive. Business, even so, was slim. A year after the move my father started looking for a second job. Unbrawny, ill-at-ease around machinery, he was in trouble from the start; but eventually he secured a slot on Mayor Meadows's geothermal research team. Reading maps, digging holes, he could do, and the impossibility of advancement suited his constant nature. In this manner we mobilized upward. Starting from poverty, we topped out at bare subsistence.

Despite themselves, my parents began to think of New York nostalgically, even wistfully. My mother had come to the opinion that there wasn't much to the wilderness that couldn't be experienced adequately through nature magazines. And the artists—true, their tips had been small, their demeanor condescending, but at least there had been a certain standard of conversation. The artists had never spat chaw or slapped my mother's rear, and when they cursed it was in the service of wit. Their every rudeness seemed, in retrospect, like charm. But there was no money to go back now.

When I was old enough I was put to work in the restaurant, in charge of the grill and the fry-o-lator. I spent every afternoon engulfed in a miasma of singed Crisco, tamping down patties the size of drink coasters, sullenly imagining myself in New York, where I was certain that I belonged, and where hamburgers, I was equally certain, were not cut so liberally with wheat germ that whole unalloyed pockets of it spilled out from the meat onto the grill and charred there, with a smell like a burning barn. Since, to my mother's way of thinking, the grill was strictly a sidelight, I was the waiter too. In fact, my cooking constituted the majority of what we sold. Her carrot manicotti, billed as "famous"—it had been in poems—languished. Apparently the people of Chandler City didn't care for fame. Nor did they care for her mock-Caesar salad, her several plates of crudités, her soy and brown-rice paella, any of the sugarless, dairyless, yeastless cakes that rested flat and foreboding in our display case like defunct UFOs. Mostly she sat at the window, glowered, and smoked. I often told customers I was not my parents' son, but an orphan midget, away without leave from the Dutch national circus. Some seemed to believe me.

Taped to the wall beside my Murphy bed was a snapshot of my mother, in the original Grape Arbor, setting a platter of sprouts and wax beans in front of Gregory Corso. The poet was smiling, his head cocked just noticeably to the left, and I liked to think he'd just said something sly and outrageous to my mother, that her affectless expression marked the moment just prior to understanding, that just after the shutter closed she would break into the laughter of shared sophistication. It was the best kind of laughter, I thought then, although I had never heard it.

I used to get up an hour before I needed to for school, shut myself in the bathroom, and mimic Corso's wry, one-sided smile in the mirror. Once I had reproduced it to my satisfaction—I was twelve—I tried it out in the schoolyard. I suppose I imagined that the other boys, observing the tiny questioning lift of my brow, my lips' world-weary tilt, would in unison reassess me as a sort of playground guru, would direct to me henceforth their questions of fashion and social arbitration.

Instead they took me for palsied. I endured their jeers, their intermittent blows, with Corso's smile—or my grotesque imitation of it—

fixed on my face. After that day I never had many friends at school; I spent my time with a loose confederation of playmates, most of them stigmatized by one physiological defect or another. The defective boys tolerated my attempts at drollery; and each day at recess, when I would inveigh against our classmates, our teachers, Chandler City, the entire American West, they listened to me dutifully. From time to time they played cruel tricks on me, but I never complained. I recognized that it was the closest thing to wit I was likely to come by for some time.

My career in high school was undistinguished. The demands of my teachers were unbearably mundane, and my peers' opinion of my intelligence meant less than nothing to me. All I could think of was getting my diploma and striking out for the East—more specifically, for the New York of my zealous imaginings, the symphony of taxicab horns, the murmur of education and wealth, starlets on my arms, and so forth. From a news magazine I had clipped out a sentence reading: "In the 1980s, New York City remains the cultural center of the Western World." I taped the clipping below the bathroom mirror and forbade my parents to take it down. As before, I spent each morning before the mirror; but now, instead of smiling, I scowled, imagining the clipping as the caption to my head shot, tallying the days before I could depart.

But my applications to Columbia, NYU, Pace, Fordham, and Cooper Union came back with purported regrets, and the few lesser schools there that did accept me were unable or unwilling to forgive my tuition. And this, my parents informed me without ambiguity, meant it would be Chandler State for me. I was stunned. In my essay I had explained at great length that it was impossible, at this point, for me to live anywhere but New York City, and that my unimposing record was clearly (and it *was* clear to me, then) a matter of my frustration at remaining entrapped in the ludicrous, backwater city-if-that in which I'd had the misfortune to be born.

For a while I dallied with the idea of giving up college altogether, and booking my own passage to New York. But none of the traditional means of free transport applied to me. Hitchhiking was out—as a man alone, I was invisible to truckdrivers and frightening to vacationers, and no one else drove through Chandler City. I considered becoming a hobo; but a little research convinced me that a life of flattering housewives for scraps, of nights spent hanging inches over hurtling, sparking tracks, violated all my standards of acceptable privation. I wasn't even sure there still *were* any hoboes. Even if I were to get to New York, I had no way of making a living. There was no musical instrument I could play soulfully on the corners; I knew no powerful insiders who would guarantee me work. I couldn't type and I was certainly no boxer. There was nothing to be done about it. I had four more years, at least, before I could become expatriate.

There was always suicide, of course. I thought of it often—decided, in fact, that I would certainly go ahead with it, weighed the available methods each time I bent, sweating, over another grillfull of the restaurant's awful hamburgers. But, having gotten through the decision, I felt there was no hurry, and September, to my mild surprise, found me living. Undefiantly, I registered. I consoled myself with the assurance that, although I had been forced to enroll at Chandler State, I could not be forced to conform to its ways. I would piece together what counterculture I could. Having abandoned the idea of becoming a hobo—please forgive me—I set out to become a Boho.

My fellow skeptics were easy to locate; they were the ones pressed grimly into the corners at mixers, draining their gaily-named cocktails one after another, remarking cuttingly on passers-by, always claiming to be about to leave. We formed a clique of sorts—Bick Wickman, who claimed to be from Liverpool, Marinet, Barberie the thereminist, the supercilious Kack, Charlie Hascomb, I, the others . . . We called each other by our last names and swore ourselves to total and eternal honesty—this meant meanness. At odd hours we could be found gathered in someone's dorm room, or in the recesses of Happy Clappy's, smoking pot, laughing hollowly, devising cruel nicknames for the basketball players and the fraternity presidents, constructing various drastic schemes (pipe bombs, excrement, itching powder) toward the impairment of the university's function, and eventually releasing the balance of our scorn on whatever members of our group were absent. From time to time the directions of our enmity would converge on one of our number, and before long that one would be driven away, to be spoken of thereafter with a venom otherwise reserved only for the most popular and well-connected students.

Charlie Hascomb, a local like me, was my "best friend" that year (certainly we were not friends in the lay sense.) His straw-blond hair was meticulously groomed and hung down below his shoulders; his face was long, too, and droopy at the eyes, giving him a permanent expression of aristocratic glumness. Without any visible exercise he maintained a credible imitation of an athlete's physique. I envied this, and, angry with myself for my envy, spent most of my time with him, by way of punishment.

Charlie's only weakness was a terrible fear of insects, and, by extension, of contamination in general.

"Good goddamn," he would say, gravely, shaking his head, whenever he walked into Happy Clappy's. "This place is a filth hole." He was always peering at the floor, starting at peripherally glimpsed motions, rubbing at the underside of a table and gazing mournfully at whatever came off on his finger. His clothes smelled of bug spray.

"I see it this way," Charlie told me once. "Basically every living thing either looks like it shouldn't be able to think, and can't, like a worm, or a tree; or looks like it should be able to think, and can. Dogs, birds, higher life-forms in general. But then look at a bug. It's got arms, legs, eyes, everything; but no personality, no *reason.*"

"What's scary about that?" I asked him.

He frowned at me, disappointed. "If it doesn't bother you," he said, "I can't possibly explain."

Ordinarily anyone with such a fetish would have been hooted from our set at once, viciously and with glee. But Charlie was safe from that. For one thing, he was our dealer; although in those days there was nothing easier than finding a new dealer. More important, he possessed an uncanny talent for mimicry, which he used mercilessly against all those who fell from his favor. An incident in which he'd impersonated a sorority vice-president in a late-night phone call, and the subsequent abjection of the former friend of ours who believed himself summoned to her service, inspired in each of us a proud kind of dread. It was not worth anyone's risk to take him on. And allied with him, I knew, I myself would never be outcast. The two of us used to sit in the back of Happy Clappy's until closing time, Charlie "doing" the other members of our circle one by one, until I was weak with laughter and the pleasure of being included.

I find it almost impossible now to identify myself with the vain, unpleasant undergraduate I was. But to my annoyance my memory of the period is thorough and detailed—I can recall each act of mean-spiritedness, each self-righteous slur, every one of my embarrassing affectations. I grew my hair long and wore a hideous beard, which tufted out from the sides of my jaw and across my neck without ever impinging on my face. An ordinary beard, at least, would have covered my acne. All the marijuana I was smoking made me break out more severely than I ever had in high school. I was always changing majors in response to imagined slights from my professors. I wore a long black raincoat wherever I went, inside or outside, winter or spring, and I fancied that the people who whispered at my passing were inquiring of each other what my mysterious story might be, what I knew that they didn't; and so on.

On the east side of campus, in a little copse of elms, stood a statue of Tip Chandler. Our founder, immortalized in bronze, must once have struck a noble figure. Under one arm he clutched a stack of books—Homer, Virgil, Ovid—and with the other he gestured grandly toward the west, his palm open and flat as if he were offering something to the Pacific; but that hand was empty. A goldpan was slung from his belt. His sandaled feet were spread wide apart on his

pedestal, as if he were trying to keep his balance on an unsteady surface. And perhaps this pose represented one last burst of prescience on
the old prospector's part, for, as it turned out, the weight of the
memorial was too much for the less-than-solid clay our school was
built on. So Tip Chandler came to resemble his name. By the time of
my arrival he had developed a list of about twenty degrees in the
direction of his outstretched arm, so that his gesture of manifest destiny took on the aspect of a lunge; he seemed to be diving like a grace-
less ballerina into the elms.

This was where I liked to sit: on the high edge of the canted
pedestal, behind the statue's back, my raincoat tucked between me
and the cold marble. It was not at all comfortable. My back rested
against Chandler's unyielding calves, and the tilt of my seat forced my
knees up awkwardly toward my chest. But many footpaths met at the
statue, making it a particularly visible place to settle myself; and it was
so uninviting as to guarantee that no one else ever sat there. It suited
my imagined reputation that there should be a location associated
with me, and only me, in the public mind. It made me, I liked to
think, a sort of landmark unto myself.

All this by way of explaining my dismay when, one afternoon in
the fall of my junior year—having by this time D-plused my way
through eight majors, alienated myself from most of my original
cadre, and proceeded not an inch toward the manifestation of my
own destiny, whatever it was—I arrived at my station to find that
someone was already sitting there. It was a girl.

"I sit there," I said dumbly.

The girl was no one I recognized. This alone was strange. By virtue
of my endless disapproving contemplation of the people walking by
me, I had come to know almost everyone on campus—if not by name,
then by some offensive habit of bearing or dress. But this girl was new.
She was wearing a long black sundress with a pattern of ivy that coiled
up to the scooped-out neck. Her face was pale and scattered sparsely
with light freckles. She was pretty, I guessed—her prettiness was the

matter-of-fact brown-eyed kind that is usually agreed to be unintimidating. I found it nerve-racking. She smiled in a hard but serene way. She was looking at me as if I were about to say something.

"But now you're sitting where I sit," I explained.

"I know you sit here," the girl said. "You're Sam Grapearbor. We have psychology together." She swung her legs gracefully over the pedestal's edge and let them dangle almost to the ground.

Now I was beginning to place her; she sat in the front of the class and left as soon as the lecture ended. I hadn't recognized her because my attendance in psychology had lately been poor. I had hoped the course would feature more murderers and outcasts. I was about to switch to criminal justice.

"Jenny?" I tried.

"Julia," she said, and hopped off the statue. She smoothed her dress with the heels of her hands. The day was unseasonably warm; the wet smell of the already-fallen leaves had risen over the campus, and the students had brought out their bright shorts, their flip-flops, for one final outing. All except me. I was wearing my raincoat, as always; and inside it I was starting to sweat.

"I've eaten at your restaurant," Julia told me.

"You have to be kidding."

"Nope," she said. "I liked the carrot manicotti. It's justly famous."

"It's not really famous. It's a ploy."

"So why do you always sit here?"

The question I'd been waiting two years for, and it caught me by surprise.

"It's nice," I told her, which sounded weak even to me, so I tried again. "It's suitable. Nobody bothers me."

"It's uncomfortable."

"You get used to it."

"Really?"

"Sort of."

She smiled. Her gums showed. "You're the expert."

I was trying to find something wrong with her, to help me regain my usual footing. She was skinny and I could just make out the cords in her neck. That and her washed-out coloration made her look, I supposed, a little tired.

Was that the best I could do? I who'd called a linebacker a name that made him weep?

"OK," I said, "here it is. What I like about this statue is its very vulgarity and ludicrousness and the fact that it's about to collapse. Which I think is deeply symbolic. Which I think sums up my feelings toward this—" I waved my arms around, unable to come up with a grand enough gesture; it would have to encompass practically everything I'd ever heard of. "This situation," I concluded. "In which we find ourselves."

"I think it's gross," she said, and smartly, without warning, took my arm. "Let's go someplace else. Walk me to class."

"To class," I repeated. "Let's go."

The two of us walked a little ways across the campus, not talking. Julia had put on a pair of sunglasses; she turned her chin up and watched the sky, while I met the eyes of the people passing us, trying to convey by my unconcerned expression that it was ordinary for me to be strolling with an attractive stranger, that were it not for the feather-touch of her hand on my elbow (steely, I refused to look down at my elbow, her hand) I might veer away, not noticing her absence until I deigned to turn my head.

"What's your game?" I said, finally, trying to sound tough; but I was melting, melting.

She looked at me over her sunglass rims. "I don't have a game," she said. "I'm just a curious person. I'm wondering why you're so disaffected all the time."

"Why aren't you? That's what I'm curious about. You don't seem brain-damaged. You're sober."

"I like it here."

"You must have an unusual definition of 'like.' You don't like a place just because you can tolerate being trapped there."

"I wanted to come here," Julia said. This stopped me in my tracks.

She had transferred from Bryn Mawr, it turned out. She'd grown up in Greenwich Village: backdrop of my daydreams, the place where I was going to share joints and bon mots with scat singers, painters, and the attractively poor. She had come to Chandler City of her own free will, bound to it by no necessities of blood or finance. I couldn't believe it. I was fascinated—intellectually, I told myself—by this challenge to my ordering of the world.

"New York is bullshit," she said.

"But come on," I said, "the culture."

"Culture is wasted on liars and slobs," she said. She seemed suddenly a little peeved. "And New York is ninety-five percent liars and slobs."

"In Chandler City it's ninety-nine. Point nine repeating."

"The difference is, I like the slobs here."

The place where we'd come to a stop was on the western edge of the campus, where the agricultural buildings stood at discreet distances from one another and the browning grass was a yard high, fizzing with gnats.

"What class do you have here?" I asked her.

"I don't have a class now," she said. "I actually just wanted to get away from that statue."

At the next meeting of my psychology course I sat down, for the first time ever, in the front row. From this vantage the blackboard was huge and foreboding. It turned out all kinds of material pertinent to the course was written there. How could people take their education this close up?

A minute later, Julia came down the aisle and sat beside me. She drew from her military surplus bag a neat spiral notebook with graph paper pages.

"Buena mañana," I said, with, I thought, a touch of ironic style. It was 2:55.

"Viva la revolución," Julia replied in kind. "I'm supposed to ask you, are you going to the thing tonight?"

The thing was a college dance, one of the dreary events my group and I tried to make more dreary by our presence. That game had gotten old long ago.

"I'll go," I said. That seemed too quick. I recalled that a certain diffidence was asked of me.

"Right, why not," Julia said.

"You've been to one of these things before?"

"Not here. But my friends are going."

"It'll be completely appalling," I said. This seemed to strike a better note.

"So you don't want to go?"

"But I might as well go."

She just nodded again. My brief sensation of know-how had spiraled away, and I tapped my pencil on the desk while I waited without much hope for it to return. The professor had arrived at the podium and was taking his time about his sheaf of notes.

Never had I anticipated so keenly—never before, in fact, had I anticipated—the beginning of a lecture.

Julia came to the dance with her friends, and I brought the few friends I still had: Charlie Hascomb with his girlfriend, Bick Wickman, and Barberie. Julia's friends were a tight group of girls I'd seen before and begrudgingly failed to disdain. They were angry girls, in ripped-up pink T-shirts, black lipstick, and pocket chains; one of them, tall and awkward, even wore a smart three-inch Mohawk. Next to them, Julia in her ponytail, in her unobtrusive slacks, looked cut out from a box-lunch social.

The Chinese American Club had sponsored the dance in honor of some holiday of theirs—there were about fifteen members and they danced in a bouncy little knot at the front of the half-empty fieldhouse, near the speakers. Our group stood in the back and made sparse conversation. We hated Depeche Mode, they hated Depeche Mode: that was all we had in common. Bick Wickman gazed up with longing at the Mohawked girl; Barberie, the fattest and the baldest of all of us, had given up, and transmitted to me with his baleful glances his resentment at my having brought so forcefully to his attention the sexual intercourse he would not be having with these women, the Chinese American women, any women. The beat of the synthesized bass failed to fill up the hall. Whenever I looked at Julia, she was cultivating a small smile; I wanted badly to know whether she was smiling, too, when I wasn't looking. It seemed right to get her alone; but there was no avenue I could think of that did not involve having to dance.

Instead I took Charlie aside to ask his advice.

"Nice girl," Charlie said, with a manner that somehow both acknowledged and belittled the man-to-man moment I'd been after. "But it doesn't look good."

"No?"

"She's playing with you," he told me, gazing affectionately at the roof, the ancient championship banners barely aflicker with the strobe light. "It's what women like. She tracked your abject vulnerability with her secret radiation beam."

Charlie's girlfriend returned from the bathroom—I've forgotten her name now. Charlie had unreckonably many girlfriends in the time I knew him, all identical: athletic, straight-haired, flat-chested girls who appeared to brook no nonsense and smelled like talcum.

"Don't listen to him, he just hates women," the girlfriend said chummily.

"Secret radiation beam," Charlie repeated firmly. "And from New York . . ." He shook his head. "They've got versions of gonorrhea there even radiation can't kill. She's probably totally microbial. My advice to you is to stick with the homegrown."

Charlie knew perfectly well that I had not enjoyed even the most modest success with the "homegrown" women of Chandler City. So his advice was either optimistic or needlessly cruel.

We rejoined the group as it was about to break up. Bick had said something too forward to the tall, awkward girl; he beamed at me and Charlie as the girls gathered to go.

I meant to say goodnight to Julia, also to avoid saying goodnight to her in order to convey a certain immunity. Superimposed, these impulses caused my upper body to lurch toward her while my legs—is this possible?—began their retreat from the dance floor.

"See you, night," I said, and backed at top speed out of the hall.

The five of us gathered outside and watched our classmates proceed home with their dates.

"She wanted me, mate," Bick said in a sad and dreamy way, when Julia and her friends came out. "She wanted me, but she didn't know how to tell me."

Who knew what they wanted? Who knew what they knew how to tell? Charlie was right—it didn't look good. Earlier that day I'd dropped psychology, so there was no reason I'd see Julia again. At home, sober and annoyed, I set myself to the long, solitary task of making sense of what I'd learned.

But the next day I found her again at my statue.

"I thought you hated this place," I said.

She hopped down. "I do. So let's go."

This time we walked east, to the cliff. We stood on the grass behind the little house there—Higgs's house, of course, though I knew it only as the building that stood where Chandler's spring had allegedly gushed—and looked out over the crumbly verge. Before us, at the cliff's farthest jut, there was a short section of fencing and a yellow phone mounted on a sturdy post.

"It's for suicides," I told her. "You pick up the phone, it calls the hotline, and they tell you why not to jump."

"Does it work?"

"I don't know," I said. "I've never tried it."

We both looked over the edge.

"I'm sorry about Bick," I said. "He's not really from Liverpool."

"We guessed that."

I put my hand over her hand. I hadn't forgotten Charlie's advice. But look—I'd seen sentimental movies, like anybody else. If I saw

someone I knew at the theater I claimed I was there for the air con-
ditioning. But I'd paid very close attention. I knew approximately
what to do; first you put your hand over her hand. She smiled again.
There were her gums again.

"My friends all said you were a geek."

"Charlie said you had gonorrhea." At this she looked less pleased.
So I kissed her; not much of a kiss, no more really than a brushing of
her lips with my own, a momentary contact of foreheads, but still the
first kiss I'd had in more than a year, and the first ever from which I
had not been gently and with mortifying concern for my self-esteem
pushed away. Julia's body rested warmly against mine with what I
experienced, even with my movie-watching experience, as startling
frankness. When I kissed her again I let my fingers rest lightly on her
right shoulder, at the scratchy neckline of her rough cotton dress.

"I really thought you didn't like me," she said.

I could feel the rusty poles of the suicide fence against the backs of
my legs. "You thought wrong," I told her, feeling brave.

There at the cliff we spent the remainder of the afternoon. Julia
told me about leaving Bryn Mawr; it hadn't been, as she'd let me
believe, a grand put-down to her schoolmates, the liars and slobs.
She'd followed a man out here—a raffish carnie with a little rose tat-
tooed on the back of his shoulder, whom she'd met at the
Pennsylvania State Fair, at the Fool the Guesser booth. He'd guessed
she was twenty-three. Two days later she was in his car, heading for
California and the lucrative circuit of agriculture fairs: the Garlic
Festival, Eggplant Carnival, Artichoke Days. . . . But somewhere
around Chandler City he'd revealed that he wasn't a carnie at all. He
was an attorney for the outdoor lighting company that kept the carnival running at night; the real carnies let him run a booth as a favor
to his bosses. There was, naturally, a fiancée. Julia got out and hitch-
hiked to the closest town. That was us.

"Why didn't you go back?" I asked her.

"Are you kidding? It's humiliating. I'd rather die."

"I'd rather die than live in Chandler City," I said, a touch of my usual self-righteousness returning to me like an old, irritating friend.

"Okay," she said. Without further warning she wrapped her arms around my chest, pressed herself against me, and made as if to lever me over the side.

"No, no," I said, "I potentially have so much to live for."

"That's more like it," she said.

Julia had expected Chandler City to be a city full of simple, wise people, brimming with aphorism and household advice. Instead she found me—poor girl!

But, then again, it was inevitable that she would find me, or someone just like me. Julia had a passion for impossible causes. In the last election she had rung doorbells for Carter all the way to the end. (I had loudly declined to state a preference.) She was eternally trying to get people to read difficult novels. Her favorite movies (she admitted to me, after we'd been seeing each other for some time) were those in which some former sports hero, alternately crippled, ruined by drink, or betrayed, battles back into condition, steps back alternately onto the field, the ring, the court, the alley, or the rink, and against colossal odds beats the unsympathetically portrayed opponent, thus regaining the love of, alternately, a woman grown cynical or a towheaded, neotenic orphan. At the climactic moments of these movies I would lean over to Julia and whisper cruel insinuations; for instance, that the boastful champion was throwing the match, or that the hero's interest in the orphan was something more than paternal. She ignored this, as she did all my uglinesses.

I'll speed through the months that followed, since they followed a conventional script: introduction to my startled parents, first quarrel, salvos of tenderness, second quarrel, the awkward but gratifying disposal of my virginity. I bid farewell to Charlie Hascomb and the remaining members of my set, shaved my terrible beard, gave up marijuana. At the semester break Julia and I moved into a low L-shaped apartment in a cheap part of town, where the streets were named for natural philosophers. We lived on Lucretius. Our building had been converted from a soap factory, and the smell of industrial lubricant had sunk into the walls and floor. We spent all day inside and saw nobody; I had given up all my friends, and Julia's stayed away. Apparently they found me a bit hard to take. I changed my major to art history, the same as Julia's, so that even our brief time outside the apartment was spent together. And each night, at my insistence, she would tell me stories about New York. She had compiled an inexhaustible catalogue. Her rendition of the city was a grotesque inversion of my parents' misty recollections. In Julia's New York, the art world had gone sour and corporate, the air was particulate and soggy, good poets went hungry and bad ones taught in college, every taxi was taken up by cokehead debutantes, who would shove you off the corner without a word or a look back. I listened to Julia's stories with mingled horror and desire, like a housewife reading about the wretched improprieties of soap opera stars.

After a while the balance began to tilt in horror's favor. Maybe New York had once been as I'd imagined it; for all I knew, my parents' restaurant had been the last bulwark against the forces of vulgarity and boredom that had triumphed everywhere else, and the city had succumbed on their departure. In any case I found it increasingly difficult to summon up my old fantasies. The kowtowing doormen disappeared; the grand sweep of society folded its skirts and retired. I had no further desire to light out East. I knew enough now; if there were any further disillusionment to be gained by going there in person, I could do as well without it.

Which is not to say that I had gained any affection for my hometown in the process. It was the same backwater it had always been— no more glittery, no smarter. My dissatisfaction remained constant, a dull whine, but I no longer had any particular ambition to distract me; that is, I had come around to a more or less ordinary way of life. In a way, of course, this was a kind of despair, but in a way it was a relief. I had been freed of the responsibility to make it anywhere.

So we settled in, and summer was pulled over us. I worked nights at the restaurant and spent my days lying supine on our ancient bed, a damp towel laid square over my chest and two fans aimed at me from either side. I was bored. But boredom was a welcome change from ceaseless hatred. I no longer fantasized about the university's destruction, and my loathing for my classmates had diminished to a bearable distaste. My acne had cleared up. Julia was kind to me, and at the time I thought this to be as much as—perhaps more than—anyone could unselfishly expect. Sometimes I still think so. Had events proceeded slightly differently, I'm convinced, we would have gotten married soon enough, bought a house, run a rudimentary gallery or taken over the Grape Arbor, perhaps produced children who would in time grow up to repudiate our beliefs, such as they were. It is important to keep in mind, throughout what follows, that I came very near to leading an entirely unremarkable life. But instead, I awoke on September sixth of my final year of college with a terrific headache. I was so addled that when I arrived at Gunnery Hall at ten that morning for my first class of the semester, I stumbled into the wrong classroom, and by the time I realized my mistake, the unexceptional chain of events described above had receded into utter impossibility. But, of course, I wouldn't know that for some time.

My class was in a new wing that had been built just that summer. In my miserable state I was unable to make out the numbering scheme of the rooms, and when I saw at the end of the long, gleaming corridor a man standing half out of a doorway, beckoning me in, I assumed that I had found my destination.

The class I was looking for was Can Art and Industry Co-Exist?—a question about the answer to which I cared not an atom. As soon as I sat down I began to suspect I was in the wrong place. There was no slide projector set up, and the students were not ones I had seen in other art history classes. In fact, they were not ones I had seen anywhere. There were three men in identical oxford shirts and razor ties, who as far as I could see were unacquainted with each other; a very fat black man with a lazy eye; an impatient-looking punk wearing that T-shirt with the

64

Milky Way and the legend, "YOU ARE HERE"; in the front, a hyperglandular adolescent boy who, after some minutes of examination, I realized was in fact a woman of no less than forty. I felt as if I were at a casting call for a film whose tortured, whimsical plot I could never hope to understand. I wondered briefly what my own part in it could be.

The class was Introductory Gravinic. The man who had beckoned me in was Professor Gregory McTaggett—that same man whose broken wrist, decades before, had turned him from basketball to the life of the mind. He was the department chair now. Seeing me wandering, he'd taken me for the final student on his roll, a freshman named Bobby Trabant, who, I later found out, had tripped on a sidewalk outcropping on his way to class and split his forehead from his hairline to the bridge of his nose. Bobby never did come to that class, even after the stitches came out.

But I stayed. Why not stay? Julia had opted out of Can Art? in favor of a course for which I lacked the prerequisites. Anyway, it had recently become clear to me (although I had not yet told Julia) that no amount of diligence would allow me to graduate in art history at the end of that year. I was going to have to switch to mass communications. Consequently I had a great deal of room for electives in my schedule.

The first day was not what I expected—no hello, good-bye, my name is, I would like. Instead McTaggett outlined the history of the Gravine and its strange language, assuming correctly that the material was unfamiliar to all of us.

McTaggett's lecture began in the final, heady days of the Pleistocene, about 35,000 years past, when an arm of glacier retreated over a ridge in the Carpathians and revealed a bowl-shaped valley. Some time later, a troop of fresh-minted Cro-Magnons happened in, and, finding game plentiful and the climate to their liking, stayed. The only entrance, a narrow, snow-clogged pass, was easy to defend even with Paleolithic ordnance. So the proto-Gravinians retained the integrity of blood and territory, while clans displaced clans in violent feuds outside. Their language, too, developed without interference.

There had been attempts to link Gravinic with other pre-Indo-European remnants: Basque, Finnish, the *Tiktiksprache* of certain Baltic islands. None were convincing. As far as was known, Gravinic constituted a linguistic family in and of itself.

I found myself paying as much attention to McTaggett himself as I did to the content of his lecture. He was tall, of course, shocked with red hair, strangely wide in the shoulders and tapered thereafter. When he was speaking he paced out the blackboard side of the classroom, almost stomping, like a coach facing an inevitable loss. I noticed with some embarrassment that the students around me were all writing furiously. I had not even brought a notebook.

Gravinian folklore had it (McTaggett went on) that the country had been founded by two ancient monarchs, called King Speaker and King Listener. Listener was perfectly attuned to the needs and desires of his subjects; a single word, it was said, would suffice for any petition to him. Speaker's gift was to issue royal decrees in language so stirring and precise that it was considered a privilege to obey them. There was no archeological evidence for the existence of this colorful pair. The going theory had the Gravinian state developing gradually out of the usual communalistic sentiments, without the intervention of any individual figures worth noting.

The Gravine's modern history was no less placid. Now and then an aspiring emperor would lay claim to it; but the valley was mineral-poor and unstrategically placed, and no foreign ruler had ever exerted sovereignty there in more than name. At the time of McTaggett's lecture the Gravine was a semiautonomous district of the U.S.S.R. The Soviet government had changed the name of the capital to Beriagrad but had otherwise left the place alone. That was where it stood.

That night I told Julia I was quitting art history. She took it well. The fact was, I hadn't been much good at art, and both of us knew it. When I told her I was taking Gravinic she wrinkled her nose.

"Just so long as you don't speak it in the house," she said.

It was months, it turned out, before I could speak it at all. The Roman alphabet had arrived in the Gravine too late to exert much normative force on the spoken language. Pronunciation was governed by a staggering collection of diacritical marks, haphazardly applied. But the pronunciation was simple compared to the task of constructing a grammatical sentence. Gravinic, like Latin, had its cases: its nominative, genitive, accusative, dative, and ablative. But then, too, there was the locative, the transformative, the restorative, the stative; the operative and its tricky counterpart, the cooperative; the justificative, the terminative, the reiterative, the extremely popular pejorative, the restive, the suggestive, the collective, the palliative, the argumentative, the supportive, the reclusive and the preclusive, the intuitive and the counter-intuitive, the vocative and the provocative, the pensive, the defensive, the plaintive . . .

As the declension of the Gravinic noun dragged on, the enrollment of our class declined alongside. One morning in December, I found myself the only one left. The boy-woman, my last classmate, had left the field.

A little self-conscious, I sat in my usual place, opened my notebook, and cocked my pen just as if a roomful of students were following along.

"Don't be embarrassed," McTaggett said. "This happens every year. Shall we just call it an A minus and go home?"

For a moment I was tempted. I had never had an A minus. But I wanted to continue. True, the forced march through the Gravinic inflections was grinding, thankless work. But I had never before submitted myself to grinding, thankless work, and the hours spent at my desk—really just a card table with a forty-watt lamp clipped to the back—conferred on me a novel feeling of virtue, whose unrewardedness was a kind of reward in itself. Certainly I preferred it to the mock sportscasts I was obliged to deliver each Tuesday afternoon, trying to keep up with the action of that weekend's contest on videotape while the dullard basketball players, my fellow mass communicators, hooted at my stammering and my ignorance of the rules.

McTaggett responded to my decision with frank dismay. In all the time he'd been teaching, he admitted, no one had ever stayed on past Thanksgiving. He had no more lectures prepared. So he started me on translation right away. My source text was the sentence, "I kicked the dog." McTaggett's idea was that I would acquaint myself with the mechanics of Gravinic by producing a complete list of possible translations. The tally would run into the tens of thousands. One had to know, first of all, what sort of kick was involved—was it a field-goal swing, a sidewise foot-shove, a horizontal sweep involving the entire leg? All these, and more, called for different verbs. Was the kicking of the dog habitual, or a one-time action? Does the speaker mean to imply that the kick is apt to be repeated? And whose dog is it?

My initial interest in the language had by now transmuted itself into something like awe. Gravinic was a perfected vehicle for meaning—*exact* meaning. All the shadings I'd lived by, all the little contradictions, were exposed in its vocabulary, drawn apart and fixed in place like moths on pins. Had I spoken Gravinic from the start, I thought, I could never have been so vain. Precision was vanity's enemy. And while I knew that my heart still harbored certain pretensions, the occasional self-delusion, I was certain these too would disintegrate in light; as soon as I'd learned enough words.

English, by contrast, was a rough and debased slang, a rickety, jury-rigged cant thrown together in a historical instant for less-than-noble purposes. When I spoke English it seemed impossible to get my nuances across, and so I spoke less. The Gravine and its language consumed my imagination as nothing had since my old dreams of New York. And the Gravine was better—for how likely was it that I would ever find a Gravinian to disillusion me?

Julia didn't know what to make of my newfound diligence; but she seemed guardedly pleased.

"I like seeing you so worked up about something," she said. "Maybe you've found your calling."

My calling! Lofty ideas like that made me shivery and nauseous. If I thought too long about them I broke out. But it was true that I had little inclination to do anything else.

"Could be," I said.

I fell into a strict routine. Each night at six o'clock I would walk to the carryout at the corner and order from the scowling Greek there an egg salad sandwich for myself, and another dinner—it varied from night to night—for Julia. Then I returned to the apartment, settled myself at my makeshift desk, ate one half of my sandwich, and got down to work. On the left side of my desk was piled my output so far: hundreds of sheets of rag bond typing paper, twelve Gravinic sentences written on each in my narrow, exacting hand. I kept my page-in-progress on the right side of the desk, and my blank typing paper stacked on the floor to the right of my chair. My copy of Kaufmann's *Gravinic Philology* lay heavily in my lap, the space on my desk being exhausted. And on the floor to my left sat the remaining half of my egg salad sandwich in its wax paper. This is how I worked: I would foray through the creaking, gold-bordered pages of Kaufmann until I came to whatever grammatical nicety I was wrestling with at the moment, and then, having settled the syntactic point, turn to the dictionary at the end of the book to retrieve the appropriate words, if they were there. If, as was often the case, they were not, I had to twist myself in my chair to consult the heap of supplementary dictionaries behind me on the floor. Finally I returned to the first section of Kaufmann to determine what morphological adjustments would be necessary. When I was satisfied that I had produced a grammatical Gravinic sentence declaring (or intimating, postulating, regretting) that its speaker had, at some particular moment, kicked in a particular manner a particular sort of dog which stood in some particular relation to the speaker, the kick, and the generalities of time and space—in all, a process of about five minutes' duration—I committed my work to the sheet of paper at my right, with a red ballpoint pen, leaving enough space so that the page would hold just twelve sentences. If the sentence happened to be the twelfth, I would pause in my work to read the whole page aloud, quite slowly, so that I had time to recall the exact phonetic value of each umlaut, hook, and slash. I added the page to the finished stack at my left and replaced it with a blank sheet from my pile on the floor. Then I rewarded myself with one bite of my sandwich. At the resulting rate of approximately one bite per hour, I finished my dinner at around midnight, at which point it was my custom and Julia's to go to bed.

There, she asked me about my night's work, and made me recite from it; she laughed delightedly at my struggles with the unfamiliar consonants.

"You just said one twice," she'd say, and I'd go back, repeating, trying to illuminate the difference between the dental and semipalatal *t*, the proper position of the tongue.

Or: "What does that one mean?"— although of course she already knew.

"I kicked the dog," I told her, pretending to think about it, playing along.

"That poor dog," she said. "Every single night."

"It depends on the translation. Tonight the dog deserved it."

She pursed her lips like a skeptical child; but what followed was adult enough, and any doubts I may have had were put aside.

I'm wondering now what sort of impression I've given of Julia. I had taken her at first for a free spirit, a carpe-deist—mostly, perhaps, on the basis that she was willing to sleep with me. I had thought we'd always be doing foolish and impressive things, things she'd have to drag me into but that afterwards I'd agree we couldn't have missed. But she was not exactly that type. I had assumed—on the same basis—that she had been promiscuous; but in fact, I was only her third lover (how I hate that word) and by far the one she had least made to wait. She had withheld herself, I learned, even from the carnie who'd made off with her. "I think I meant to do it," she said, "but somehow my back hurt from all the driving and there was never a convenient time." No barefoot cartwheels through the sprinklers for Julia, no sudden changes of hair color, never a ludicrous purchase. She wasn't shy, but only duty made her really sociable. With my parents she was easy and deferent; she praised my mother's couscous and seemed, even to me, to mean it. At heart, I'd learned, she was deeply domestic; she seemed happy enough staying home with me, sitting at her desk in the opposite leg of our L, writing her thesis as my egg salad waned.

She must never have imagined we would stay together so long. I think her idea, conscious or not, was to do something about my awfulness; and that, by now, she had accomplished. But something made her stay. I do not want to exaggerate my charms. It may be that I was still more awful than I thought.

Thinking back now, it seems to me that those dog-kicking weeks were the happiest time I have known. I have it absolutely clear: the comforting hum and clack of Julia's electric typewriter from around the corner, so sharp I imagine I can reproduce the rhythm of it, whole sentences at a time. Effortlessly I can call to mind the taste of egg yolk and mayonnaise lingering on my tongue and on the ridge behind my teeth; and I could describe, if I chose, every flaw in the bricks of the wall I faced. On that wall, just above the edge of my desk, someone (a long-ago line worker, I supposed) had chiseled out the words, "THIS IS THE LIFE." At the time it must have been ironic. But for me—my hyperextended tantrum of an adolescence forgotten, my meeting with Higgs and all that followed still ahead—it was the plain truth. What could I do but agree? Guilelessly, with all my heart?

CHAPTER 3

LITTLE BUG, LITTLE BUG

One morning in January, McTaggett asked me about my plans for the future. We were sitting in the shabby coffee shop where we had shifted our meetings some weeks before. Our relationship, removed from the classroom, had grown informal. As often as not we would pass over the elided ultrasubjunctive entirely and devote our hour to departmental politics, the day's news, the generally degraded status of the college and the state. McTaggett always looked unhappy; on occasion he visibly despaired, and the best mood he ever mustered was downcast. At the same time he took a frantic interest in my own good cheer. Whenever I showed any reaction to one of his gloomy anecdotes, he seemed startled and ashamed.

"Hey, but no," he'd say, "don't let this old man get you down. Hang in there. Buck up. Smile and it seems like the whole world's also smiling, what do you say? Let's get back to work. Good Lord, I'm a bore." Then he would release a thin chuckle, to forestall any earnest contradictions I might offer. I began to think of us as friends.

So when McTaggett asked what I expected to be doing after graduation, I took it as an off-hand query, one friend to another, and therefore—instead of replying so as to impress him, or at least so as to avoid embarrassment—I answered him honestly.

"I have no idea," I said. "I'm a mass communications major. I'll probably go work in my parents' restaurant."

It was not, actually, the strict truth. I had some idea of writing, which was partly a vestige of my youthful idealization of New York and the poets, partly a long-nursed desire to correct the follies of my former acquaintances by satirizing them, transparently disguised, in print. But I had never worked very hard at writing, nor had I displayed much ability when I had worked at all. So I'd mostly given up on literary immortality. My expectation of waiting tables at the Grape Arbor (and in no restaurant had that job more accurately been called "waiting") had, by that time, hardened to a near-certainty.

"Mass communications," McTaggett said. "With the basketball team."

"Most of them, yes."

"All of them," he told me. "We keep track of these things."

Up on the counter next to us was a glass case in which a blistery corned beef sat half-submerged in its own juice, like an island where a horrible test had taken place.

"Have you given any thought to graduate study?" McTaggett asked.

Strangely, I hadn't. Graduate school was certainly the first refuge of the directionless, in those days as always. But I had started college with the idea that school was to be gotten through at top speed, with head down; and despite all that had changed I had never really let that idea go. It had not occurred to me to stay a moment longer than was necessary to be certified a bachelor of arts.

McTaggett went on: I did not, of course, possess the ordinary qualifications to enter a doctoral program in Gravinic. He assured me that in my case the department would be willing to waive the requirements. I gathered their cooperativeness was related to the fact that there was just one graduate student left in the department, and he was receiving his degree in June. Even so, McTaggett insisted, I was an excellent candidate on my own account. Simply by virtue of attendance I was the most promising undergraduate in years.

I raised the question of my finances. Through a series of part-time jobs which do not rate mention here I had managed to pay my rent so far. But I was often fired; and I could certainly not afford tuition for graduate school. McTaggett coughed. There were no teaching fellows in Gravinic, the faculty being embarrassingly adequate for the courses offered. And the professors, given the slightness of their pedagogical responsibilities, needed no assistance with their research. However, there was one job available, a position about to be vacated by the graduate student now departing, and which, McTaggett told me, I was already qualified to take on. That job, of course, was listening to Higgs.

"I can understand if this all sounds dreary to you," McTaggett said. "Go ahead and say no."

"I'll take it," I told him.

He brightened; that is, his mournfulness became briefly less intense. "Wonderful," he said, "that's just wonderful." Then, as a sort of afterthought, earnest and final as a deathbed conversion: "Welcome to the family!"

Julia took the news well. We agreed that she would apply to the doctoral program in her own department, where she, like me, had become something of a favorite. In fact, she had already considered staying on; but knowing my feelings about the university, she had not yet broached the subject. She was delighted at my change of heart.

"But this Higgs," she said doubtfully.

"What about him?"

"Don't you think it's a little creepy? Thirteen years without saying a word?"

She had a certain way of tucking in her lower lip that meant she was being practical.

"I wouldn't worry," I said. "I doubt he's going to *kill* anybody."

"That's not necessarily what I meant."

"If he tries anything funny I'll be ready. I'll kick the knife out of his hand. I'll get physical with extreme prejudice." And by way of demonstration I seized Julia around the waist.

"What if he resists?" asked Julia, crooking one arm behind my neck.

"I'll sacrifice myself to save the world." And together, tussling, we plunged to the mattress.

Later, awake before dawn, I reconsidered Julia's question. Did I think Higgs was creepy? Honestly, I'd hardly thought of him at all. Stanley Higgs, my charge, was little more to me than a name I'd seen on the flyleaves of translations, in bibliographies, in the earlier issues of the *Journal of the Henderson Society;* although once, as a freshman, I had telephoned his house.

An acquaintance of mine from high school, a year older than I, had prevailed upon me to rush his fraternity. I had repeatedly explained to this acquaintance my feelings toward the university's social organization in general and Greek life in particular; but in the end his pallish persistence overcame my surliness—or, as I would have put it then, my principles. So I went to the rush party, eager to detest everyone and everything I saw. I had decided that I would stand in a corner and speak rudely to everyone who approached, so that my acquaintance would suffer a social blow for having brought me. I was a success at standing in the corner; but no one approached, so there was not much to do but drink cup after cup of the sweet, rummy punch that was back there with me, and about an hour after I arrived, following a sequence of events which I am unable to reconstruct, I found myself standing before a battered Princess phone, surrounded by a circle of cheering fraternity men and men-to-be. My acquaintance took me by the shoulder.

"You gotta call Higgs," he said. He handed me a beery scrap of paper with a telephone number on it.

"Who's Higgs?" I asked him, but he had vanished into the crowd. A rhythmic chant set in: *Go! Go! Go! Go!* And nothing would have pleased me better than to go. But the men in the circle were by and large large, much more so than I, and I did not believe I had much chance of breaking through. So I picked up the phone. At this, the crowd grew quiet. I dialed the number and after three rings a woman answered, not *Hello?* but *Yes?* Behind her there was country music playing.

"I was wondering if I could please speak to Mr. Higgs," I said weakly. I realized I sounded even drunker than I was. I had no idea what I might say next. But the woman just put down the phone.

"She hung up," I said, turning to my audience, managing a smile. And the crowd swept over me, pounded my back, handed me a beer, within seconds forgot about me. My acquaintance found me just as I reached the front door.

"You're a lock," he said. "They loved you." But I never went back.

My project throughout the winter and spring was to translate a collection of Gravinian nursery rhymes into English. These were different from the little verses I had known as a child; they were more like aphorisms, or, speaking loosely, haiku. Most of them concerned a character named Little Bug, a generalized figure of youth and folly. There was one of these that stuck doggedly in my mind. In Gravinic it formed a series of perfect dactyls, which by an unfortunate chance coincided exactly with the endless TACK-eta of something inside our radiator; so I seemed always to be hearing it, whenever the nights got cold. My English version of the rhyme went as follows:

> *Little Bug, Little Bug, my son Little Bug,*
> *It is time to do your lessons for school,*
> *Hurry, hurry, hurry, Little Bug!*
> *Or Mama will throw you to the jackals.*

This was typical. Gravinian nursery rhymes were all alike in their earnest didacticism, their brevity, and their termination in sudden, usually unpleasant surprises. As I shouldn't need to point out by this time, my translation fails to capture the full meaning of the source text. The original, for instance, strongly implies that the jackals in line

77

4 are not a vague and distant threat, but rather a specific set of jack-als, probably nearby, very possibly inside the house. In English all this is lost—and with it, I think, the verse's special charm.

Late in May, as the term and my desultory college career limped to a close, the Department of Gravinics held a party. It was the first pleasant day after a week of rain and threats of rain. I'd been told to come at 2:00; when I arrived, with Julia in tow, at quarter-past, the party was already well underway. The whole of the faculty was spread out across the patchy lawn. I pointed them out to Julia one by one. There—I gestured—was Rosso, emeritus now, and there beside him on an iron bench, Lionel, Prince, and Treech; there was Jervis, the social historian, waving his hands a little fearsomely at a pair of musicologists; there was a knot of medievalists beneath a hungry-looking tree; there was Little, the dialectician, standing thoughtfully alone.

"Where're the wives?" Julia asked me. "At ours we have wives."

"I don't think there are very many," I said. "These guys are like nuns. They're married to it."

Tip Chandler, too, had been a lifelong bachelor, a fact of which certain elements of the faculty had recently made much.

"Like nuns," Julia said. "I suppose it's a living."

McTaggett was bustling over a hastily erected hibachi. When he caught my gaze he released the meat to someone else's charge and hurried over to where Julia and I stood in the building's shade.

"It's always the same," he said, grandly morose, "burnt on the out-side, raw on the inside." He wiped his forehead with one big hand, then offered that hand to Julia. "I'm Greg McTaggett."

She shook his hand a little longer than was necessary, giving me a look: *See what I go through*. "So can I ask you a question?" she said.

"I'll do my best."

"Why are there so many professors in a department without any students?"

One of the professors nearby was saying, "Yes, yes"—as if this question had been bothering him too, but until now he had been unable to put it precisely into words.

"Good question," McTaggett said. "We have a grant from the Henderson Society to keep the positions filled. Mr. Kosugi takes a personal interest in our department, fortunately for us."

"The radio man," Julia said.

"Well," I announced, "a hamburger for me is great. Anybody want anything?"

My interruption, though calculated, was not insincere. The Grape Arbor's legacy to me: I find an ordinary hamburger difficult to resist.

"Nothing," Julia said.

"Be careful," McTaggett said. "They're raw on the inside."

The man McTaggett had left tending the grill stuck out a hand at my approach.

"Sam Grapearbor?" He was a thin, grayish man of an indeterminate middle age. The wide set of his eyes and the tilt of his brows made him seem on the verge of panic.

"I am that man," I said, shaking his hand; it was unpleasantly warm from the heat of the grill.

"Frank Slotkin," he told me. "I'm the one whose job you're taking." His voice was papery, reminiscent of seclusion.

We exchanged pleasantries about our work: me about my nursery rhymes, he about the revolutionary bread-factory poet, the subject of his dissertation. Then a silence fell.

"The job's not bad," Slotkin said finally. "It's dull. But if you don't mind dull it's not bad."

"I wouldn't think so."

"Ellen—his wife—she can be a little off-putting. But in the end it's not a real problem."

"That's good to hear."

He nodded; I nodded. Off-putting? The smell of burned meat hung thickly between us.

"You can get a lot of work done," Slotkin said. He nodded again. I had the feeling he was trying to warn me of something I couldn't quite make out; maybe something *he* couldn't quite make out.

"After a while it's like being alone," he said. The wind picked up and seemed to blow something out of his face. "Hamburger?" He chiseled one off the grill.

"Actually, maybe later," I said. I turned back toward Julia and McTaggett. Slotkin followed my gaze. Julia waved to me with half her hand. The wind was buffeting her dress back into a triangle, extending behind and away from her like low wings.

"Your girlfriend?" Slotkin asked.

"Yes," I said, strangely giddy; as if I were getting away with some three-quarters-truth. I started to go.

"Oh," he said.

I turned around.

"He likes checkers."

Checkers, I thought, as I walked back, hamburgerless. Everybody likes checkers. I like checkers. How could he have said it would be dull?

"I see you met Slotkin," McTaggett said. "Did he give you some useful advice?"

"He said Higgs's wife was off-putting."

"Did he?"

McTaggett clasped his hands behind him, considered.

"I'm not sure I'd be willing to go that far myself."

"It must be hard on her," Julia said.

He started, as if he'd forgotten she was there.

"Well, yes," he said. "I imagine it must."

I still didn't know what "off-putting" meant. But I found I was unable to keep my mind on it for long; something about the steady wash of sun, the smell of the drying ground, the drizzle of smoke that jaunted crookedly up from the grill, forbade all thoughts but the simplest. It's warm, I thought. McTaggett's here. Julia's here. I turned my face up to the sun and shut my eyes, staring out into the red of my lids as endless as a new sky. I smell grass, I thought. I'm hungry.

"Wasn't so bad, right?" I asked Julia, as we walked home, down Anaxagoras. On the corner ahead of us an old man with steel-wool hair was selling hurt books off a table.

"I liked Professor McTaggett."

"He's likable."

After a while I said, "So you're glad you went?"

"As the saying goes, I'm not sure I'd be willing to go that far myself."

"Fair enough—glad's a strong word."

"Glad," Julia said, "is a strong plastic bag."

It was only when Julia felt weary that she came out with nonsensical, unanswerable jokes like that. Since we'd settled on staying in Chandler City she felt weary more often than before; though staying had been her idea all along. Next her mood would turn cold and she would make a remark. I could see it warring in her face with her natural disposition toward kindness and pluck. Her skin absorbed the late light, reddening to match her freckles and the bricks of the warehouses.

"Those guys are weird," she said, without inflection. "Are you going to get like that too?"

At these moments I felt—well, stomach-churning fear, yes, the kind I was used to at any danger or rebuke, but, too, a cheery, vigorous, obligatory lightness. I'd grab her under the shoulders and haul her out of despond; if it took a low distracting joke, if it took a pratfall, if it took a spray of apologies. Even if I had to resort to sentimental compliments, I'd buoy her up.

"What—weird? Obviously not, not me."

"They remind me of your college friends."

"Oh, no," I said. "They could be the way they are now, and also eat baby harp seals, while listening to Depeche Mode, and they would not be as bad as my college friends."

But I knew what she meant. The professors had something in common, something I couldn't place. Not the same as my college friends, whose afflictions were simple, nasty things. With the professors it was something subtler: there was a shared insubstantiality, a harried look, a way of talking as if the words they were saying had been selected and conjoined years back, and were just now finding their exhausted way out. Sometimes their feet seemed insecurely attached to the earth. I could have told Julia all this. But I didn't think I could make sense of it. And I felt it would be better, now and in the future, if she thought it were all in her mind.

Julia's face lightened a little and I saw she'd accepted, for now, my offer of repair.

"You're right," she said. "They could all have Hitler mustaches and they wouldn't be as bad as your college friends."

"Maybe as bad as Wickman; Wickman wasn't so bad." And as I mentioned his name I was visited, against, you must believe, my will, by a vision of Wickman, engaged with Julia's Mohawked friend in the very sex act he'd invited himself to perform upon her, these many months past. With pleasure I shared this grim and hilarious picture with Julia. We forgot the professors, her weariness, and my forced charm, and cheered by this impossible reminiscence we progressed home in a spirit of tenderness and sport.

Shortly afterwards, I graduated. Julia and I spent commencement day in bed, playing Sink, a game of our own invention. One of us would propose a place—Greenland, say—which the world, in our opinion, would do as well without. Then we would focus our psychokinetic powers and by the combined force of our thought send the chosen place to its watery rest.

"Trinidad," I suggested; Julia made no objection; down it went. Julia countered with Kentucky. Just like that, a new Great Lake. "Sink Los Angeles," I said.

"We already *sunk* Los Angeles."

"Sink it deeper, then. Make it a trench."

We pressed our fingers to our temples, ground our jaws; it was so.

Our diplomas came in the mail two days later. "Isn't it exciting?" Julia said, hugging me. "We're adults now."

And it *was* exciting. My four years of imprisonment were over; I no longer had any institutional ties to Chandler City. I still had no money, but I was certified as educated, and was somewhat wordly-wiser. I could leave any time I wished.

But—here's the exciting part now—I didn't want to go. Without my noticing it the prospect of staying put had become not so terrible. In our low, oily L Julia and I had constructed our own miniature city-state. The striped, porridgy mattress at the room's elbow served as our seat of government; our respective desks became a pair of companionably feuding baronies; and the lone window on the east-facing wall was a view through a mountain pass to the vast disorderly world of life-sized countries. Who needed that world? Not me, not us. Aside from the sandwich-selling Greek at the corner we were entirely self-sufficient.

I visited Higgs's house for the first time three weeks later, on a Saturday, the fifteenth of June.

"Ides," I told McTaggett. He had thought it best to come along and introduce me.

"No," he said, "you missed them. The ides of June are the thirteenth."

"I guess that's a good omen."

"If you insist," McTaggett said.

A flagstone path ran down to the house. The lawn on either side looked like a haircut abandoned halfway through.

"Ready?" McTaggett said.

He rang the bell; through the heavy mahogany door the sound was soft and queerly unresonant. There was music in the house, but I couldn't make out what.

When Ellen Higgs opened the door the music swept out and smacked us like a palm. I took an involuntary step backward, almost tripping, and pressed my hands against my ears. It was a Latin song playing—marimbas loud as wrecking balls, trumpets like eighteen-wheelers skidding to a stop. McTaggett remained on the doorstep, apparently unaffected.

Experimentally I angled my hands a bit outward, so that my ears were slightly uncovered. The music was loud, but not so painfully loud as before. The initial surprise had been the worst. Bracing myself, I dropped my hands and stepped up to meet Mrs. Higgs.

She was not what I had expected; that is to say, not a harridan, a cleaver-wielding harpy, Clytemnestra in a housedress. Instead I saw a mild-looking woman of about fifty, in a checked blouse, her eyes a pale surprised blue. She seemed to have been unexpectedly called away from something—but I learned after a while that she always looked like that.

"Mrs. Higgs," McTaggett shouted, "I want you to meet Samuel Grapearbor."

"He's the new one?" Her voice cut through the racket like a bell—like a disapproving bell, a schoolbell. Now that my ears were adjusting I was beginning to discern other sounds beneath the din of the radio: a clattering fan, a Spanish newscast, a straining, grinding whine that I thought might be a malfunctioning blender. McTaggett put his hand on my shoulder and guided me through the door, into the dim and empty foyer.

"Is Professor Higgs downstairs?" McTaggett asked.

"Where else?"

McTaggett turned to me. "Then down we go."

So the two of us started down the stairs; and when we reached the bottom I forgot the noise, forgot my nervousness. Neither Slotkin nor McTaggett had bothered to prepare me for my first sight of Higgs's astounding basement.

I have already mentioned that the house had once belonged to the university's anthropology department. The move had been hurried, and the anthropologists had used the excuse of haste to leave behind everything they didn't want: specimens which were duplicates, or demonstrably forged, or simply poor examples of their kind. In all the years the Higgses had lived there, they (I mean Ellen) had never seen fit to get rid of it all.

The basement was a little, stuffy room, packed halfway up the wall with the anthropologists' unsorted leftovers: flint blades and arrowheads, fat daikoku, fertility dolls, chipped pots and fragments of pots, Kachinas of various provenances, tiny woven mats, handleless vases, noseless statues, chisels, pestles, adzes, scattered across the concrete floor, heaped in the corners, without regard for function or origin. A few exasperated-looking masks hung from sills beneath a row of half-height windows. In places the floor was three deep in tattered prayer rugs. It was as if the world's forgotten cultures had pooled their meager resources and mounted a garage sale.

Across from the stairs there was a richly filigreed sarcophagus, wide open, and inside it a wrapped, mummified corpse. ("Twentieth-century forgery," McTaggett explained to me later. "A couple of Belgians dug up an Arab and pickled him. A real one wouldn't last a month in this climate.") Next to the Arab was the only evidence of modern times: the bank of tape recorders which were to capture Higgs's remarks, when and if they came.

For the second time in five minutes, I stumbled backwards in dismay.

"I should have told you," McTaggett whispered, shaking his head. "Stupid of me not to have thought."

I mention Higgs himself last because, to be honest, he was the last thing I noticed. He was sitting in the far corner of the room at a round card table, facing us, apparently unperturbed by my novel presence. He looked much as he had in the newspaper photographs from thirteen years before; older, of course, but the architecture of his face was the same, his haircut, even the musty-looking shirt he wore.

(But there was one difference, one I didn't know about. Higgs's gaze, by the time I met him, no longer flickered from person to person, near to far; instead it was steady, fixed on an unexceptional point in space, a few feet in front of his sheepdog eyes.)

"Professor Higgs," McTaggett said, "this is Samuel Grapearbor. He'll be sitting with you from now on." McTaggett inclined his head toward the chair opposite Higgs; dutifully, I sat.

"I'm going," he said. "Well. Good luck." He clomped upstairs. Faintly, under the music, I heard the front door open and shut.

So this is it, I thought. Postgraduate education.

I slid my chair over to what I estimated to be the focal point of Higgs's gaze. "Hello, Professor Higgs," I said, experimentally. "I'm a great admirer of your work."

His fixed stare and the unrelenting calm of his expression made me nervous, the way a defective child makes one nervous, but worse in this case because I knew he was *not* defective; I had to keep reminding myself that Higgs was no doubt executing a mental description of me, even as I was of him. And what must he have thought of me? Probably not much. To him I was just another entry in the long undifferentiated series of young men who had shared his cluttered basement, waiting for him to speak.

Of course, I was special; I was the last one. But even Higgs could not have known that yet.

My duties were simple. I was required to stay with Higgs from nine in the morning until eight o'clock at night, when Ellen would take him up to bed. The tape recorders were staggered, so that reels ran out at every even-numbered hour. When a tape ended, I was to remove it from the recorder, label it with date and time, and replace it with a fresh one from the cabinet behind the mummy. Were Higgs actually to speak, I was supposed to move into my position across from him at the table and record, in a stenographer's notebook provided me for this purpose, whatever gestures and expressive actions accompanied his words. Barring that, all I had to do was wait. It was dull, all right. I wished now that I had brought some work to do.

At half-past eleven Ellen came downstairs dragging an electric vacuum cleaner behind her like a reluctant dance partner. The machine
set to a furious screw-loose clattering the moment she turned it on. She
took care to cover every part of the floor, some more than once; often
the fringe of a rug or the end of a flax rope would catch in the nozzle
and the noise would excite itself to an even higher, more discomfiting
pitch. When she was finished, not having spoken a word, she disappeared upstairs. An hour later, she came back down and started over.

"This place must collect a lot of dust," I said, as congenially as I
could.

Ellen ignored me. She kicked aside a pile of eccentric grindstones
and vacuumed the immaculate floor underneath. I was struck suddenly
by the absurd fear that she had recognized my voice from my drunken
phone call, three years before; that she was waiting for me to apologize,
or worse, that she had no interest in my apologies. I pushed it aside.

"Saturday's a good day for housecleaning," I offered.

She lifted up a stack of thatch something-covers and a dozen or so
insects leaped out, bouncing into far corners and disappearing before
I'd gotten a good look.

"You've got crickets?" I asked.

"Grasshoppers," she said. "They've been down here since we
moved in. We tried poisoning them." Then her face closed up. She
seemed angry that I had gotten her to speak.

Later in the day I went upstairs to look around, on the pretext of
needing to use the bathroom. I was desperate for something to do. I
had picked up, looked over, and set down every slingshot and bridle
in the place—some twice. I had made my egg salad sandwich last an
hour and a half.

The above-ground portion of the house, now that I had seen the
basement, was stirringly ordinary; although in isolation it might have
been a bit unnerving. The light filtering through the poured-glass
window was gray and cool, more like March than June, and the house
had a shut-in, bookish smell, although there were no books anywhere.

In fact, there was not much of anything anywhere. By means of some slow gravity the upstairs was as empty as the basement was full. There were no tables in sight, no coatrack; no chairs, no shelves, not even any lamps. The only furniture I could see was Ellen's stereo, which squatted at the center of a Stonehenge of speakers, its equalizer lights fluctuating now to the beat of an auto commercial. I'd been in the house eight hours and already it didn't seem so loud.

I nearly collided with Ellen in the foyer.

"Yes?" she said—hostile, frank.

"The bathroom . . ."

She jerked her head leftward at a door I hadn't noticed.

The bathroom, unsurprisingly, was bare; but tucked under the lower rim of the mirror there was some minor ornament, miraculously left in place. Looking closer, I saw it was a remote microphone. McTaggett had explained this to me. There was a pick-up in every room but the bedroom, wired to the banks of recorders downstairs. Wherever Higgs decided to hold forth, the apparatus would be ready.

Even the water was loud. When the toilet flushed it sounded like a jetliner launching through hail.

Back downstairs, no vehicles for amusement having sprung up in my absence, I suddenly remembered Slotkin's last piece of advice.

"You want to play checkers, Professor Higgs?"

Not even a flicker in return. But I was too bored to be deterred. I found the checkerboard propped up by the sarcophagus.

"We're going to play some checkers now, okay?" It comforted me to keep talking. "Here we go . . . I'm setting up the board now. I'm going first."

During my preparations Higgs's gaze had not once deviated from its position; but as soon as I had made my opening move, his eyes snapped down to the board. He moved his man. Within five minutes he had beaten me handily. We played six more games and I lost every one.

"You're very good, Professor Higgs," I said, and although his expression did not, of course, change, I postulated a slow inner smile, imagined him luxuriating in the idea of a new opponent, someone else to teach, slowly and by example, working upward through the levels of strategy, postponing as long as possible the despairing moment when both players' knowledge of the game was exactly equal. With Slotkin that moment must have been years past.

When I came home that night there was a lasagna on the bed. It was piled into a stewpot, a little lopsided, and under its weight our sad mattress sagged almost to the floor.

"Hi, breadwinner," Julia said. "What do you think?"

"It looks great," I said, a little guiltily; guiltily because my first reaction, when the startling smell of a cooked and actual meal had met me at the door, had been to think, *I'm in the wrong place.*

"I got the recipe from our secretary. And the pot is from the kitchenette in my old dorm."

We sat down on either side of the bed and dug ambitiously in. "How was the first day?" Julia asked me. Beneath the first layer of noodles the cheese was waxy and cold. Strangely, this touched off in me a little hubbub of affection.

"I couldn't wait to get home," I said.

Meanwhile, I was learning more about Henderson. By the time I came to the subject, his life story had been scavenged and glued into something that almost made sense. It turned out Henderson was the terminus of a somewhat noble English line, which had been reduced by the end of the nineteenth century to landlessness and progressive politics. In 1895, his parents, reckoning correctly that no proletarian revolution was imminent in Britain, picked up their meager stakes and moved east. They settled in the Gravine as party organizers, and, when the revolution finally came, were rewarded for their efforts by being purged. Henderson left for Berlin a month later. He stayed there until 1940, when, having somehow run afoul of the Nazis, he fled to London.

In the intervening years he wrote, and he published; mostly, that is, he copied out his verses in his own painstaking hand, and passed them out at streetcorners, or in parks, or in front of churches and banks. On one occasion he released a hundred copies of "Vile Mouse Conspiracy" from the roof of an apartment house in Potsdam. (That was what had gotten him the littering citation.) His poems, which he carefully marked with the date of composition and his initial "H," formed a more or less complete record of his time in Berlin. The only break of any size was a six-month interval in 1932, which time, Henderson intimated later, he had spent in Holland. He never said why.

McTaggett had me working on a short story of Henderson's that had appeared, with the author's own impenetrable translation alongside, in a 1922 number of an agrarian-feudalist monthly called *Tractor*. Each day I brought the story with me to Higgs's house, where I sat in the chair across from him, translating, my copy of Kaufmann on the table between us, trying to ignore the racket from upstairs. I had hoped that the sight of Henderson's text in the original Gravinic might catch Higgs's attention—in vain. Only the checkerboard could stir him. We played fifteen or twenty games each afternoon. I had gotten into the habit of making a running commentary as we played, partly to hear the sound of a voice, and partly to convey the idea that my attitude toward the game was one of detached amusement, that it was nothing more than a mildly entertaining respite from my work, one about which I maintained a healthy sense of humor, and that it certainly did not matter to me when I lost—which was every single time.

"A costly miscue by Grapearbor," I'd say, as Higgs laid me open with a triple jump. "The champion wastes no time taking advantage of the upstart challenger's childish blunder." Then, a little later: "Grapearbor's defense is in disarray. Ladies and gentlemen, the desperation is palpable. It appears Grapearbor has no chance . . . and Higgs jumps Grapearbor's final man. This one is history. Higgs is the winner."

When Higgs played checkers, he made a small continuous sound, deep in his throat, a bit like a growl but with no connotation of menace. It was as if the checker-playing segment of him had grown noisy with age and overuse, like Ellen's vacuum cleaner. I noticed the sound only after a few days; it took me that long to pick it out under the general din from upstairs. Ellen would change the channel on the radio now and then, to keep me distracted, I supposed, and some days would leave the tuner between stations, besieging me with static and the distant, panicky voices of churchmen. Even so, I learned in time to hear the smaller noises: Higgs's sound, and the collective murmur of the grasshoppers, which was loudest in the morning and faded as the day wore on. Each day Ellen came down four or five times with the vacuum; each time I tried vainly to engage her in conversation. I was no longer trying to be friendly. Now it was one hundred percent spite.

"Take it easy on her," Julia advised me, "you can't blame her for not wanting you there. You wouldn't want you there, if you were her."

This counterfactual gave us both pause.

"But I *am* there," I said. "It's just my job to be there. It's not my fault Higgs doesn't talk."

"Maybe it's her husband she's really angry at."

That made sense, in the abstract. But I'd been there, and I knew—it was me. Though angry wasn't quite the word; people had been angry at me, for good reasons, my whole life, and I knew what that felt like. Ellen wasn't angry; she *endured* me, as if I, McTaggett, the tape recorders, the scholars, were just another alien presence sharing space in her house, like the grasshoppers. Not even worth poisoning.

Three weeks into my tenure, Professor Treech came to the house for the first time. He announced himself with a quick double knock: RAT-tat. Ellen was in the basement with me, vacuuming. When she heard Treech's knock her face folded for a moment into something quite terrible. She looked as if she had something unpleasant in her mouth but were someplace where it would be inappropriate to spit. She leaned the still-running vacuum against the wall and went upstairs to let him in. I followed, with no little interest. It was the first time since I'd been there that anyone had come.

Treech was the department's liaison to the Henderson Society. The Society had imposed on him the duty of visiting the house each month, looking over Higgs and his surroundings, and quizzing us as to the likelihood, in our opinions, of a break in the case. Ellen responded to his greeting with a silence even frostier than the one she used on me. I would not have thought it possible. With a little sniff she vanished into the kitchen.

"So you're the new man," Treech said to me, giving me an up-and-down look. He was nervous, thin, knife-nosed, a bit pocked. His hair fell in slack wings on either side of his head, giving him, as a whole, the shape of an arrow. He had a reputation as a facile and unoriginal thinker.

"That's right," I said.

Treech had nothing more to say on that subject. He clapped his hands for punctuation. "Then let's stop down and see the good Professor, shall we?" His voice took on a desperate upward lilt which might have been his attempt at jollity. I wasn't sure Treech was talking to me. But I followed him downstairs.

He checked the tape recorders first, making sure each set of heads was spinning freely. Then he asked me a few obviously memorized questions: any unusual behavior on Higgs's part, any action I could read as mute complaint, mute enlightenment, mute despair . . . No, I told him, no, no, and so on, feeling, despite myself, a little chirp of competence—this was my job, I was doing it.

Finally he came to Higgs. Treech felt his forehead, tugged at his lower eyelids, pulled up his shirt and listened to his breathing with a cheap-looking stethoscope. Higgs accepted all this impassively.

"Healthy as a horse," Treech pronounced. "Will you listen to that clapper." Here, suddenly overtaken with fellow-feeling, he walloped my shoulder with his cupped hand. "Clean living!"

"You'd have to think so," I said.

"We should all treat ourselves so well," Treech said. He deployed a sort of leer in my direction. "But, you know . . ."

I was still trying to construct some suitable reply when Treech changed the subject again. "We're going to take pictures," he said, pulling a camera from his satchel. "Mrs. Higgs!"

Ellen descended warily. "What is it?"

"Is it going to be all right if we just take some photos here? It's for the newsletter."

"It is not," she said. But Treech had already started shooting. He took one picture of the three of us, another of Ellen and Higgs, and one last shot—as Ellen reached out angrily for the camera—of her alone.

"Get out," Ellen said.

"Right away, Mrs. Higgs. See you next month."

After Treech left, Ellen vacuumed the basement for two hours straight, as if he'd left some trail that only her detective eyes could see, that only her rattling vacuum could erase. To my surprise I felt almost sorry for her.

I tried catching her eye. "Hey, what a jerk, huh?"

She straightened up.

"What Professor Treech is," she said, "is not important. I'd like it much better if you wouldn't speak to me, now that you know your way around the house."

Then she bent to her vacuum cleaner again, leaning her whole weight on it as if it were a broom. She moved behind Higgs to clean the corner; she tapped the back of his chair gently and he scooted up to give her room. No; it wasn't Higgs she was mad at. The two of them were still in league.

"The last one didn't talk at all," she said.

"All right," I said, with a hardness that unnerved me. "All right. I tried."

I was no tenderfoot; in my social career I had annoyed, and been annoyed in turn, by hundreds of people of all temperaments and stations. When my irritation with one acquaintance grew too keen to be borne, I'd move on to annoy someone else. After a week or so, I'd feel a twinge of forgiveness toward my first partner; then I knew it was time to reestablish contact, make up, and experience the slow and enjoyable build-up to antipathy once again.

With Ellen it was different; there was no decay. The moment she opened the door in the morning I was just as inflamed as I'd been the night before. Was she doing this to me on purpose? I couldn't tell. Somehow, that made it worse.

Julia suggested deep breathing. Ha! I could have chuffed like a racehorse with an "Om" on each exhale; it wouldn't have made a dent. I couldn't walk past Ellen without wanting to punch her; but I didn't punch her. It wasn't that I wouldn't punch an old woman. It was that I was afraid I might lose. She seemed like a woman who might know karate, or something more secret than karate; or who could just take my forehead in her palm and force me whimpering to the ground.

Anyway, I had another way of getting back at her, a slicker, more satisfying way. McTaggett had told me, in rough, the story of Higgs's retreat into silence, the Society's installation of the listening devices, and Ellen's futile resistance. So I knew that the absence of a microphone upstairs was a special favor granted Ellen by her father—and that seemed hardly fair. What if Higgs *did* talk in his sleep? What if Ellen's selfish desire for privacy was, all by itself, holding up the progress of human knowledge? It was only right, I assured myself, that I should take whatever steps I could to undo Dean Moresby's nepotistic leniency. If I succeeded in getting the bedroom wired up it would make Ellen furious; and at the same time it would advance the cause of learning.

Of course, I had no say in the matter. I was just a student, and a new one. I possessed no influence; I held no sway. But Treech did.

I arranged to meet him one evening at his office. The walls were covered with unimpressive-looking prizes and citations, neatly framed. On his desk there was a photo of his dog.

"My good man," he said, skinny palms pressed together. "I'm glad we're having this meeting." It did not seem quite right to shake his hand—unsure whether I was meant to come forward, I halted just inside the doorway and stood clumsily on the spot until Treech motioned me to sit in the rattan chair across the desk from him.

"You're a Henderson man," Treech said.

"I'm working on one of his stories."

"That's good," he said. "It should always be a Henderson man. So he'll feel among his own. Slotkin wasn't one."

"But there wasn't really any choice."

"No," Treech said, then was quiet for a very long time, as if the possibility of there being no choice had just occurred to him for the first time, and he were faced with the abrupt and unpleasant necessity of counting out those instances of choicelessness which he might have still to endure. "There was no choice."

"There's something I have to talk to you about," I said. At this Treech retreated from his reverie and grew businesslike. "It's about Higgs."

Treech nodded. "Naturally."

I was trying to remember everything I'd read in spy novels about how to lie. I had read spy novels mostly for the sex scenes and my memory of the actual spying was sketchy at best.

"I've been having concerns," I said.

"And bringing them to me is the right thing to do."

"About the bedroom."

"Ah—the *bed*room."

"I think"—I steadied myself—"he's talking up there."

This gave Treech pause; but only a little.

"That's potentially quite serious," he said.

"I thought you'd think so."

"Of course, the Dean's wishes on the subject are very clear. We're not in a position at this time to make any change."

"So I understand."

"If you don't mind my asking a question?"

I nodded, shoot.

"What brought on these—concerns?"

As darkly as I could: "I've heard things."

"You have."

"I think so. Just very quietly. Sometimes I get there when he's still upstairs."

"Things that sound like talking."

"Very much so."

"But the actual *words* of which you are unable to make out."

"That's right."

"Well," he said. "But if you had something more concrete."

But I wouldn't, of course, and plainly my allegations alone were not enough to spur Treech to action. Some Iago I turned out to be.

"Perhaps we'll look into it," he told me. And that was the last I heard of the matter for some time.

"How was Treech?" Julia asked me when I got home. I'd told her I was meeting him about an independent study.

"I couldn't get him interested," I said.

"You tried," Julia said, coming up behind my chair and resting her arms on my shoulders. She gave the back of my head a rub, briskly, like a Little League coach. "That's what's important."

Once, telling venial lies had been fun—where were those days now? I just felt foolish and ill. "No," I said, "trying is not important. Succeeding is important."

Her hands lifted from me, and I heard her retreat to the bed. I'd spoken more sharply than I'd meant to. Apologies bloomed in me but I tamped them down.

"Back to work," I commanded, and opened the book before me.

The story I was translating was Henderson's rendition of a traditional Gravinian folktale, "The Four Wives of Little Bug." Because so much of my time as Higgs's companion was spent translating this piece, and because an acquaintance with Little Bug's unlucky career is necessary for the understanding of certain parts of my own story, I will reproduce it here.

Once, very long ago (the tale begins) there was a boy named Little Bug, who lived on a farm with his two very wise grandmothers and his two very wise grandfathers. One day Little Bug decided that it was time for him to take a wife. His grandmothers and grandfathers attempted to dissuade him.

"If you leave us," they cried, "we will starve, for we are not strong enough to sow the harvest by ourselves. Besides, Little Bug, there is nothing to be gained from marriage but pain and heartbreak. Stay with us!"

But Little Bug was as foolish as his grandparents were wise. Unfortunately, he had gotten hold of books of a certain kind, and these books had instilled in him the idea that to have a wife was an altogether fitting and pleasant thing. So Little Bug ignored his grand-parents' pleading and set off down the road.

Little Bug's farm was in a sparsely settled part of the world and he walked for a very long time without seeing any other people. (Meanwhile, his wise grandmothers and grandfathers starved to death, just as they had predicted.) After fifty days Little Bug came to another farmhouse. In this house there lived an evil widow, her two cruel sons, and her wicked daughter Clarissa. When the widow saw Little Bug coming down the road, she rushed out to meet him; for her favorite thing in the world was to play spiteful tricks on voyagers who came that way.

"Hello, stranger!" the widow shouted cheerfully. "What brings you to our humble farm?"

"I am looking for a wife," Little Bug said.

The evil widow saw at once that Little Bug was very foolish, and in an instant she had hatched a fiendish plan.

"What sort of wife were you looking for?" the widow asked.

Little Bug thought for a long time. The question had never occurred to him before. He thought back to his books and remembered that the wives he had read about had all had long, flowing hair and long, slender legs.

"I would like a wife with long, flowing hair and long, slender legs," Little Bug replied.

"Well, you have come to the right place," the evil widow said, rubbing her hands gleefully. "I think I have just the wife you want." The widow led Little Bug into the farmhouse, then went out to the back and returned with an old mare. Her two cruel sons and her wicked daughter, Clarissa, laughed behind their hands when they saw the trick their mother was playing.

"Here she is," the widow said. She pointed out the mare's long, flowing mane and its long, slender legs. Little Bug was proud of himself for having remembered what sort of wife to ask for.

"This is the wife for me," Little Bug said. "When can we be married?"

"I'll marry you now," the evil widow said. "Fortunately for you, I happen to be a district magistrate." (About this matter she was telling the truth.) The evil widow spoke the applicable formula and pronounced Little Bug and the mare man and wife.

"You two can live in the shed out back," the evil widow said. "Now that you're part of the family, you'll do your share of the chores. We're all a little old for heavy lifting."

"Yes, ma'am," Little Bug replied. He was so happy to be married that he was hardly listening to the evil widow's words.

That night the two cruel sons crept out to the shed and peered through a crack in the boards. There they saw Little Bug coupling with the mare. The mare's legs were so long that Little Bug had to stand on a crate. It was the funniest thing the cruel sons had ever seen. They laughed and laughed, but silently so that Little Bug would not realize he was being tricked.

From then on, Little Bug did all the chores on the evil widow's farm. He tilled, planted, and sowed; he fed the goats and milked the cattle; he walked the beans; he reshuttered the windows and unstopped the chimney and sanded the splintery floors of the house. After a year, Little Bug came to the evil widow with a complaint.

"I have heard," Little Bug said, "that a wife is supposed to produce a son. Now, my wife and I have been married a year—and no son! I am beginning to wonder if you are trying to trick me."

The widow allowed a look of great contrition to overtake her features. "Why, Little Bug," she said, "you should have told me sooner. This is certainly not an acceptable state of affairs. By my authority as district magistrate I declare you divorced."

The evil widow sent one of her cruel sons out to the shed to fetch the mare. Then the son took the mare over the rise and slaughtered it.

"Tonight we will have a great feast in honor of your divorce," the evil widow said, "and then we will find you a new wife."

So that night the widow and her two cruel sons and her wicked daughter, Clarissa, and Little Bug sat down to eat Little Bug's first wife.

"This is delicious," Little Bug said. "What is it, may I ask?"

"Steak," said the evil widow.

After they had finished dinner the widow asked Little Bug, "Tell me, Little Bug, what sort of wife would you like now?"

This time Little Bug thought even harder than before. He did not want to make another mistake. Then he remembered that the wives in his books always had round, pink flesh. Perhaps this was the crucial detail.

"I want a wife with round, pink flesh," Little Bug said.

"You happen to be in luck," the evil widow said. "I have just the wife for you." And she went out back and returned with a sow.

"Notice the flesh," the evil widow said.

"This is the wife for me," said Little Bug.

That night the two cruel sons crept out to the shed once again, and once again peered through the crack in the boards, in order to see Little Bug coupling with the sow. This spectacle was even funnier than the one provided by the mare. Little Bug was chasing the sow around and around the shed but could not get a grip on her smooth sides. This time the cruel sons had to press their faces against the boards to keep their laughter in.

So Little Bug went back to doing all the chores of the farm. After another year had passed, he came back to speak with the widow.

"It has been another year," Little Bug said, "and I still have no son. Once again I am beginning to wonder about the wife you've given me."

The widow's face whitened. "Why, Little Bug, this is terrible. You should have told me sooner. By my authority as district magistrate I declare you divorced." She sent one of her cruel sons out to the shed to fetch the sow. Then the son took the sow over the rise and slaughtered it.

That night the evil widow and her two cruel sons and her wicked daughter, Clarissa, and Little Bug sat down to eat Little Bug's second wife.

"This is delicious," Little Bug said. "What is it, may I ask?"

"Veal," said the evil widow.

After they had finished dinner the evil widow asked Little Bug, "Tell me, Little Bug, what sort of wife would you like now?"

Little Bug thought and thought. He thought as hard as he had ever thought. Finally he remembered that the wives in his books were always smaller than their husbands, and that none of them appeared to be very smart. Perhaps that was the problem, Little Bug thought: his previous wives had outsmarted him.

"I would like a wife who is smaller than me and not too smart," Little Bug said.

"Very wise words," the evil widow replied. "I have just the wife for you." She went out back and returned with a hen.

"This is the wife for me," Little Bug said.

That night the two cruel sons crept out to the shed for a third time. The sight of Little Bug coupling with the hen was so hilarious that they could not control their laughter, and the two of them fell backwards and rolled noisily down the hill to the house. But Little Bug was so absorbed in his task that he didn't notice.

Almost a year later, Little Bug was outside repairing a fence when a traveling salesman came down the road.

"Hello, friend," the salesman said. "Tell me, why do you look so sad?"

Little Bug sighed. "It's just that I am already on my third wife and I have not yet fathered a son. Oh, why did I ever want to marry at all?"

"What does your wife have to say about it?" the salesman asked.

"Oh, she doesn't say anything; she's a hen."

"A hen!" the salesman exclaimed.

"That's right," said Little Bug. "My other wives were a sow and a mare. But they were too smart and schemed not to have sons."

"Why, what a little fool you are!" the salesman cried. "Don't you know that if you want a son you must take a girl for a wife?"

After the salesman left, Little Bug thought for a long time about what he had said. Then he packed his meager things and went to talk to the evil widow.

"A traveling salesman has just explained how you've tricked me," Little Bug said. "I am on my way to the city to lodge a complaint with the chief provincial magistrate."

The evil widow knew that even a fool like Little Bug could bring trouble on her head if he complained to the chief provincial magistrate. She was furious that her plan had been upset. Quickly, she thought up a new one.

"Oh, my sweet Little Bug, surely you don't think we meant you any harm! Why, we just knew you weren't ready for a son yet. But now I see that you are. In fact, to show there are no hard feelings, I will give you my own daughter, Clarissa, for a wife."

Now Little Bug did not entirely trust the widow; but her explanation seemed logical, and Clarissa, while wicked, was not unattractive. So he agreed to the match. The widow divorced him from the hen and married him to Clarissa on the spot, and to celebrate they all sat down to eat Little Bug's third wife, which the evil widow told him was duck.

That night when the two cruel sons crept out to the shed they were dismayed to see Little Bug coupling with their sister. They did not find this funny, although it was, in its own way, of interest. Then they saw Clarissa reach into a hay bale, pull out the carving knife the widow had hidden there, and stab Little Bug in the back until he was dead.

The next night the evil widow and her two cruel sons and her wicked daughter, Clarissa, who was now also a widow, sat down to eat Little Bug. They all agreed that this was better than all the other feasts, and each one expressed the fervent desire that the future would bring more foolish boys like Little Bug down the lonely road to their farm.

"Nice story," Julia said, after I'd summarized the plot for her.

"It's a cautionary fable against marriage," I said. I was lying on the bed with my head tilted back so that I could see the Chandler City sunset upside down, a bloodied lake. "It's about how women always get you in the end."

"Maybe it's a cautionary fable about how you shouldn't kill and eat your wife."

"Henderson calls 'em as he sees 'em," I said, sitting up, too fast.

"He must have been a real Mister Sunrise," Julia said. And that was what she called Henderson from then on, at first to tease me, and then, after a while, because she started to think of it as his real name. Even I said it, sometimes, because it always made her laugh when I did ("You sound so *serious,*" she'd say, "like it was an *epithet* or something.") Because of the job we had not been spending so much time together as we had during school, and it was good to have a joke between us.

One day, shortly after my visit to Treech, Julia asked me if she could meet Higgs.

"Of course," I said. "Tomorrow, if you want. If you don't still think it's creepy."

"I do. But how else will I get over it, right?"

"Right," I said, overcome—her magnanimity, her kindness, and so on. She looked staunch, like a solo pilot.

"Just remember," Julia said, "I'm counting on you to take action if he does anything strange."

"Bam!" I assured her. "Biff! Whack! Pow!"

⚞ CHAPTER 4 ⚟
DOUBLE DATE

When Ellen, opening the door the next morning, releasing the now-familiar blast of music and appliances, found both me and Julia on the stoop, rather than, as usual, only me, her forehead creased and her mouth drew into a tight, questioning frown. It was her response, I'd learned, to any unexpected occurrence—and who could blame her? Everything unexpected in her life had been more or less catastrophic.

"This is my friend Julia," I said. "Julia, Mrs. Higgs."

"Hi," Julia shouted. "Hello. Good to meet you." Her hand tightened on my wrist.

Ellen nodded. She looked from my face to Julia's, then back. The fingers of her two hands worried at each other as if she were silently adding up columns. It was the most recognition she'd given me in weeks. I felt I'd won some puny victory.

"We're going to go downstairs," I told Ellen. She shuffled backwards into the loud gloom of the foyer to make way. She made no move to follow us down.

"God," Julia said when we came out into the basement. "This place."

"I told you."

"But still," she said. "Actually seeing it. It's not the same." She picked up an acromegalic idol which lay overturned on the floor and

103

set it down upright. "Wouldn't you think somebody'd want some of these things?"

"I'm not sure anyone even knows it's all here. Maybe some very old anthropologists. Treech and McTaggett. Ellen and Higgs."

"Speaking of whom," Julia said. "Introduce me, dummy."

"Professor Higgs? This is my girlfriend Julia. She's been looking forward to meeting you."

Julia let go my wrist and proceeded to Higgs, her right hand out.

"I don't think he shakes hands," I warned her. But her object was the checkerboard on the table. Higgs's black pieces remained in their victorious position; my jumped red ones were neatly stacked beside the board.

"You want to play?" she asked me.

"You play checkers?"

"I know *how*."

She arranged the men in their zig-zag ranks. She seemed already to be considering her opening move.

"Why don't you play Professor Higgs?" I suggested. "I could use a break. And he's probably tired of me already."

She looked at Higgs doubtfully. He dropped his eyes to the board, began to make his sound, and without hesitation moved a red checker one step into no-man's-land.

"See?" I said. "Everybody likes variety."

Julia took one of Higgs's checkers early, then fell back to a grim defense of her king line. Now and then she muttered, "Good, OK."

"He's got tricks in store," I told her.

The two of them traded captures for a while, neither gaining any clear advantage of position. When Higgs's force was reduced to two and Julia's to three, Higgs stopped making his noise. Julia stood up from the table.

"What's going on?" I said, a little panicked. "Why didn't you finish?" I had been rather expecting a last-minute comeback.

"Look at the board," she said. "He's got no way out. He resigned."

I looked, considered, couldn't make out the hopelessness. But I trusted Higgs.

"Go again," I said.

Higgs won the next game, and Julia took the one after that. Higgs responded with two commanding victories ("He's tricky," I counseled) but in the sixth game, trying the same opening, he fell two men behind in the early going, and never recovered.

"Rubber match," Julia said coolly, and began to set the checkers up again. She seemed to have forgotten her initial discomfort with Higgs, with the basement, with my job. As far as I could tell she didn't even know I was in the room.

But before the tiebreaker could start, Ellen came downstairs with lunch. Without ceremony she moved the checkerboard aside and laid in its place a platter of vegetable sticks, potato chips, and sandwiches: sliced turkey on rye, cut into quarters, a cellophane toothpick driven into each section. Next to the platter she set down a snack bowl filled with sesame sticks and cashews. The cellophane ribbons hung stiffly over our lunch like tiny flags.

"Ellen," I said, trying not to sound shocked, "you didn't have to. We brought lunch."

Julia stepped on my foot.

"But thank you—of course. It looks delicious."

Ellen shrugged. "I had all this around." Suddenly I realized she hadn't vacuumed all day. And Higgs had lost at checkers. . . . Dizzy, I ransacked my memory—were the planets all on one side of the sun today? Was the Mayan calendar about to flip?

No: so it had to be Julia.

The two of us set to eating. It really was good; I hadn't known it until that moment, but I was tired of egg salad. Ellen stood in the corner and watched us, rustling her feet unrhythmically, her eyes focused on some point well beyond the wall. It made me terribly nervous. I hurried through my lunch, swallowing half-chewed bites of sandwich, not pausing to lick the potato chip residue from my palate and the backs of my teeth.

"Oh," Julia said.

"What?"

She glanced at Ellen. "Nothing. I had a chill."

I followed Julia's eyes to the corner and the little crack there between the molding and the floor. "There's a grasshopper problem," I explained.

"It's the water main," Ellen said. "They bollixed up the survey or some such thing and built the house right over it. That's what draws them in. And there's always more when it rains."

"That must be a nuisance," Julia said.

Ellen—was it possible?—sighed. "We've tried everything," she said. "But nothing."

Once we'd finished eating, Julia offered brightly to help Ellen with the dishes, then, equally brightly, refused her demurrals. The two of them trooped up the stairs. Just before Julia climbed out of sight she turned, ducked so I could see her face, and blew me a kiss. I held up my hand to catch it, then, feeling foolish, brought it down. The kiss shattered against the wall behind Higgs's head—whatever that meant.

When I heard the water go on in the kitchen, I leaned over Higgs's table, palms planted where the checkerboard and lunch had been. He stared past my shoulder.

"Don't you see?" I said. "Your men are getting logjammed on the perimeter. You're letting her control the center squares. Keep playing like that and you don't have a chance."

The next day, Ellen came down at eleven, as usual, with the vacuum cleaner. But this time she worked efficiently, covering the floor just once, not bothering to move the larger heaps of artifacts aside, and after ten minutes she snapped the power off. I looked up from my translation, startled by the sudden relative quiet.

"You're engaged?" she said.

"Not really. Did Julia say . . ."

She shrugged. "No. But maybe you were thinking about it."

"We're in the planning stages," I said, and dropped my eyes

ostentatiously back to the page. I knew Julia would have been annoyed with me. This is an offering, she would have told me. You have to respond.

"You ought to get her a ring," Ellen said.

I looked down at my bare fingers. "My finances are a little uncertain right now."

"I know how much they pay you."

"Well," I said, off-balance, "still. One doesn't want to . . ."

Why were we talking about this?

"Suit yourself," she said. She sounded angry and I thought she would start vacuuming again. But instead she hoisted the machine with a grunt and marched upstairs.

She came down again, an hour later, empty-handed.

"The last one didn't have a girl," she said.

That was her way of starting: no salutation, no preamble.

"No?" I said. I could hardly say I was surprised.

"He only cared about his work."

"There's something to be said for that," I said, feeling obscurely annoyed.

"Every man," she said, "needs a woman by his side. That's the truth."

I nodded.

"And when I say woman I mean anyone who'll stand by you. I'm open-minded."

"Of course."

She seemed satisfied that she'd gotten something across to me. But she didn't leave. I wished she would. I was a little afraid of Ellen for the same reason I was a little afraid of dogs. When the cards were down one couldn't rely on them to do what made sense. I was afraid that the language Ellen thought in was different, in subtle but crucial respects, from my own. I thought that the occasions on which I thought I understood her were unfortunate chances which would lead me, if I trusted them, to ruin.

"Well," I announced, "I guess I'll get back to my story."

"When I think of what would have happened to Stanley without me . . ." Ellen said. Both of us turned to look at Higgs. He was sitting as quietly as always, his eyes two ciphers, unintent. What *would* have happened to Higgs without Ellen? What calamity could she possibly think she had spared him?

Higgs dug two fingers into the snack bowl and rooted around, not looking down, until he found a sesame stick. He put the whole thing in his mouth, and forcefully, deliberately, chewed. A signal? If so, it was in a semaphore I did not yet understand.

I went to talk to my parents about marriage. I rode my bicycle along the empty upward-slanting avenues of the west side, my twilit childhood streets, and thought of what I'd told Ellen. Was it true? Were we in the planning stages? Were we, as certain hateful girls at school had put it, "engaged to be engaged"? Julia and I had spoken of it, of course, but only jokingly, in the way of manufacturing silly names for our offspring, or thinking of where we'd settle: Samarkand, Antarctica, the San Diego Zoo, no more real to us than the places we sank with our brainpower. In fact they were often the same places. Whenever I tried to consider it more seriously I shied away; it was like thinking about cancer, or the exhaustion of fossil fuels. I had a feeling that marriage—which seemed, on the face of it, like little more than a codification of the life we already led—concealed some secret, unknowable in advance, which would change everything. I didn't think it was necessarily something bad. But I hated surprises.

I could see the Grape Arbor coming from three blocks away, a hubbub of green and white light between two warehouses. My mother's idea had been to bring to Chandler City a little of that Edward Hopper equipoise they admired so much: twilight, cool neon, hardened faces seen through drapes of coffee-steam. With the mood of quiet desolation we'd had no trouble; but the neon had proved our downfall. My father, thorough as always, had ringed every window with it, and the door, and the rain-gutter. He'd planted grapevines,

too, at my mother's direction, and these—as if to make up for everything else my parents had ever set out to do—had flourished. They
grew over the tops of the trellises and lay in tired ringlets on the roof.
The lights, shining through them, took on a foreboding tint of jungle.

Inside, my mother sat alone at her window table, a great rectangu-
lar oven trough before her. Like many Jewish women of a certain age
she was beginning to resemble Ayn Rand.

"Samuel," she said, "try this."

"What is it?"

"Something new. I burned it. Chicken tetrazzini."

"What did you use for the chicken?"

"I used chicken."

"You never use chicken."

"Now he tells me," she said tragically.

I sat down across from her. The substance in the tray gave off a
doughy, acrid smell. It was the deep nuanceless green of a public
swimming pool.

"Why's it green?" I asked her.

"It's cilantro paste."

"I don't think you put cilantro in chicken tetrazzini."

She crossed her arms, produced a snort. "Somebody's full of good
advice tonight."

"Sorry," I said. "I'm somewhat harried."

"Why? Julia leave you?"

"No," I said crossly. "As a matter of fact I'm trying to decide
whether we should get married."

"Don't get mad, I was just guessing. She wants to marry you?"

"I don't exactly know."

"You're my son and I love you," she said, "but you recognize you're
not much of a catch for her." She dipped a spoon into the chicken
tetrazzini and slid it between her lips. "Aagh," she murmured. Slowly
the tetrazzini closed over the spoon-hole and erased it.

"Mom."

"I burned it," she said.

"I don't think that's actually the point. Whether or not I'm a 'catch.'"

"She's a very personable young woman. With potential."

"I have potential."

My mother reached out with one slightly greasy hand and swatted me lovingly on the side of the head. "Of course you do."

"So you think yes," I said.

"I think you're a lucky boy," my mother said.

"I *know*. Where's Dad?"

I found I'd had enough of the restaurant, of the nauseous-making buzz of the neon and the enveloping smell of my mother's casserole, which may indeed have contained chicken but to which textured vegetable protein, my nostrils told me, was not a stranger.

"He's working late," my mother said.

"I actually have to go," I told her. "I'll let you take care of things here."

There was only one customer in the restaurant, a spattered housepainter in his seventies, who was sitting by the door, gumming with all his power of concentration at a mouthful of mixed greens.

"I'm bored," she said. "When you see him kick him in the ass for bringing me here."

My mother had long since modified that part of our history. If my father wouldn't bother to correct her I didn't see why I should.

"Come on," she said. "Stay. We'll play Scrabble."

"I'll see you, Mom." I stood to go. The old housepainter looked up; his eyes shimmied on either side of my face for a moment and then locked on.

"Be nice," he said, "you've only got one."

I hurtled out into the evening.

My father worked in a trailer even farther out of town than our restaurant. I set off uphill again, laboring, not letting myself slow until the green-white reflected smear of the Grape Arbor had vanished from my handlebars and the casing of my front wheel. As I pressed toward the city limits, the cross streets gave over to foreigners. I passed Cambyses, Nabopolassar, Shih Huang Ti, Xerxes—the last red light, which I blew through like a ghost. The road turned to thin gravel that champed at my tires. In a few more minutes I passed through a chain-link gate and was there.

The trailer was no larger than a few elevator cars laid abreast, and there were five people inside. Four of them sat in a rough circle of vinylized chairs, playing canasta. My father, the senior member, was the only one who had a desk. He was behind it—not sitting at it, I mean, but behind it, kneeling on the floor, scrabbling around for something he'd dropped. Above him, on the back wall, a framed photograph of Mayor Meadows peered down at us with bleary self-satisfaction. He was now very old.

"Dad," I said.

One of the canasta players turned and gave me a long look. "He's your dad?" he said. I had not been to the trailer in almost a year, and none of the men were familiar to me. No one but my father stayed at the station very long. It was agreed to be the lowest and most embarrassing position in the whole Department of the Interior, which offered a wide spectrum of low and embarrassing positions. Enforcing grazing violations on speed crazed ranchers, counting the used condoms in the Hudson—these were promotions from the spring-finding project. It had been a long time since anyone (again, I mean anyone but my father) thought there was a spring to be found. The other men mostly played cards and searched for loopholes in Indian treaties while they waited for their transfers to come through.

My father clambered over the desk and lowered himself heavily on the other side. The desk occupied the whole width of the trailer and it was the only way he could get out.

"Son," he said. "I happen to have a minute."

His eyes had retreated a little in recent years, and the lines from his nose to the corner of his mouth had grown much deeper. I had to admit it; even he was starting to look like Ayn Rand.

"I think I may be onto something," he said. "It's still tentative."

It was what he always said.

"I wondered if we could talk," I said.

"I'll bet we could."

He steered me outside, into what was now night. We were at the western rim of town; there was ten more feet of gravel past the trailer, and past that just the sand-shot soil of the mesa. In the other direction, down toward the cliff, the lights of town were coming on. The Grape Arbor glowed greenly in the middle distance like an indicator light.

"How did you decide to get married?" I asked my father.

"I think your mother decided," he said. "Or at least she was the one who brought it up."

After a while he said, "Has she?"

"Excuse me?"

"Has Julia? Brought it up?"

"Not really," I said.

"Do you love her?" my father asked.

I had considered this question before.

"Sure," I told him.

But I wasn't sure. My life had improved since she'd joined it, that was certain. We spoke to each other in sweet tones of voice, and kidded as I'd heard other lovers do; and in our physical relations we acted out what I understood to be the healthful exertions of average young people. But love? I was hampered here by my refusal to admit I didn't know what it was, or whether it was in my repertoire. Those men of my acquaintance who "didn't know if they could love" were, without exception, the basest seducers of the campus, and their prey, the callowest, the weakest-willed of girls. That wasn't Julia; that wasn't me.

Henderson had said this about love: "Lovers stick to my shoes/ at which time my shoes stick to the street/ Between the street and my shoes the sticky lovers sweat upon each other."

I had told Julia I loved her, and it didn't feel like a lie. But it did feel like an approximation. Something in the sentimental movies was missing for me; this visible selflessness the heroes experienced, as they emptied themselves utterly into their romantic trials. Take a look at me now—there's just an empty space—could I speak those words with the conviction that was necessary?

Something, I thought, had gone wrong with me, my parents' healthy habits notwithstanding. My mother had eaten a bad helping of seitan, in the crucial early weeks of my gestation, or been struck in the belly by a tragically well-aimed gamma particle from a black light, or maybe one night's bowl of hash had done it. I didn't know what had done it. But the tragic and self-sacrificing part of me, the loving part, was missing—perhaps stunted into uselessness, perhaps never formed. The only time *I* was selfless was when I was asleep.

My father, with a strange seriousness, took a stick of gum from his pocket, carefully unfolded the paper and the foil wrap, bent it double, and put it in his mouth. The gum migrated to one cheek, where it sat, like a nut.

"What I think," he told me, "is that it's just something that happens. I mean it comes over you like a . . . like a cloud. A rain cloud. And no matter who you're standing next to, you're bound to get wet."

"What if you've got an umbrella?"

"What? I don't know."

"I was just kidding."

"It's a *comparison.*"

"Never mind. Sorry."

"Umbrella."

"Okay, Dad."

He shook his head, roughly, as if a bit were attached to it. "What if there were a drought? What if rain fell up instead of down? What if you were made of sugar and when water hit you you just melted into the ground?"

"Okay."

"What if you could dodge the raindrops?"

Julia began to accompany me regularly to the house.

"Otherwise I hardly see you," she said. "And I can work just as well there as at home." Her work, these days, consisted of searching eighteenth-century English folios for images of women's stockings, her advisor's special research interest.

"Look here," she'd say, when she turned up a particularly well-concealed example. "There's a little piece of leg. There, behind the haywain."

What her advisor was after was the earliest instance of the stocking fetish in British painting: what he called "The Primal Lingerie Scene." His most recent book, *I See England's Underpants,* had been a great success in the relevant circles. Julia had made me read it.

I didn't think much of Julia's project, and I told her so.

"Somebody's got to lay the groundwork," she said. "I know it seems silly. But how can we talk seriously about the representation of stockings before we know where all the stockings are?"

How, indeed, I thought, but didn't say it. I was not inclined to argue the point too strenuously; the last thing I wanted was for Julia to change her mind about spending her days in the basement with me. If stockings behind the haywain would keep her there, then I was all for stockings.

I'd like to say my motivation was founded wholly on my affection for Julia; but in fact it was just as much for the effect she had on Ellen. When Julia was with me, Ellen vacuumed just once a day, and the frequency of clanging pans diminished to a level commensurate with reasonable use. She kept the snack bowl full. I was pretty sure she had even turned the radio down—although I thought it would be ill-advised to ask.

And I, too, was quieted, I hardly ever wanted to punch Ellen anymore. That, by my standards, was something very close to friendship.

Ellen began to spend more time in the basement. The four of us, engaged in our respective pursuits, made up a sort of grotesque double date: I translating the story of Little Bug, Julia hunting stockings, Higgs staring, and Ellen just sitting, in a luridly faked Louis xiv chair that smelled of wood rot. Sometimes she knitted. Other times she wrote letters. I could see her handwriting from where I sat: plump, mild letters in perfect schoolgirlish rows. She wrote to her nieces in Tulsa and Seattle, of whom, from time to time, we saw snapshots.

Ellen still unnerved me. For all her noisy appurtenances, she was herself rather quiet, and tended to disappear into corners, so that sometimes I would find myself meeting her distracted, bluish stare before I'd known consciously that she was in the room. That was bad; but not as bad as it had been before. At least now she was willing to talk. Often she would launch without warning into a story of her youth. "At Vassar I attended Friends of Labor meetings on several occasions," she'd say, or "My father and I enjoyed fishing in the arroyo where Thales Road is now." It was never clear what Ellen intended us to take from these stories. Sometimes she would stop in what seemed to be the middle, and pick up the thread again only after some weeks, or not at all. Other times she started mid-stream, repeating to us something that, say, Margaret had said, without giving any indication who Margaret was, in what relation she stood to Ellen, and whether we might ever hear of her again. It was as though she were telling one endless story, down in her mind, which through some sporadic malfunction surfaced now and then into speech.

Sometimes she read to us from Higgs's letters. These consisted mostly of sentimental flattery, school advice, and off-hand scholarly remarks—although it was from one of them that I extracted the story of Higgs's introduction to Henderson, plucking it from among the blandishments and declarations of intent just as Higgs himself had plucked *Poems Against the Enemies* from that long-ago trashbin in Düsseldorf.

Whenever Ellen read from the letters, I watched Higgs carefully for any sign of indignation. I wondered if he were embarrassed; certainly I was embarrassed for him. I cringed whenever I thought of his hand scripting out the pet names and nonwords, the occasional heart drawn at the bottom of a page—or worse, his face, his attentionless gaze, turned to secret contemplation of the charms of young Ellen, goopy Ferris-wheel fantasies . . .

Julia, on the other hand, thought it was sweet.

"You see?" she said. "Not everybody's repressed like you."

"He was young."

"*You're* young."

"You're right," I countered, "but is that how you want me to get old?"

My stomach tightened a little, as it always did when I inadvertently alluded to a shared future for us.

"I think it's possible," Julia said, "to be romantic in your youth and yet not eventually stop speaking and withdraw from all human inter-action forever."

"Anything is possible," I said.

In any case, there was no sign of indignation from Higgs, nor did he appear to be embarrassed; and while this, of course, meant noth-ing, I liked to think we had his permission to hear the letters. After all, hadn't things improved since my arrival? Didn't Ellen seem hap-pier? Wasn't Julia the most challenging checkers player he'd faced in years? (Yes: Ellen attested to this.) I read gratitude in Higgs's blank expression, seemed to hear him say, "Samuel, though I didn't know it, it was you I've been waiting for."

Same to you, I said silently back. I had always been a bit of a deter-minist. Now—just as I had once believed myself fated to join the end-less after-dinner drink of my parents' New York—I felt that destiny had brought me to Higgs, with whom I shared a secret, possibly supernatural bond. I tried to analyze the process by which I constructed the thoughts I ascribed to Higgs—half-suspecting that there was no process, no con-struction, that the thoughts were real and I was receiving some dim transmission available for whatever reason only to me. I reflected often on the series of coincidences that had escorted me to my present posi-tion: the new wing at Gunnery Hall, Bobby Trabant's fractured skull, the timely departure of Slotkin. Forces, I thought, were at work.

It was my custom to stop, on my way home from Higgs's house, at a little restaurant not far from campus, the same one where McTaggett had first broached the subject of graduate school. As I sat there in the back, mashing a cinnamon bun about in my mouth (theirs were swollen and uncannily heavy, like sticky meteors) I felt myself sunken in the easy pleasure of regularity. The waitresses knew me, if not my name; the pattern of varnish-lumps and fork scars on my usual table had grown familiar to me, likewise the faces of the usual patrons.

On one of these stops, I found myself staring at someone I did not recognize—or not quite. He was a neat-looking young man in a blue blazer with a steaming cup of tea in front of him. The man caught my eye, then turned away. A moment later he shot a furtive glance in my direction. It was impossible to tell whether he was recognizing me or simply unnerved by my staring. Rudeness didn't bother me—this was my familiar place. Familiarity meant license to stare, or what good was it?

Suddenly the man's brow cleared. He sprang from the counter and strode at me, down the aisle, extending one long hand, shouting, "Sammy Grapearbor, good goddamn!" And by this I knew at once that the neat young man was my old friend from my college days—already, a month out, I was thinking of them as "my college days"—it was Charlie Hascomb, the impressionist, the enemy of vermin. His close-cropped hair had fooled me.

"Charlie," I said weakly, "sit down, man."

My relief at recognizing him quickly gave way to apprehension. I had little desire to remind myself of the ugly, disaffected days that Charlie and I had spent together. But Charlie made it immediately clear that he too had abandoned the company of our erstwhile set, and thought no better of them than I did. We spent a pleasant half hour exchanging bad news of our former comrades. Bick Wickman, the purported Englishman, was serving time on vaguely reported interstate charges; another of our circle had gotten a girl pregnant and was living with her and her extended family in a tattery commune where animal products and carbonated beverages were forbidden.

"His first time!" Charlie told me, frowning hilariously.

And Barberie was writing pornographic science fiction novels to make ends meet, and there was Kack's aborted career as a stock car racer, and peccadillos, and botched suicides. And some of them were still undergraduates, and this, we agreed, was somehow most piteous of all.

Charlie, for his part, was working at his father's record store, which, he gave me quietly to understand, was also a head shop. "So if you need anything . . ." he said suggestively; and when I told him I'd quit marijuana, he cackled. "I noticed your zits had cleared up," he said, and at that I had to smile.

"Do Bick Wickman," I said, on impulse.

"It's been a long time. You're asking a lot of my talents."

But with hardly any more encouragement Charlie dropped into Bick's wobbly British accent, his foppish intonation, and began to admit to a sequence of crimes, each more unnatural and defiled than the last.

"I'm *so bloody sorry* for all that I've done," he wailed, his voice stopping up with simulated guilt.

"Stop it," I begged him, teary, choking with laughter. "It's too cruel."

"Okay," he said, himself again. "But what about Beemish?" And he went on in this way, mimicking each of our old acquaintances, confessing in their earnest voices to every kind of perversion, iniquity, and bad faith. I felt almost nostalgic.

Finally Charlie looked at his watch and grew serious.

"I'm late already," he said. "But let's get together soon. I want to see the famous Julia again. I remember her well." Then he took on her voice. Even after all these months, he had it down. "Come here and take me, you big, brutish man!" he said. At another table a slight trucker looked up hopefully from the menu.

"You warned me off her, remember? You said she had a secret radiation beam."

"Radiation beam." He grinned, dazzlingly. "Sounds like something I would have said. But I don't remember it."

"Now I'm not sure," I said—and why I told this little lie I really don't know—"maybe it was somebody else."

Charlie wrote his phone number on my napkin, paid for his half-consumed coffee, and left. I tucked the napkin in my pocket, thinking that perhaps I would make plans to see him, that there were, after all, drawbacks to the joined hermits' lives that Julia and I had taken up. As I drank the rest of Charlie's coffee I resolved that I would call him. It might do us good—who could say?—to entertain.

Ellen's stories, as I've said, were almost always concerned with her youth. About the thirteen years since Higgs had fallen silent, she seemed to have nothing to say. Sometimes I wondered whether she knew how much time had passed. Once, unable to sleep, I considered the shopworn idea that time was a road. If it were true, I thought, the Higgses' carriage had caught a wheel in a rut, or the horses had broken their tethers and run; or they had simply slowed their pace further and further until finally they had come to rest, settling there in the dust, the rest of the world's wagon train having long ago passed out of earshot. That was why the front door was so thick. Otherwise the accumulated pressure of time would break it down, would flood in and kick out the walls, sweeping everything away and off the cliff.

Even in the dark, I knew this was nonsense. That door was opened every day—no flood. But the fact remained that she showed a peculiar unconcern for what any reasonable person would consider the distinguishing feature of her life: her husband's silence. In all the time I spent there, she spoke about it only once.

Julia had brought that month's *Cosmopolitan* to the house. She was fond of all the women's magazines; she read them fervently and with mock-disregard. Now she sat in her chair (a three-legged Shaker) and flipped efficiently through the pages for something that would amuse her. The perfume samples, meant to be activated one at a time by a more deliberate reader, mingled uneasily in the air of the basement. Together they smelled fruity and dank, a little spoiled—strangely, I thought, like meat. Maybe it was ambergris.

"Listen to this," Julia said. "Forty-three percent of American women have had a sexual fantasy involving President Reagan."

"Define 'involving,'" I said.

"And thirty percent with Bush." She looked up from the magazine with her lower lip tucked in. "Who reads this stuff?" she said.

"You do," I pointed out.

"You know what I mean."

I shrugged. "I don't know. Maybe Reagan. Maybe Bush."

"I doubt that."

"Never assume."

I was looking down at my text, and Julia was facing my direction, so neither of us saw Ellen lift herself with unprecedented quickness from her chair; and when her palm slammed down on the open magazine, nearly upending Higgs's spindly table, Julia screamed, and I leaped from my chair in alarm, spilling my papers onto the already cluttered floor. Ellen snatched the magazine off the table.

"Were you reading this?" she asked Julia—all tranquility.

"Oh, no," Julia said, clasping her hands. "I was through."

The quiet, perfumed air had swallowed up Julia's scream; it was already hard to believe that she had screamed at all. I sat back down and bent to collect the pages of Henderson's story. Ellen stayed standing, peering closely at the magazine's jaunty type. I wondered what her interest in it could be. I found it impossible to imagine her fantasizing about any government official, past or present. Then I saw that she wasn't looking at the article Julia had been reading. Her eyes were fixed on the facing page. It was some sort of questionnaire.

"Is your marriage in a rut?" Ellen said grandly. "Is . . . your . . . marriage . . ." She glanced at Higgs. "In a rut?"

"I think those questionnaires are more for newer couples," Julia said apprehensively; but Ellen's momentum would not be deflected. She had already begun to read.

"Do you and your mate go out less often than you once did?" she said. She took a moment to consider. "Yes. Do you find that your day has settled into a fixed routine? Yes."

Her face was held tightly, and her jaw worked, as if she were engaged in some awesome concentration, as if the questions were not yes or no but formulas to be solved, equations to be balanced, a final examination in some difficult science.

"Do you and your mate have trouble communicating? Yes. Do the following aspects of your life lack variety: meals? leisure? career? sex?"

"Honestly," Julia said, sounding panicky now, "nobody puts any stock in these things. They're entertainment."

"Yes," Ellen said. "Yes. Yes. Yes."

She continued down the page, reading every question aloud, answering each with a toneless affirmative. Finally she came to the end, where the tallied-up scores were interpreted.

"It says here," she announced, "that my marriage is in a rut."

"Oh, no," Julia said. "We don't think so."

"Julia's right," I told her. I tried to drag out a comforting maxim; but before I could remember one, Ellen began to speak.

"I've been called all kinds of things," she said. "People"—here she held up the magazine, "feel they have a right to comment."

She spoke haltingly, but with forceful inflections, as if reciting a well-memorized speech in a language she only partially understood.

"My own father believes Stanley to be in some way ill. As you can see—" she gestured at the bank of recorders, "he is not at all solicitous of my feelings. He feels quite strongly that Stanley ought to speak— that it is always better to speak than to refrain from speaking. As if some sort of moral *axiom* were involved. Of him, if we ourselves were on speaking terms, I might ask: what about 'Silence is golden'? What about 'Forever hold your peace'?"

"I will concede there's something to be said for variety; but then again there is something to be said for the lack of variety. Death—that's variety. Beating—variety. Adultery—extreme variety. You read about these things. My marriage lacks variety—all right, why shouldn't it? What about domestic tranquility? It's in the Constitution. And we have it."

She closed the magazine—releasing a final exhalation of perfume—and set it back on the table.

"And Stanley agrees with me," she said. "One hundred percent."

We fought all the way home, scattering pigeons with our passage. It was Saturday, and the streets, except for the pigeons, were empty. Without the background of traffic, our voices sounded strangely earnest, and our pauses unnaturally long, as if we were acting in a movie with artistic ambitions.

"She's deranged," I said.

"Don't be ridiculous."

"I'm being sensible. She needs to see somebody. It's her you ought to be scared of, not Higgs. She's the one who'll pick up a knife someday."

Julia folded her arms. "If you ask me, she made some pretty good points."

We walked a few blocks without speaking. This was the kind of trifling, unworthy argument that either one of us could have shut down with a word. I could have told her that I was overreacting, that I'd been tired lately, or sick, that the steady toll of my work had made me raw-skinned and quick to see threats. All of these things were more or less true. But it would be just as easy for her to make equivalent admissions; and so I was reluctant to give in. I waited her out, as the pigeons fled before us. I knew that in the end she would speak. It was part of her being better than me. We'd played this game before.

"Listen," she said, finally. "Do you want me to stop coming?"

"Of course not."

"I'd hate to leave Higgs."

"Really?"

She turned a little upward and away from me, as if she were expecting something in the rooftops, a face behind the crumbled cornices. "It's hard to explain. I guess I'm starting to find him—I don't know. Appealing."

"Should I be worried about this?" I asked her, joking.

"I don't think so. It's weird. But he *is* sort of sexy."

I stopped dead, underneath a streetlight.

"What?"

"Not that I'd ever let anything happen. It's purely mental." She twirled her hands as if trying to gather something up from the air. "It's sort of fun, not knowing what he's thinking. Not like you—I know you by now."

"I can't believe this," I said.

Julia toyed with the bottom of her shirt. "I wonder what I'd have to do," she said dreamily, "to make him talk . . ." I gaped at her; she met my gaze evenly. I was short of breath, as if someone was sitting on my chest: someone with a cruel face and a mocking laugh, a little goblin in spurs. I tried to tell myself it was nothing to worry about. Just as she'd said, it was purely mental, abstract. But I couldn't force down the taste of catastrophe. What now? I thought. Just walk home? Or take off gibbering into the streets?

The lamp above us cracked and hummed into light. Both our heads jerked up; then we looked at each other. The light jaundiced us, made our skin waxy and grooved, turned our eyes the color of parchment.

"I'm *kidding*," Julia said. "You are the stupidest boy ever."

"Oh, ha ha."

She looped a companionable arm over my shoulder. "Seriously," she asked me, "is there *anything* you can't believe?"

That night, we settled into the saggy center of our bed, supine and pressed together; and Julia let one of her hands twiddle in my hair while the other roamed down my flank; but I picked up that hand and put it back on her side of the bed. I was one-third asleep and my thoughts were bubbling down into a confused and unappealing stew—

like a stew my mother would have made. Sexy Higgs was in my mind, and the long and tedious haul of translation that waited for me in the morning, and, still, the voice and the portentous drumming of Phil Collins: *You're the only one who really knew me at all* . . . With a delicate renunciatory thrill, I turned myself to face the peeling wall.

"Are you OK?" Julia said.

Instead of answering her I issued a small and worthless mumble: I'm asleep, no talking. And within a few minutes this lie was true.

The next day Ellen was herself again: hospitable, shifty-eyed, and unforthcoming, which was as I preferred it. We returned relievedly— anyway, I was relieved—to our ordinary routine. The four of us worked silently all morning; then Ellen brought us lunch; and once the plates were cleared away we got down to checkers.

We had all long since grown tired of playing the usual way. We experimented with the Spanish and Italian rules; we played Damenspiel, Russian shashki, and loser's draughts; Ellen taught us several nameless variants she'd learned in childhood. All these felt like gimmicks, and all lost their luster in time. It was Julia who suggested a tournament; and it was this idea that finally proved to hold our attention. Our schedule was a simple cycle of the six possible pairings: first Julia and I, then Ellen and Higgs, Julia and Higgs, Ellen and I, Julia and Ellen, Higgs and I, and around again to the start. Ellen established a cumulative scoring system. A victory against the first-ranked player counted four points, beating the second-best earned three, and so on. We kept a running tally on a blackboard which Ellen had propped next to Higgs's seat, under the row of windows.

Higgs held the top rank permanently, maintaining a comfortable if not insurmountable lead over Julia in second place. Ellen and I were far behind; the two of us traded the third and fourth spots every few days, since whichever of us was ahead had to win two games of every three to keep from losing ground. Neither of us ever beat Higgs. I had a few successes against Julia, but I suspected she was letting me win, and after I alerted her to my suspicions, though she denied any leniency, I never defeated her again. That was all right with me. I enjoyed checkers much more when there was no doubt about the outcome. A close game seized me up, especially at the end, when there was room for nothing but response to my opponent's moves, trying to pull my men away from the threats in every direction, looking for the one adequate move in the heap of sure disasters. Losing was a relief.

Sometimes we lured Treech into a game, during his monthly visit. He was ludicrously bad; even I had no trouble against him. Whenever he jumped one of my pieces, even when it worsened his position, he cackled, thumped my back, and shouted, "Chalk one up for the old man!" I abided the games solely because his tenacity gave me a weird pleasure; it seemed each time as though he thought he actually might win. There were no points for beating Treech.

The matches between Julia and Higgs became the center of our afternoons. Higgs's style was one of ferocious, omnidirectional assault, while Julia preferred to hang back, holding two checkers on the king line as long as possible and protecting her double corner. When she was able to king a man before Higgs, she almost always won. During their games the two of them seemed to share an obscure understanding. Higgs's throat-noise took on a patterned (I thought) variation of tremble and pitch, about which I imagined Julia knew more than she was letting on. I despaired of ever decoding it myself; and when the two of them were playing my supposed bond with Higgs seemed a vain product of my hopefulness and folly.

He and Julia played from a tournament deck, a collection of one hundred and thirty-seven laminated cards, each of which displayed one of the three-move openings that gave no immediate advantage to either side. When their turn came around, Julia drew a card from the deck and laid it face up in the center of the board. Then the two of them took a moment to contemplate the game into which they were about to be thrust. When I recall those afternoons of checkers it's this moment that comes to mind: the caesura between consideration and play, the respite of Ellen's knitting needles, the slow graduation of the noise in Higgs's throat, and at the end of it the punctuation of the checkers clicking against the board, three times, as Julia and Higgs carried out their predetermined moves, three full stops, or—I should say—an ellipsis.

Around the end of August a heat wave settled into Chandler City, a high-pressure system, a heavy, grayish air mass squatting over us like a sweaty giant. It was the kind of heat a thunderstorm would break up. But there was no sign of a storm. Outside it was impossible to tell morning from evening. In the evening peoples' clothes were wet through; that was the only difference.

In Higgs's house, built before central air, Julia and I stripped to our undershirts and gulped for breath like lungfish. It was eighty-five degrees in the basement by noon, and the slack breezes that made their way in through the half-height windows only served to remind us of other, more refreshing breezes. Ellen carried down an ancient box fan which, thanks to some old sabotage of hers, clattered like a wooden rollercoaster car when it was at full strength—and we always kept it at full strength. I was in a terrible temper. Ellen had built a commanding lead over me in the contest for third place, and my work on "The Four Wives of Little Bug" was going poorly. The traveling salesman's part was rendered in a soupy provincial patois which I was unable to translate. I was waiting for some papers from a dialectologist at Cornell; until they arrived I could not proceed. I resolved to spend my enforced sabbatical studying the finer points of the Gravinic postconclusive. There were many relevant points, and they were very, very fine. The work, even by my standards, was difficult, uninspiring, and slow.

Julia was having troubles of her own. A team in Leeds had succeeded in programming a computer to scan paintings for pictures of stockings. The machine was not perfect, but it was much faster than Julia—faster indeed than a hundred Julias. Her advisor, not to be outdone, had rushed a paper into print declaring that, in all sensible constructions, stockings would have to take a second place to handkerchiefs. It would be months or years before the hated Leedsians could have a new program ready. In the meantime, it fell to Julia to return to all those volumes of paintings she'd counted as complete, now with an eye toward handkerchiefs, and moreover—as a precaution against greater-than-expected versatility on the computer's part—for ascots, tippets, chemisettes . . . Week by week her advisor added to her list. She could study the paintings for, at best, an hour at a time before her attention began to flag, and the too-familiar images began resolving themselves into brushstrokes and fields of color.

At home she'd lay herself across our bed with a raft of art books and a magnifying glass; but before long she'd flip on the little television set she'd bought for ten dollars at a yard sale. The set had color; but not the right color. A light green Julia Child wavered across the screen, hoisting a saucepan whose contents were impossible to make out through the snow.

"I've seen this one," Julia—my Julia—said.

I crouched behind her and watched as an intricate deglazing began to take shape. The fan chilled the sweat on the back of my neck in an unpleasant way.

Julia rolled over to look up at me. "I feel like a lump."

"You've got to have a system," I told her. "You can set a number of paintings to do and give yourself a little reward when you finish. Like ice cream or a gold star."

"And yet I cannot," Julia said.

It was not the first time—not the tenth time—I'd made this suggestion, which I'd learned, long ago, from a pallid guidance counselor in my high school, a kindly and awkward woman who'd mistaken my disobedience and sloth for frustrated promise.

"Lumps don't have boyfriends," I pointed out.

The night after Ellen's speech, I'd again kept Julia on her own side of the bed; and the night after that, and the succeeding nights, she'd stayed there on her own. We didn't speak about it. But each night I felt

a strange, thin, pride—like a hungry cross-desert driver, like a monk
whacking himself with thorny branches. How far—the unspoken
question—could we go?

As summer approached its technical conclusion, Julia took on a new
project, which seemed to me more hopeless than handkerchiefs, more
unrewarding than undershirts; but she wouldn't be dissuaded. She was
going to organize the Higgses' basement. She tacked hand-lettered
signs to the walls, one for each continent except Antarctica, and set
herself to the task of sorting the heaped artifacts by landmass. North
America was pinned up on the back wall, to the right of the tape
recorders; South America in the corner beside the mummy; Europe
next to the blackboard where we recorded our day's wins and losses,
with Africa occupying the remainder of the windowed wall; Australia
behind the false Louis xiv chair, on the staircase side; and Asia on the
wall across from the windows, where Julia was wont to sit. Within each
continent she separated the pieces by function: ornamental, household
use, weaponry, devotional, other, and unknown.

Julia's project made me uneasy. In its doggedness, its zeal for tax-
onomy, its stubborn attention to things ignored by all reasonable people, it was altogether too familiar—too much, I mean, like something
I would do. I didn't want Julia to become more like me. Our romance,
I suspected, would founder.

"Why?" I asked her. "Nobody's ever going to use these things.
They're trash."

She looked me over, weighing a confidence.

"Actually," she said, "I'm doing it for Professor Higgs."

I was unable to conceal my bewilderment.

"I know," she went on, "but it just seems as though he wouldn't
want everything all mixed up this way. I keep thinking maybe it's
distracting, sitting in all this mess. Maybe that's why he doesn't say
anything."

"I doubt that's what it is."

"I just thought I had a sense. I've been here practically as long as you have."

I had to concede that —and, if only inwardly, that Julia could after all be right. Did I have any better explanation? Maybe it *was* the disarray of the basement. Nothing could be ruled out. Maybe it was a rite of some kind, or a political statement, as Harry Reasoner had thought; maybe a lost wager, or a rare and unnamed neurological syndrome; maybe nothing but a prolonged mulish sulk at some unintended insult perpetrated on him by the world. Or maybe the Henderson Society was right, and he was still en route to some revelation that would make up for it all. I had no way of knowing.

Nor, strange as it seems, had I given the question much thought. After the first few days Higgs's silence had begun to seem immutable, part of the world, even ordinary. It was hard to imagine that he had ever spoken, impossible to imagine that he would ever again speak. Why was Higgs silent? I couldn't exactly make sense of the question. It was like asking why I was five-foot eleven and pigeon-toed, or—better—why Julia was a woman. He just was. All I knew for certain was that whenever Julia claimed to know what Higgs wanted I felt helpless and a little ill.

"I suppose it can't hurt," I said. I started to set up the checkerboard; it was my turn to be beaten by Higgs.

Just then there was a sound that it took both of us a moment to recognize; it was one we had not heard (and would not hear again) the whole time we stayed in Higgs's house. It was the telephone ringing.

Neither of us knew where the phone was, and Ellen was upstairs; but finally, by following the sound, I turned it up in the back cupboard, encarceled behind a stack of back-up tapes. The man on the phone asked to speak to Higgs. Behind him I could hear music, furniture moving around, girls talking.

"Who is this?" I asked him. "Alpha Chi Beta? Sig Sig?"

"I'd like to speak to Professor Higgs, please," the man said again. I heard him swallow hard. He was far gone.

"This is he," I said.

There was a pause on the other end. Someone was asking the caller a question. "He says it's him," the caller told the someone. He sounded almost indignant.

The man came back on the line.

"I just called to tell you you suck!" he said.

"Good luck," I told him. "I hope you get into whatever house this is." But he'd already hung up.

"Don't they have anything better to do?" Julia said, a little peevishly.

I rose up from the cabinet.

"Almost certainly not," I said.

My unease with Julia's endless sorting and shuffling began to shade into anger. Sitting at the table, my back and behind sweat-stuck to my chair, my gaze resting heavily, immovably, on a sentence of Kaufmann, I could not help but take her diligence as a reproach. Every time she set an object in its continent I lost my place, and my eye floated slowly, resentfully, back to the passage I'd been reading; if indeed I could be said to be reading at all. For weeks I'd been stuck fast on one page, the one that started, "The dual manifestation of the Gravinic postconclusive is easily conducive to the apparent misinterpretation." The sentence galloped hectic through my mind, a lumpy stanza: "The dual manifestation"—bum bum—"of the Gravinic post-conclusive"—bum bum—"is easily conducive"—ba da bum—"to the apparent misinterpretation"—bum *bum*. To this day I don't know exactly what it means.

Worse than the distraction was the apparent calm lightness with which Julia carried out her task, seemingly unaffected by the heat, by her now-constant defeats at Higgs's hands, or by her abdication of her academic responsibilities—for it was a rare day now that found her at her folios. There at my table, I fumed, and was quiet. Smoldering silence was a tactic that usually worked well for me; after a while, Julia would ask what was wrong and I could proceed from the strengthened position of not having broached whatever subject I was smoldering about. But this time she seemed prepared to ignore me indefinitely, despite the undue vigor with which I permuted my papers and the many pained upturnings of my eyes.

Once it was clear that my behavior would not have its intended effect, I began to see that it was inappropriate and childish. One afternoon, in a spasm of high spirits—I had just unraveled the postconclusive in its collective manifestation, though the dual remained as mysterious as ever—I resolved that I would not only tolerate but take an interest in Julia's project. At the moment she was considering an object which seemed to be about two-thirds of a three-legged bowl, dull orange and painted with stairsteps.

"Aztec?" I asked her.

"Zapotec."

She set the bowl down in a little bramble of ceramic shards at the foot of the sarcophagus. Ellen glanced down without interest, then returned to a letter.

"But Mexican, right?" I said.

"Mm hmm." She turned the bowl over and peered at the handwritten label. "From Oaxaca State."

"So it should be North America."

"No, I've got it in South."

"Mexico is North America."

"I know that," she said. "But everything Mesoamerican goes with South America. It makes more cultural sense."

"Then the 'South America' sign should say 'South America and Mesoamerica.'"

"This is the stupidest argument we've ever had," Julia said.

"Think about what you're saying. Of all our stupid arguments . . ."

She cocked her head for a moment and thought.

"To the best of my recollection," she said, "this is the very stupidest."

"Fine," I said, and returned sullenly to my studies, feeling ill-rewarded for what had after all been an improvement, however slight, in my demeanor. To demonstrate that I was no longer available for chit chat I assumed a voice of concentration and read aloud the sentence I had just succeeded in analyzing.

"Grinto mapplethorpe watusi bah," Julia said suddenly. "Frente chico matuba hiawatha. Hepzibah barada nikto."

"What?"

"You heard me."

"I did?"

"I have my own language now," she said. "It's called Juliatic."

"And what was that you said?"

"'My boyfriend is annoying.'"

"Huh."

"The reason it's so long is Juliatic has no word for 'boyfriend.' Literally it comes out as 'he who sleeps in my bed and thinks he knows much more about everything than he does.'"

"That sounds sort of inefficient."

"But once you get used to it . . ."

"Yeah," I said, burning. "I'd imagine so."

She knelt to the floor and came up with a tangled quipu slung over one hand.

"I guess we could just break up," I said.

"Who'd get the apartment?"

"You found it."

"True," she said. "So I guess I get it."

"Then can I take the bed?"

"It's yours."

"I'd hate telling my parents."

"I'll tell them," Julia said. "They'll understand."

Ellen had been gaping at us in turn, her head jerking back and forth, her mouth growing steadily rounder and wider as if an invisible sphere were working its way out. Now she released a shrill uninterpretable syllable of dismay.

"She's kidding," I told her. "Don't worry."

"He's kidding too," Julia said.

"Did Julia tell you why she's cleaning up?" I asked Ellen.

"Oh, don't," Julia said.

"Women like things orderly," Ellen said. "Men don't care about things like that. It's a fact. In my youth I was ready to turn everything upside down—all the traditions, everything. But now I see that people are fixed into being what they're like." Some memory overtook her. "Marriage and property—we'd tear it all down, we thought—oh, and the parietal rules—how we lied . . . !"

"She says she's doing it for your husband."

"Oh," Ellen said. She put one hand to her lips. "Did he ask you?"

"Of course not," Julia said tightly.

"Well put," I said.

Julia turned back to me. "I don't know why you think you know so much."

"I'm not quite sure why I've never cleaned this place up myself," Ellen mused. "I suppose you can get used to anything."

"You can't study Henderson and care about things being neat," I said. "If you did, you would know what I mean. It's all about sloppiness and ruining things."

"Oh," Julia said, "so I'm unable to participate in this discussion because I haven't read the collected works of your third-rate poet. Mister Sunrise. *Fourth*-rate."

"I'm just saying—"

"You're the worst checkers player I've ever seen," Julia said.

"I'm better than Treech."

"Treech likes you. I think he lets you win."

She brought the quipu over to South America.

"Can you not do that now?" I said.

"Why not?"

"Because it's distracting."

"It's not as though you're really working," she said. "Not until your papers come from Cornell."

I tried to look at my book again; that was a lost cause.

"I'm sure you'd find somebody else right away," I said. "You're young and attractive."

"I'm sure you're right," Julia said evenly.

"You know how to be aggressive with a man," I said. "We respond well to that."

"I had to be aggressive with you," Julia said, "because you were a pathetic dipshit."

"And this is convenient, it's almost time for the state fair."

Julia raised her eyebrows.

"I think I heard the guy running the Whack-A-Mole's available."

"Oh," she said. "That's really nice." She threw down the quipu, which landed among the spoils of the Taino and the Nahua, their sacrificial knives, their carvings. All at once I was acutely conscious of being in a room full of weapons. Ellen stared at me with terrifying interest, as if I were a stranger who had opened my coat to her and revealed some novel deformity. It struck me suddenly, and with some force, that I had at last reached the end of Julia's kindness and the end of her kidding. She was serious. Following just behind that thought, a little slower and not so forcefully, but hugely, sickeningly worse, came the understanding that I had been working toward this moment all along.

But, of course, this realization—like all the other epiphanies in my life, large and small—had come too late.

That night I slept at my card table, my head resting on the x of my crossed forearms, the workman's legend—"THIS IS THE LIFE"—grinning down at me from the wall. The next day, to my surprise, Julia wordlessly gathered her things and accompanied me to Higgs's house. Along the way I attempted a rapprochement, filled with thin hope and self-recrimination; I spoke jauntily of the day's news, various of our former acquaintances, even the weather. I listed and repudiated my unappealing qualities, one by one, with a grit-toothed likeness of cheer. I flung apologies like candy from a float. None of it availed me anything. When we arrived at the house, Julia started immediately on a stack of jugs and pots that occupied the corner by the stairs, taking care to set each object in its place as deliberately and noisily as possible. I opened Kaufmann and closed it again, unable to bear the sight of that same page: bum-*bum*. I rested my chin on my joined hands, clenched my eyes shut, tried to pull myself inward to some clear, meditative state, where the route back to normalcy would be apparent, a bright portal. But I couldn't concentrate; couldn't not notice the chalky scrape of pottery on pottery, the radio from upstairs, the chattering grasshoppers. I was trapped in the sensory world. I was sweating. I began to succumb to a matter-of-fact despair.

Who knows how long this might have gone on, had Ellen not interrupted us with news of the most startling kind?

We heard her shout from upstairs. Immediately she came barreling down, agitated into speechlessness, waving a fat blue envelope in her right hand. It was a letter: the first of two we would receive that week, in a house that didn't see much mail. I stood up from my chair.

"A letter for Stanley," Ellen forced out, catching her breath in whoops. "It's a letter for Stanley from Germany."

All of us looked at Higgs. I knew already of the letters Higgs had posted to Berlin in his attempts to uncover Henderson's biography. But what sort of reply could take thirty years to compose?

"Open it," I said. "He won't mind."

Ellen tore the envelope open and withdrew a neatly folded sheaf of papers. "It's in English," she said, flattening it out, and then—glancing once more at her husband—she began to read.

CHAPTER 5

HENDERSON BETWEEN THE WARS

September 10, 1985

Dear Professor Higgs:

Excitedly am I responding to your letter concerning the tall man with the cough, which you have sent to various addresses in Berlin during approximately the first week of April, 1951. I know this Henderson! Also have I often wondered what has become of him! If I am correct, he was a poet, some sort of Russian, whom I knew for a time in my youth. Please accept my very heartfelt apologies for the slowness of my reply! Let me explain. Three months ago passed my sister Ulrike away. She was a fine woman, but it must be said that in her whole long life she had never thrown a thing in the rubbish. So it was, that in the sorting of her many papers, which has occupied me every day since my dear sister's funeral—we old men are always grateful to find ways to fill up the time!—as I was saying, while sorting yesterday morning I turned up a page to find your old letter. Imagine my surprise at seeing there a perfect description of my old friend Henderson! Well, at once put I aside my task and sat myself down to recall as much as I could about that funny character. Henderson! If you know where he may be now, then must you tell me where to find him! I am certain, that he and I could spend a few marvelous hours talking over all our memories, as we old men love to do! Well, you know this? If you are still alive and reading this, Professor, you must be an old man too!

But enough about me!

I met your poet Henderson in 1932, when I was a boy of eighteen. Though my father was a humble cabinetmaker, we were related on my mother's mother's side to the Schönaich-Carolaths, wherefrom came the Empress Hermione, the second wife of Emperor Wilhelm. Well, as you know, life in Germany was not so good under the Republic! Many people were trying to get away for a while into another country. So it was very good luck, that through my family connections was I offered an appointment as a stable boy at the Emperor's court in exile at House Doorn, in the Netherlands.

The night that I met Henderson—it was March or April of that year—was the Emperor hosting a tremendous banquet. Great people of all sorts were there, barons and baronesses, dukes and duchesses, and artists; they had been arriving at the estate for days. All of us servants, even those not ordinarily allowed inside the house, had been brought in to assist with the party. What an affair! Even now can I recall the glittering jewels of the fine German ladies, also their rich gowns. You see, the Republic was not so bad for everybody!

Outside, there was a terrible storm. Now and then would a thunderclap shake the whole house, and the ladies would fearfully gasp. But the food and wine were very good and they kept everyone from worrying too much about the weather. Then suddenly there was a howl: a very loud howl! I remember saying to my friend Heinrich, whom all of us called Hieronymus—how we remember these little things after so great a time!—that the howl sounded like some terrifying thing from the grave. Now began all the guests to look nervous and set down their silvery forks.

The chief butler gathered the servants around. "Arno has caught something," he told us. "Some of you boys go out and quiet him."

The howl was coming from the garden. When we got there, we saw that the chief butler had been right. (That was why he was chief!) Arno, the Empress's German Shepherd, had something up a tree. A man! He was up there in the highest branches, which with his weight rose and fell, bringing him closer and closer to where Arno could reach him with his high leaps. He made no sound at all. He just stayed hanging there.

"Hah, Arno," I said, and the dog came to my hand. Warily climbed the man down. He pulled his rain-hood away from his face. This was my first sight of Henderson. That queer fellow! I remember him well. He was very tall and thin—just as you have said, Professor. Also had he a sort of nervous way of looking about, which reminded one of a schoolboy. He was all wrapped up in a poor sort of rain-coat, in one pocket whereof—which you have also mentioned—was a writing-tablet. There was water pouring down his face and out of his sleeves. I recall this because good old Hieronymus joked, "Look! Arno's treed a fountain!" And how we laughed!

As I write this, recall I also that Henderson had a great gold tooth, on the left side of his mouth, a very bad one that stuck out in a funny way, which I am surprised that you have not put in your letter, for it was what one would notice first of all about him.

Anyway: I stepped forward. (Though it's just me saying it, I was a sort of leader of all the boys.) "Who are you?" I asked the stranger quite commandingly. "Don't you know you're trespassing on the Imperial Court of Germany?"

"I need to see the Emperor," said the man. Then we shared a good chuckle! Ha! This wet beggar who no doubt had gotten himself lost on the road from Amersfoort! "You're surely a joker!" I told him.

"No," he said, seeming confused. "I am a poet."

Well! A poet! I didn't know whether to believe him or not. I had thought of all poets as looking like my uncle Walther, who was very fat, a bachelor, his veins always breaking and thereby making blue lines on his face: and he wasn't even a proper poet of the sort found in books. He only made up little rhymes about the girls in town. You can see I haven't much education! Well, it's a fine thing, a "country bumpkin" like me is writing to a Professor about a poet! Chance is a funny trick player!!

Of course, we should have turned the intruder away on the spot. But as I have told you there was a very terrible storm. The stranger seemed harmless. And after all hadn't he given us a bit of fun? So we brought him back to the servants' quarters and made up the spare bed for him. This was all quite against the rules—but we were the boys! I think boys are never any different than we were, isn't that right? Then afterwards returned we to the party, telling the chief butler it was a squirrel Arno had caught.

"The biggest squirrel I ever saw!" said Hieronymus.

How we laughed!

After that, Mr. Henderson became a sort of secret mascot for all the servants. We brought him pocketfuls of food from our own table; the girl servants—we'd let them in on it soon enough, that's no surprise!!—sewed him a new coat out of scraps, all different colors, so he looked always like a gay marionette going about. Each day he would remind us that he needed to see the Emperor. He told us he was bearing a very important message. "His Majesty is very busy!" we'd tell him. "You're on the list! Be patient!"

Of all the boys, it was I who knew Henderson best. I was interested in him right away since I was a bit of a Communist back then (not anymore!!) as very many young people were in those days. Well, when I found out Henderson was a Soviet I was naturally excited! I wanted to hear all about "the workers' paradise." But it turned out Henderson was no Communist at all. This is what he said to me once: "The Communist Party is a wretched galleon manned by fleas, adrift upon a sea of mucus and spit." Well, what do you think he meant by that?! Have I any idea? Well, you see why he was the poet and I just a stable boy! I hope you can figure it out, Professor!

And here's a queer thing! Whatever Henderson said—sense or nonsense—captivated us! It did not matter that he was so poor at German speaking. It only made us listen more carefully. And even when we had not the littlest idea what he was saying we never became bored or wandered away. Well, somehow there was always an idea that he was saying something important and with patience we stupid boys would understand him. But we never did!

Henderson and I used to roam through the woods that grew around the edges of the estate, which was the only place, where would we not be seen. What kind of a pair of friends we were! Well, but he kept me laughing all right. He called the other servants "curs" and "locusts." The lords and ladies who visited the palace were "pustulating parasites and whore-diddlers, abomination-hawkers, nation-out-sellers." The only person to whom he gave any respect was the Emperor himself. Each day asked he me, when his meeting with the Emperor could be scheduled. "Soon," I always was telling him, "any day now. You are close to the top of the list."

Of course there was not any such list! But one day—and with no help from me—Henderson got his meeting! Well, that's quite a story!

This was in September of 1932. By that time I had moved a bit upward and at last had I gotten out of those very bad-smelling stables. Now I sat all day long in the entrance lodge, where my job was to sort through the hundreds of letters that arrived each day for the Emperor. Such tales of woe! Such misery! Germany brought low! Terrible times! I picked out one sad letter from every bundle for the Emperor to read. When he was finished—I can see this now in my eyes!—he marked his imperial seal "IR" on the top corner of each page.

Well, with my new job I had not as much time to spend walking about with my friend Henderson, you can guess it. I left him in the morning and came back to visit him in the night time. Now one day I came back to the servants' quarters and what do you think? No Henderson! Well, was I afraid! At once started I a search for him, praying all along that nobody had found him first; then were our secret all finished!

Soon enough I spied him far away on a garden path; but oh no! He was conversing with a certain Baron Pfaffenrot! I was ruined! I thought, the Emperor will certainly be done with me now! Now it's back to Germany with me! My parents throw me out! I am a beggar on the street!

But when I drew closer saw I, that the Baron looked unangry; let it be said, he was laughing! Well, this made me not so afraid, and I joined them to see what all this laughing was about.

"Hello, boy," Pfaffenrot said. "Your friend Henderson here was just explaining to me how I was like the sow that roots about in her own excrement."

"You might also," Henderson told him, "be called a two-legged pestilence. Or a bicycle whose front wheel is stupidity and whose back wheel is treason. And whose foot pedals are an idiot's love of British foppery." At this laughed Pfaffenrot all the harder.

Well, let me explain a little. Pfaffenrot was not really much of a Baron. In fact, he was the very last of seven sons and so his whole life expected he to enter a trade. But then the other six boys got the Spanish flu! And just like that he was a Baron! I've said it already—chance is a funny trick player! Anyway, Pfaffenrot was not only very bad-mannered, he was also a British spy! He was always hanging about House Doorn asking questions to the nobility. Spying on the Emperor's court was the least important of all British spying; so nobody bothered him about it. Well, those were funny times, that's all I'm saying!

So Pfaffenrot said to me, "Boy there, my amusing new friend tells me you've been putting off his appointment with the Emperor."

"Well, no, Sir," I said, "not exactly. Any day now his Majesty will be free."

"Still," Pfaffenrot replied, "since I'm seeing his Majesty in a few moments, I thought I might bring Mr. Henderson along with me."

Well, what was I to do! I stood there with my mouth fully open!

"Oh, do not worry, boy," Pfaffenrot said. "I won't expose you."

And the two of them strolled off toward the palace. Well, what do you think I did then? I sneaked along behind! When I came into the house I hid in a storeroom wherefrom I knew I could overhear people speaking in the Emperor's chambers. One of the house girls had shown it to me once, ha ha ha! Boys!

I settled myself in the little room and waited. Before long were the Baron and Mr. Henderson let in. The Baron introduced Henderson as his new manservant. Not very likely! Henderson in his torn-up every-colored coat! But as I have said, Pfaffenrot was not well known for his good manners!

Mr. Henderson kept quiet at first, while talked Pfaffenrot and the Emperor of their mutual friends in London and Berlin. I could hear the Baron taking notes in his little pad, all the while, and sometimes he would ask the Emperor to repeat himself—well, you see why he wasn't a more important spy! After some time came the conversation around to politics. This was one of the favorite topics of the Emperor; I heard him lean forward on his creaky seat, which was just his old saddle, actually, fixed upon a post behind his desk, and the two men spoke about issues of state of every kind.

And then: Henderson spoke up!

"Hirohito, that little mongoose with grotesque fangs," Henderson growled suddenly. "He will eat the eaters of spoiled eggs under the ground."

What a surprise for the Emperor, when the manservant so spoke! For one thing, it was Italy the two men had been discussing! But Baron Pfaffenrot did not seem so surprised. "My man refers to British possessions in China," said Pfaffenrot. "They are seriously endangered by Japan, he is quite correct."

"All emperors, except the Emperor, should be mashed up in the gears."

"I like the way you're talking!" said the Emperor. Then he asked Henderson what he thought of Mr. Hitler and his National Socialists.

"Pah," Henderson said, "A stupid puppy who does not know enough not to defecate in his vomit before eating it. Soon enough he will sicken and choke on his own soil."

Now, the Emperor did not care for Hitler a great deal. For at one time Hitler was every month sending us flattering notes—the Germans needed to claim again their past, the Emperor would sit again on his throne, and so forth. And at that time Hitler's name was spoken about very sweetly in House Doorn. Not any more! Now it was clear who wore the hat, if you see what I mean!

"Yes," Pfaffenrot said, "there are many people in England—I have heard—who think that Hitler is the least of the dangers that they face."

"The English are in more danger of breaking off their own noses while trying to straighten their absurd hats," Henderson answered him. I heard Pfaffenrot make a great laugh at that one.

It's a funny thing! A wandering poet instructing a Baron and the Emperor about matters of state! But that's just how it happened! As I told you, Henderson's talking had a curious effect on people!

"Surely you're no servant," said the Emperor.

"Indeed, no." replied Henderson. "I am a poet, and I have come to Doorn to deliver an important message to you."

"Well then, poet," said the Emperor, "let us hear it."

Henderson took a deep breath. "His Majesty," he said, "is a demented old ass."

"I say," said Pfaffenrot.

"By rights he ought to have expired with his hand-fantasies of world conquest. He is like a toad sick with constipation who boils himself in his own reeking fluids. He ought to be eaten from the feet up by wasps. His mind is gone and replaced by a chamberpot in the shape of a human head, which is filled with a vile soup of sweat, rotten meat, and worthless notes. He is to be pitied by idiots and pilloried by besotted dwarves. The Dutch ought to burn his house down and sprinkle the ashes with lye. Hail the Emperor!"

Well, what do you think? After all these years I remember every word! I was shocked! Even merry Pfaffenrot couldn't manage a laugh!

The next thing I heard was Henderson running out of the room, and the Emperor shouting for the guards. I burst out of my hiding spot; but I couldn't catch up with Henderson. Neither could the guards. So that was the end of the poet's visit to House Doorn! And I the last of all the boys still alive to tell about it! Lucky your letter found me when it did!

Well, anyway, I'll finish! Soon enough the trouble in Germany became worse. But, you know, Pfaffenrot was always saying from then on just what Henderson had said; that Britain should only wait and let Hitler come to his own grief. And I suppose he was saying that same thing to his employers in London too. Well, I don't want to be the one to say that Henderson's poor advice kept the Nazis around long enough to start all their trouble! You, an educated man, know better than me: things have all kinds of causes! I'm an old dullard! I'm only telling you these things I've seen!

Now I'm still not quite done. By chance I ran across Henderson one more time, in Berlin, in 1940. By then I am sorry to say had I fallen a little distance in the world—so I was quite excited to see a reminder of happier times! And you know, Henderson had not changed a bit! In fact, he still wore the rag-coat the girls had made for him! It turned out he was about to move to London; apparently something he had written had made angry the Nazis. Well, there's old Henderson, always getting in trouble with his talking! I couldn't resist having a little fun with him!

"Well, Mr. Henderson," said I, "you certainly did have it wrong about politics!"

He gave me a queer look. "It was you worthless Germans who were wrong," he said. "So it's you who will wake up with a bloody throat. Not I. I will be gone."

Well, as usual, I didn't know what he meant! But I think he was right about being gone—that was the last time I saw him! If he is dead or living I don't know! Maybe you can tell me!

Look how long now I've gone on! Well, we old men are all alike that way. I'm sure you know so! I hope this will be of some help to you. But don't thank me! It's my sister you ought to thank—for never throwing anything away!

I am yours!

Karl-Heinz Sethius

CHAPTER 6

THE IMPLICATIONS

"That's the end," Ellen said, and for a confused moment I thought she was still reading; that Sethius was assuring us we hadn't lost a page. But of course she was speaking for herself. She folded the letter up and slid it back into the blue envelope. There was silence, the heavy kind that follows a loud, startling sound, or a tremor. I found myself waiting for an aftershock; but there was none. The four of us were there in our places, just as we had been, and the earth was still.

"So Mister Sunrise started World War Two," Julia said. "Who would have thought?"

No one answered her. During the course of the letter I had turned to stare at Higgs, hoping for some reaction; I'd even brought out my Henderson Society steno pad. The silence nagged at me like slight hunger or an itchy eye. I bombarded Higgs with telepathic messages: Come on. No time like the present. Go for it.

Julia tried again: "Imagine, him finding that flyer after thirty years."

"It's some coincidence," Ellen said. Then, carefully: "Don't you think, Stanley?"

"Yes," Julia said, "isn't it strange?"

Suddenly I was swept up with anger at Higgs. Why wouldn't he speak? Why not now, with this scholarly windfall in front of him? When would he ever have a better chance?

But there he sat, silent, and confronted with his smooth and even gaze my anger dwindled to nothing. I was left with a heartful of wan resignation. The moment was fixed: our situation there, Higgs's and Julia's, Ellen's and mine, was suddenly imbued in my mind with an aura of domestic permanence, the aura that marriage has in Victorian novels, or the curses of the gods in Greek plays. We four were a tableau. Nothing from outside could touch us. The world beyond our basement, that realm of coincidences, of Henderson, of college, of countries and armies, seemed phantasmic now, a conjecture, utterly unconvincing.

"It's really something," I said. And it *was* something, I told myself: what had happened, what we'd learned, even if Higgs wouldn't admit it. Maybe, I thought dizzily, it was everything.

Then Higgs stood up. Ellen and Julia gasped. I fumbled for my steno pad. But he was only getting the box of tournament cards. Higgs looked over the topmost card, placed it on the board, and sat down again. Then he picked a red piece from the stack on the table with the eagerness and delicacy of a glutton selecting a bonbon, and set it down, with a click, on the square the card dictated. A black piece, a second click; and another red man, a third. *Click. Click. Click.* It was the sound of empty chambers, of a Russian roulettist three times fortunate. I began to consider the implications of what Sethius had told us; and Julia, whose turn it was, sat down to play.

The implications! It was not just the explanation of Henderson's time in Holland, not even the effect Henderson might have had on the outbreak of the war. No—what excited me, what made me distracted and light-headed with ambition, was not the answers in the letter, but the prospect of a whole new line of questions. Higgs, starting from the barest evidence, had brought to light Henderson's influence on the world's literary heroes. Now I would do the same for politics and states. How could no one have thought of it before? Berlin under Weimar was the crossroads of Europe, the petri dish of the Allied experiment: and there, and then, was Henderson, the blood of dukes in his veins, the uproar of Bolshevism in his past, and the beloved, despised figure of Kaiser Wilhelm in the secret spaces of his heart. He must have been an incarnate League of Nations—a human bickering. Who better than he to set the course of governments? I could already see the shape of what I'd find: one by one the yellowed headlines of *Le Figaro,* the *Times* of London and of New York, would reveal the workings of Henderson's hand, his hidden counsels. Next to him, Rasputin would come out as a harmlessly eccentric old clergyman. Madame Mao would be an ordinary henpecker. Whole countries, it would transpire, had been struck down by his off-hand remarks, and thousands slaughtered according to one or another of his fancies. I could see no limit to what might be explained. What I had in mind was no less than a new, more sensible history.

By this time I'd lost my taste for my nightly ritual of estrangement from Julia. Turning away from her no longer flattered my continence; or the flattery had grown too old and repetitive to please me. It was easier to stay at my desk until she was asleep; then I flicked off the lamp and lowered myself gingerly to the mattress, like a wayward husband. No creak, no rattle betrayed my lonely hitting of the hay. Flat on my back, arms at my side, I took my four hours of sleep.

I needed—had time for—no more. Before I hammered the twentieth century into its new shape, I had to verify the story that Sethius had told; and that would not be easy.

I gathered what documentation I could: memoirs of various German dandies; Dutch tourist guides; hundreds of ancient, spotted letters, cracking along the creases; the logbooks of the Amersfoort precinct; endless dull histories of Her Majesty's Intelligence. I felt like a movie Indian, padding silently through the pathless waste of words, searching for the one weathered footprint, half filled in with mud, that would give my prey away. My orderly habits deserted me. Up half the night, I worked in fits and starts; sometimes pacing feverishly, sometimes staring out the window, trying to pick out the squat skyline of

Chandler City, pitch dark against the almost-pitch dark of the sky. I blotted the sweat from my forehead with endless processions of tissue. My acne, psychosomatically, returned. The floor of my room was stalagmited with tottering stacks of books, letters, quartos, maps, and strewn with crumpled drifts of wax paper: the accumulated wrappers of my egg salad sandwiches. By that time I was eating eight or nine a night. And behind me, Julia slept, perfectly still, curled on her side with the covers pulled over her head; she was a long, z-shaped mound among the blankets, like earthworks.

I found out a few things. From the Kaiserin's diaries I learned that Kaiser Wilhelm had, in fact, been in a terrible temper throughout September 1932, snubbing nobles, insulting their wives, sending his supper back night after night. Hermione did not record the cause of her husband's distress; but it seemed clear from her language that she knew exactly what had brought it on. The Kaiser had indeed held a dinner party on the tenth of April of that year, and it had indeed been raining. The layout of the house was as Sethius had described it. And the Kaiserin's dog was named Arno.

Baron Pfaffenrot, too, was actual, although Sethius's estimation of him as a spy turned out to be overblown. At best, he'd been a gossip on retainer. But he'd dined with the Conservative MP Leo Amery on October 2, sharing his new opinion on the Hitler question. He'd met, too, with Arthur Henderson, Labour's tribune of disarmament, and— yes—Henderson's third cousin; and when Italy invaded Abyssinia in 1935, it was Arthur Henderson, months from his deathbed, who'd expressed in a privately-circulated editorial the prevailing opinion that Japan, not Fascism, was the real threat to England; and that Britain, by rearming, "would cut off her own nose"—surely an echo of Henderson's own assessment. And England did not rearm; and Mussolini took Abyssinia unopposed; and everyone knows what happened after that.

That was where I stood: the circumstantial evidence perfect, and perfectly circumstantial. I could find no contemporary testimony to Henderson's presence in Holland. Nor did Sethius show up on the books. The letter, to a critical eye, could still have been a hoax; one had only to postulate a hoaxer as diligent in his research as I was. As for myself, I had not a doubt that the letter was genuine; but, I was forced to concede, I was anything but an unbiased observer. The letter, if verified, would make my reputation. If it were fake I would be a laughingstock. And there—as I said—I stood.

Until: at three-thirty in the morning of September 19, my fingers clumsy from a night spent fruitlessly unfolding and refolding facsimiles of Imperial correspondence, I plucked an egg salad sandwich from my bag, my eyes still focused on the sheet before me (some soapmerchant's petty wheedle, his Majesty's sympathetic but unhelpful reply) and, as I unrolled it from its wrapping, lost my grip. I fumbled, made a futile stab; but the sandwich plummeted into the raft of papers at my feet. When I retrieved my snack, a page came along with it: a poem of Henderson's that McTaggett had given me to read some weeks ago. I peeled the poem off the sandwich. The leaking mayonnaise had left a broad, shiny stain on the page, a stain shaped suspiciously like a hand; and the outstretched finger of that hand was resting on a stanza just two words long; and the two words were "red whistle."

Red whistle—*rote Pfiff*—Pfaffenrot.

The poem was called "Sudetenland, My Mother." It was a late work, only recently discovered, dating from just before Henderson's move to London. The poem had not yet yielded to analysis, which was why McTaggett had given it to me. I'd looked it over and found it impenetrable. In the excitement surrounding the Sethius letter, I'd forgotten all about it.

The stained section read, "Examine the// red whistle// of the tea-cur which chews at its own entrail/ My uncle has lost his hat and chamberpot; it/ is my fault." The tea-cur was England; this was one of Henderson's favorite kennings. McTaggett had suggested that the "red whistle" was the dog's penis; but the Gravinic word for "dog" Henderson used to describe his parents' countrymen suggested a contemptible absence of sexual characteristics, whether female or male. The sense of the passage, McTaggett had conceded, remained unclear.

But no longer. The red whistle was none other than the spying Baron; the rise of the Nazis (i.e., the passing of the "hat" from the Kaiser, or "uncle") had left him consumed with guilt, a guilt which, in some sense, was Henderson's own. It was all obvious now. Scattered throughout the rest of the poem I could see the rest of Sethius's story. There was the storm, the dog, there a "spasmatic servant boy" that must have been my informant himself. I stood up from my chair, reeling with the onset of understanding, wanting desperately to have it all set down somewhere, publicized; I swayed like a Pentecostal, there in my circle of lamplight, transported by joy and the responsibility of being the only one who knew.

"I win," I said aloud, trying out the sound of it. Julia stirred and tugged the sheet down a bit, uncovering her still-closed eyes. She mumbled something I couldn't understand. I knelt by the bed.

"I've got it," I told her.

"Yes," she said; to somebody, I thought, in a dream.

"I'm going to be famous."

Her eyes opened a little.

"Hi, there," she said.

"Hi," I repeated; vaulted into bed, pulled the covers over me.

"Sleepy."

"Sleepy," I agreed.

And amazingly, I was. My moment of exultation was through now and I was left perfectly, serenely, exhausted. I turned my body toward Julia's back and let one arm drape over her sweat-damp shoulder. She moved neither away from nor toward me, which was as I wanted it. I pressed my face into the pillow and twisted myself deeper into the sheets. I felt capable of racing through two weeks' sleep in the three hours before morning; and in the dim light of my desklamp, my arm thrown over Julia's warmness, I got down to the business of rest.

Events proceeded quickly. I showed McTaggett my discovery, and through him the word diffused within days to the strewn Gravinicists of the world. Daily I received flattering, inquisitive letters from my colleagues—so they called themselves now! I let them stack up on my desk. McTaggett assured me that upon the publication of my paper the department would grant me my degree at once. Even my parents were impressed. We were welcome, my mother told me, to stay with them if we wanted to save some money—an offer previously extended only on the condition that I give up my academic ambitions and resume my old station at the fry-o-lator.

And Julia—Julia accepted the reestablishment of my affections without a protest, with, in fact, a fierce and cattish enthusiasm that startled me anew each evening. My petulant self-denial dropped off me like a snakeskin. I was a red, sensitive, brand-new thing.

"Isn't that better?" she asked me. She'd put her bra back on and was standing in the window's orange light, looking out at the not-much-out-there; I was resting, out of breath, against the bathroom door.

"You're right," I said.

Such a pleasure to hand over the keys.

"That's good to hear," she said, not turning around.

"You're right," I told her. "You're right, you're right, you're right."

Now and then I forced myself to recall that all my success was the result of a simple stroke of luck. Sethius's letter might have come on someone else's watch, or it might never have come at all, or I might have been more sure-handed with my sandwich. But the letter *had* come, and to me. My future was assured; once my paper was done I could quit my job with Higgs; and in my private reckoning it seemed to me that the whole sorry story of my benighted youth had come, against all odds, to an entirely satisfactory conclusion.

But it was not the conclusion. One morning, a few weeks after my discovery, I opened the door to Higgs's house only to be hit full on by a man hurtling out. His momentum knocked me backwards; my heel struck the scalloped edge of the front walk and the two of us plunged into the bushes.

I was stunned for a moment, there inside the hedge, until the stringent odor of the snapped branches tugged me back into full awareness. I could hear Julia's voice, from out on the walk: "Sammy? What happened?" But all I could see was the spiny network of branches, and my skinny assailant, heaped atop my chest in the green darkness. Shaped like an arrow. It was Treech.

"Sorry," he said, managing to lift his face up a little. "One second." Then he slumped back down, out of wind.

Into the thicket came Julia's hands; she took me by the wrists and dragged the two of us back into the light. Treech leaned on me woozily. I clapped my chest for breath. The two of us hung together like a just-finished relay team.

"Sorry," Treech repeated, panting. "Just going . . . on my way."

But this time he wasn't talking to me. Ellen had come out of the house, still in her slippers. In one hand she was clutching a crumpled sheet of paper, and in the other she held a serrated stone dagger, thrust out in front of her, its tip shaking with the shaking of her hand.

"You. Get. Out. Of. Here," she said through gritted teeth, punctuating each word with a downward chop of the knife. I had long since disavowed the idea that Ellen was really dangerous; but now, her face emotionless, her skin flushed, her hands clenched so tightly that her tendons stood out up to her elbows, she seemed fully capable of reviving the dagger's long-dormant career as an agent of human sacrifice. I wished Treech would let go of me. I felt like a hostage.

We stood frozen, a diorama. Ellen's housedress flapped in the feeble breeze. A pigeon was pecking spitefully at something in the lawn. I became acutely conscious of the scratches I had incurred in my fall; I thought I could feel each tiny pain as a distinct sensation, requesting individual attention, a cold compress, a prod. But under the circumstances it seemed best to hold still.

"What *is* this?" Julia said. And at the sound of her voice Ellen softened a little. Her face became less masklike, her grip a little looser. The dagger drooped from her hand like a rejected flower. She seemed to consider; then she held out the crumpled paper to Julia.

"Read," she said. And Julia took the page from Ellen's suddenly limp hand. When she was finished with it—her face dark—she handed it to me.

It was a letter from the Henderson Society, on stationery the color of old gauze, informing Mrs. Higgs that said Society, concerned about the continued mental degradation of Professor Higgs, and having been made aware of questionable practices in the guardianship of said Professor—I stopped there.

"Questionable practices?" I said, bewildered. "What are they talking about?"

"Read," Ellen said.

So I continued: the Society, having been made aware, etc., had filed suit for and been awarded custody of the abovementioned party, effective in one week's time—noon on Friday, the 11th of October. There followed a solid block of legal hocus-pocus, in eight-point type: I saw the word "exigency," and the names of several psychiatrists. Below the text were affixed the signatures of the Society's officers and the relevant funtionaries of the court. I recognized the judge's name. He'd been a star basketball player at Chandler State, of Coach Mahemeny's vintage.

"This can't be right," Julia said. "You can't sue for custody without a hearing or family court or something."

"Oh, there was a hearing," Treech said. "Maybe Mrs. Higgs shouldn't have skipped the court date."

"What court date?" Ellen said.

"The one you signed the summons for."

Ellen seemed to rediscover the dagger in her hand. "That's a lie."

Treech held his hands up, edged backwards. "Hey," he said, "I'm just a messenger."

"Questionable practices?" I burst out.

Treech drew himself up a bit. He was still speckled with tiny leaves. He looked at me with a little wrinkle in his brow; as if I, not he, were the one talking craziness.

"Honestly, Samuel, I didn't think you'd want to belabor the point—not *here.*" He glanced significantly at Julia.

"Let's belabor it," I said. "For my peace of mind."

"If you're determined to put it all on the table . . ." He produced three photographs from his bag and handed them to me.

I recognized the pictures immediately as the ones Treech had taken at our first meeting. But to my dismay they had somehow been tampered with. The first photo on the pile was the last one he had taken, with Ellen reaching to block the camera lens. Someone had added a rolling pin, mottled with flour, to Ellen's outstretched, clutching hand; and the annoyance on her face had been magnified, through a darkening of the brow and a tightening of the cheeks, into a feral grimace. The next picture was the one of Ellen and Higgs. Ellen had been given the rolling pin again, which she now brandished above Higgs as if about to administer a gleeful punishment. Higgs's gaze had been redirected to meet beseechingly with Ellen's. Fading bruises were laced artfully up and down his arms.

All three of us were in the final shot, which appeared, at first, to have been left alone. Ellen and I were standing against the wall, under the row of windows, facing the camera; Higgs was seated at his table. There were no rolling pins, no bruises, no suggestion of violence. But my own face, I saw after a moment, had been subtly changed; with horror, I realized that my expression was one of barely suppressed lust. And Ellen, the recipient of my painted-on ardor, had been given a proud smirk, as if to encourage me, and to mock her cuckold husband, whose oblivious stare had this time been left exactly as it was. The effect was stunningly realistic, and the implicit narrative obvious: Ellen and I had conspired to keep Higgs silent, through threats and corporal abuse, all so that I could remain available for adultery—and on the university payroll. I was almost convinced myself.

"These pictures are doctored," I said. My voice, even to me, sounded strident and guilty.

"Don't be ridiculous," Treech snapped.

"It doesn't make sense. If this were going on, why would we let you take pictures of it?"

"Your poor judgment isn't any concern of mine."

"And what about the tapes?" I asked, jabbing my finger at him. "There'd have to have been some sign on the tapes."

"Save it for the judge," Treech replied. Then he made a show of slapping his forehead. "Oops," he said. "I forgot about how you skipped the hearing."

"Ask him what they're going to do to Stanley when they take him away," Ellen said, startling me.

I turned inquisitively back to Treech.

"Well," he said. "He's obviously in need of psychological therapy. Communicative breakdown. Possible aphasia. Possible regression." He ticked off the symptoms on his palm.

"They're going to shock him until he talks," Ellen said.

"Oh my God," said Julia.

"It's an established medical procedure," Treech said mildly. "Your husband's health is extremely important to us. As I think this whole episode demonstrates."

Ellen raised the knife again. Treech dipped into his bag, came out with his camera, and squeezed off a series of shots.

"Why, you," she said, "don't you—"

"You have to admit," he said, pocketing the camera, "that's not going to look good." And he turned officiously and strode off into the campus, a bouncing arrow pointing at the sky.

There was a sharp crack. On the walk at Ellen's feet lay the dagger; the impact on the flagstone had snapped the handle neatly from the blade.

"Oh my God," Julia said again.

I had begun to form a terrible suspicion which I wanted very badly to dispel.

"I'm going after him," I said.

I caught up with Treech not far from the house, in a little tiled plaza adjoining the biology labs. He was sitting on a bench, his bag beside him, watching a loosely organized volleyball game. The sun pressed down on my shoulders; the breeze carried past me the languid cheers of the volleyball players. A tiny plane banked overhead. It was difficult to keep the gravity of my mission in mind.

When Treech saw me he shoved his bag aside and slapped the slats of the bench where the bag had been.

"Come here and sit down," he said.

I came, I sat.

"You made good time," Treech said.

"You were expecting me?"

"Well, I assume you're here demanding an apology. Of course you've got every right to be angry."

"Yes," I said, disarmed.

"You should have been notified earlier. It's not that we don't recognize your contributions. But we couldn't risk your letting something slip. He doesn't miss much."

"He?"

Treech gave me that wrinkle-browed look again. "Higgs."

"Notify me now."

"What's left to say?" Treech said. "Once we found out he was holding out on us it was just a matter of deciding on a response."

"He, Higgs. Was holding out on you."

Treech peered at me, staring into my eyes as if searching for some flaw there, a burst blood vessel that would account for my behavior.

"Don't you remember telling me?"

So my suspicion was confirmed. I was Iago after all.

"All I wanted was for you to put a microphone in the bedroom," I said weakly.

"We considered that. But he and his wife could have just gone outside at night, after you'd gone."

"He doesn't go outside."

Treech went on as if I hadn't spoken. "We could have just had you stay through the night, of course, or just hire another informant. Probably that's what we should have done all along; as in, to hell with the dean, to hell with his daughter. But who knows? He could have written her notes under cover of darkness. Thrown them in the fire when he was done, or eaten them. Even if you slept in the same room he'd have chances. Finger spelling. Things you'd never detect. Best just to get him out. That makes it simple."

"But you said—something concrete. I didn't bring anything. There *isn't* anything. I thought you'd forgotten all about it."

"You know," he said, "things move slowly. There are certain elements within the Society that were resistant. The older professors. It's sentimental; respect for our stricken comrade, and all that. And I won't say I don't understand that way of thinking."

"No, of course not." I was dazed. Behind Treech a shirtless boy leaped, hollered, spiked.

"And frankly," Treech continued, "when you first told me what was going on I didn't think much of it. After all, who were you? Honest truth here: nobody. All that's changed now."

"The Sethius letter."

"You're worth quite a bit more than you used to be."

"But listen—"

"I know," Treech said, "the photos." He waggled his head slowly. "An unavoidable measure. We needed it for the hearing; the judge wanted some cover. In addition to what we paid him. You can't believe how much these guys ask for! Thank God for Kosugi."

Then he glanced at me slyly. "Oh—but *I* know what you're worried about. Nobody thinks that you and Ellen—you know! I hope you're not in too much trouble with your girlfriend!"

He clapped his hand to my shoulder, like a comrade. The volleyball game was breaking up; I imagined one of those tanned and bright-toothed players catching sight of us on the bench, and I realized with a little horror that we would look perfectly natural, Treech and I. We made sense together.

"I noticed that the girl seems to have developed an attachment to him," Treech went on. "Well, that's the way. You know women; they go for the vulnerability. *Woundedness.* She'll get over it. Buy flowers, that usually works."

"There's been a mistake," I said.

"Yes?"

Confessing was easier than I would have thought.

"I made it up," I told Treech. "I didn't hear him saying anything. I just wanted to get back at Ellen."

Treech stood up and began to pace out a slow, wobbly circle.

"I'll tell you what, Sam; I'm inclined to believe you."

I buckled a little with relief. "I'm so sorry for all the trouble this must have caused."

"And I *will* believe you—as soon as our results at the clinic back you up."

"I'm serious!"

"How did he get to you?" Treech asked sharply.

"He?"

"Higgs!"

"Higgs?" I said. "Higgs doesn't get to anybody!"

Treech gazed back at me, coolly.

"I'll find a way to stop this," I said.

"That's easy enough."

"What do you mean?"

"All you have to do," Treech said, "is get him to talk."

That night I sat on the bed, unable to concentrate, trying to force down an egg salad sandwich that tasted like dirt, like accusation. My gaze crawled from the yolk-flecked wax paper to our swaybacked, sweat-yellow mattress to Julia at her desk, her back to me, bent ostentatiously over a stack of folios. I'd told her I hadn't been able to find Treech, no better lie having occured to me. And she'd believed me; no surprise. Hadn't I already proved myself a liar of the first class?

"Stop staring," she said, without turning around.

"Let's go for a walk," I said. "It's too hot in here. You're not working."

"I *am* working."

A little while later she stood up, set her hands on her hips, and stretched backwards, cracking her waist.

"Well, let's go," she said.

We walked up Epimenides into what had been the industrial section of town. It wasn't any cooler than in our apartment; but outside, at least, one could dangle before oneself the false promise of a cooling wind, and the scenery was somewhat less familiar. The sun was still up, barely. It wouldn't start to cool down till well past dark. We walked, hand in damp hand, past the empty warehouses with their painted-on pediments and columns, over the cracking streets, through intermittent clouds of gnats and flies. Julia was reading the faded emblazons of commerce off the bricks, one by one: McHenry Bros. Joseph Parson Sinks. Dry Goods. Sons of Jacob Henneman. The column of quiet smokestacks ahead of us seemed part of a gigantic municipal pipe organ, three-quarters submerged, poised to explode at an appropriate moment into song.

"Do you think we should get married?" I said.

"You mean now?"

We walked another block.

"I mean eventually. Sometime specific."

"Maybe." Another block, then: "Why do you ask?"

"It's obviously of some interest to me." Wry was what I was going for but it came out stuffy, as if we were negotiating a bank loan.

"I mean why do you ask *now,*" she said. "Because of Treech?"

Honestly, I wasn't sure. I had proposed, if proposal it was, almost before it had occurred to me that I was going to speak. But it must have been Treech; because all day I'd been thinking of his hand on my shoulder. And *You know women,* he'd said, as if admitting me with these words into some unpleasant fraternity with him, with the Society, with garreted, scheming men everywhere. I didn't want any part of it. I wanted to marry Julia; wanted to move away somewhere, maybe take up psychology or art history again. I could learn to respect that. What I wanted most of all was to drive down the conviction I'd felt, there on the bench, bubbling up in me like crude oil, that Treech had me pegged; that at my cloistered heart I was one of his. I nodded: it was Treech.

"What do you think will happen?" she said.

"I think Treech'll take him away on Friday. I guess I'll have to get a new job for a while. Maybe work in the restaurant. My mother said we could move in."

"We are *not* moving in with your parents."

But she must have known we would have to; our rent had gone up again, and there was no way I could make enough at the restaurant to pay my share. Not even if I worked nights at the copy store besides. That and my plasma wouldn't be enough.

"Anyway," she said, "what I meant was once they take him. With the shock treatment."

I knew, of course, what she'd meant.

"I don't know anything about it," I said. "Could be he'll be brain damaged. Could be he'll die. I guess there could be no effect at all. Could be he'll talk."

"You're awfully calm about it."

"There isn't much we can do."

It was true; Julia had talked to every lawyer in town and none was inclined to take us on, not for what we could pay. Not that it mattered; I didn't doubt the Society would buy as many judges as they needed to, if it came to a fight.

Julia laced her fingers up behind her and lifted her gaze to the tiny, faraway clouds. "It's terrible," she said.

Once we'd laughed about suicide: remember? And not just that, but floods and earthquakes, girls down wells, the situation in the Middle East, widow-burnings and ritual mutilation, the way a teenager might shoot you for a parking spot. We'd sent half the world down to Davy Jones. There wasn't anything awful enough to sober us up—until now. With a little perspective it made no sense. One old man and a few thousand volts against the great parade of suffering we'd already allowed to go by: it was nothing. And yet there she was, cloud-gazing, pronouncing it terrible, her lips set without a trace of joking. It's my fault, I thought suddenly. Not the whole catastrophe with Higgs, though that was my fault too, but her seriousness. I'd exhausted something in her. Whatever it was that was meant to lift me up had dragged her down instead, to the gloomy, hot, humorless land of me and people like me.

Anyhow, it was clear enough what I had to do. I took Julia's hand and ordered myself to commiserate, with all the gravity that I owed her. But what I said was "Although."

"Although?" she said, stopping, letting my hand go. "Although what?" We had come into the shadow of the cloverleaf; ahead of us, a finger of road swung upward and traced a dramatic gesture over our heads, on its way to join the interstate on its charge to the Pacific.

"Although there's not really anyone to blame," I said. "When you look at it rationally. It's not as though they *want* to hurt him."

"But?"

"But he's getting old. That's all it's about. What if he dies without saying what he's going to say?"

"Somebody else would figure it out."

"Not necessarily."

"And so what anyway?"

"I'm not trying to defend it," I said. "All I'm saying is that they want the same thing we want; for Higgs to talk again."

"The same thing *you* want."

"So what do you want?"

She shrugged. I felt duplicitous, weak as a reed. How had it come out this way?

"To get married?" I suggested.

"I said maybe."

I was sorry I had brought it up again. It would now be more difficult to raise the next point at hand.

"I hope you understand Treech changed those photographs," I said.

"That's obvious."

"At this point I feel very close to Ellen," I pressed on. "But you can't think that anything's gone on between us besides what's natural."

At this Julia made a noise very much like a gargle.

"Could you not," she said, "be a *complete* idiot."

"I worry."

"Just don't say anything."

And the rest of our walk passed in silence. The air was as thick and soggy as hot milk.

When we got to our door, Julia said, "What if he talks before Friday?"

"Then they won't take him."

"And do you think he will?"

I sensed the opportunity, a drab consolation, to be reassuring. "I do."

"You really think so?"

"In his situation," I said, "wouldn't you?"

But he didn't say anything: not the next day, not Sunday, not Monday, and my optimism—forced, let's face it, even at the time—began to seem ill-considered, even meaningless. "In his situation," I'd said; but what *was* Higgs's situation? How could I, or anyone, begin to guess?

Of course, I had theories. Here was the simplest one: the Society was right, and Higgs was still wrestling, after thirteen years, with the Henderson problem. Maybe he was too proud, even in this extremity, to admit defeat. It was noble, at least; and it admitted the possibility of a last-second turnaround. Or: he'd forgotten about Henderson altogether; maybe from boredom, maybe from some tiny and irreversible malfunction. There were embolisms no bigger than a flea. All those thoughts we'd been ascribing to him were creatures of our own desire, as phony as the faces people see on Mars. This smacked of easy irony and I rejected it.

But what if he'd succeeded? That was the idea that started looking better as the week trickled on. He'd found it: the truth about Henderson, distilled into a few neat sentences, or words, or, who knew, one word! Certainly he'd had enough time to pare it to the kernel. I didn't know why he wouldn't tell us, unless his conclusion was so disappointing that he thought it better not to release it on the world. Or *dangerous*—that idea appealed to me a little. The order of things upset, all bets off . . . In any event it did not seem likely that the threat of the electric therapy would change his mind.

But Ellen and Julia, less susceptible than I to theory-making, were sure that Higgs would save himself; and I was eager to be proved wrong. So over the harried days that followed we tried everything we could think of to spur Higgs into speech.

On Tuesday it was arguments. "He'll listen to reason," Ellen insisted; and we offered him reasons, we pelted him with reasons.

"All you have to do," Julia said, pacing out the room's perimeter, "is say something—anything. It doesn't have to be the final say-all. Just to let them know you're still working on it." I was sucking sullenly from a can of too-sweet lemonade.

"A reassurance," Ellen said.

"You don't even have to tell Treech yourself," Julia pointed out. "The tape recorder's on. Just tell us what you're thinking."

We held still, neither breathing nor swallowing; lemonade pooled brackishly around my teeth and the bottom of my tongue. But nothing. Higgs seemed to be listening to a different station, and intently.

We presented him with ever more fanciful cases. Ellen unearthed photographs of long-forgotten family, nephews and nieces and in-laws of Higgs who had long since severed all ties with their silent, embarrassing relation; she entreated Higgs to believe that missing the Society's deadline would condemn them en masse to crippling years of grief. Julia reminded Higgs that his prominent position made him a role model, and that were he to submit without protest to the Society's treatment he would be endorsing a dangerous precedent for any other professor judged to be underproductive. (Did Higgs have a single colleague at Chandler State who could not reasonably be so judged?) We trotted before him the demands of finance, of Christian ethics, of national security. Higgs did not budge.

The next day Julia and I were greeted at Higgs's door by the unmorningish smell of raw meat. Ellen rushed out of the kitchen as we entered, and at the sight of her my first, aghast thought was that we'd lost track of the days; that Higgs had already been taken away, strapped in, shocked down to a smoking ruin before his wife's horrified eyes; because Ellen smelled like something charred, and her hair was pure white.

But it was only flour. It was all over her arms and hands as well. "I'm making Beef Wellington," Ellen said cheerfully. "Stanley's favorite. It's been years since we've had it. I just thought . . ." She waved one floury hand, vaguely, as if dismissing a social unequal.

"Sure," Julia said, "it's a special occasion." I nodded uneasily. It was a special occasion all right; but so was an execution, and the parallel was a little closer than I liked. She might as well have invited a priest.

Julia went downstairs. On impulse, I followed Ellen into the kitchen. It was a bare, bright room with windows looking out over the mesa's edge; just in front of us the sun was blazing its way upward through pink mats of cloud. The meat lay raw on the counter. Ellen leaned down and pulled open the oven door, releasing a billow of hot, bready air.

"This part's done," she said, lifting the tray of pastry to her eyes. And there, in the sunny, white-walled kitchen, among the reassuring knocks and clatters of the ancient oven, there with Ellen in her apron, I was able for a moment to imagine that it *was* done; not the pastry shell, I mean, but the whole story, my grand mishap, all the study and worry I had known thus far. I thought I had slipped mysteriously and permanently beyond it into some fixed domestic space.

"I've been up since five," Ellen said; then her face contracted and drew backwards as if caught in a bright light, and she began to cry, silently, without sobbing or shaking. She turned away from me so that her tears, falling, struck the hot surface of the stove and hissed away.

"I'm an old woman," she said. "I can't be expected to adjust to changes like this. I am an old woman now."

"You're not old," I said. I had no idea how I could reassure her, and I wished that Julia were there. But then I thought: just as well.

"I was Stanley's first girl," she said. "Did you know that?"

I shook my head.

"Before he met me . . . well, he wasn't much to speak of with girls. Is that an awful thing to say? But it's true—he told me. When he was in school here, before he found out about Henderson and Gravinic and everything, he was just a nothing. That's the way he put it to me and that's the only reason I say it—a *nothing*. Nobody thought he'd be a genius then or ever amount to anything and for sure you wouldn't have thought he'd ever leave Chandler City. We've had a good marriage."

"Of course you have."

"I'll be a *widow*." Her voice took on a flavor of wondering contempt.

"Don't think about that. He'll say something."

"One way or the other," Ellen said bitterly, "he'll say something."

I couldn't stand it: what I'd done, my hypocrisy. I felt the truth hot in my throat like bile, wanting out. It *was* bile. I thought I might be sick.

"It's my fault," I said.

"Don't be silly."

"No, I mean it. It's because of me."

"'Because,'" Ellen said, "is a very difficult word to use correctly. A because of B equals Not B implies not A; is that what you mean?"

This sudden turn to the abstract distracted me, then made me wonder if, in fact, a strict adherence to propositional logic might not moderate my guilt. Had all this happened because Stanley was born? Because Henderson was? Because Chandler City was founded in the first place?

Ellen, changeable as always, was back in the universe of things. She turned her head so she was looking up at me. "I don't want you blaming yourself," she said. "All those other boys sat down there, too. He didn't talk for any of them."

I placed one hand on her shoulder; I meant by the force of physical touch to keep up my resolve. But my resolve was already fading. What good would it do to confess? It wouldn't change anything; it wouldn't save Higgs; wouldn't, that is, redeem me. It would only make Ellen and Julia hate me forever. Why put that on top of everything that had already gone wrong?

"I'm sorry," I said lamely.

"I'm aware," Ellen replied, "that you're trying to help."

There was an uncomfortable silence. The raw tenderloin was stretched out before us on the counter like a prop for the Old Testament, an offering. I could feel the jutting, sail-shaped bone of Ellen's shoulder, straining against her skin and the thin, rough cotton of her dress. And that was how Julia found us.

"It smells great," she said.

"It sure does," I agreed. I felt a sudden, desperate need to be hearty. "You've got that right. That's going to be quite a breakfast!"

And so it was; although by the time the meat was ready it was almost time for lunch. We ate in the basement, exchanging appreciative murmurs, sopping up the juices of the roast with spongy hunks of sourdough bread, drinking glass after glass of iced tea from crystal tumblers. Ellen had broken out the good china, and covered our little table with a yellowed, creased cloth that smelled of naphthalene.

Higgs ate methodically and carefully, chewing each bite with the deliberateness advised in bygone health manuals. He displayed no more relish for Ellen's meal than he did for the packaged sesame sticks.

"Is it good?" Ellen kept asking him, her voice more tremulous each time. "Isn't it good, Stanley?" Higgs did not even turn to face her. When the meal was finished, he tilted his head up and allowed Ellen to wipe his lips; that was the extent of his response.

Discouraged but undissuaded, we pressed on. Julia tried taking away the checkerboard. He was not bothered at all. Ellen presented him with a selection of whiskeys and cordials, all of which he refused. By turns we leapt out from the stairwell, shouting like savages, in vain attempts to startle him.

There were still two days left, but I was beginning to resign myself to Higgs's upcoming removal; at the same time I couldn't stop rummaging around for stratagems. Those were two stages of grief; but which ones? I wished I'd stayed a psychology major longer. My legs were achy, I felt like snapping at Julia, and I had to go to the bathroom. What stage was that?

Just before nine, Ellen came downstairs, smiling nervously, a thin leaf of paper in her hand.

"Stanley," she said, "a telegram's come from London."

"Let me see that," I said, but she waved me away.

"My goodness, it's from Henderson!" she exclaimed. "He's heard about this trouble you're in." She looked down at the paper. "He says, Dear Professor Higgs, stop, I must ask you, stop, to break your silence, stop, for the sake of scholarship, stop, and your own well-being, stop. I look forward, stop, to your reply, stop." She looked hopefully at Higgs. "Did you hear that, Stanley?"

A cold rush of irritation invigorated me.

"For God's sake," I said.

Ellen shushed me violently.

"You can't seriously think he'd fall for that."

"Why don't you leave if you don't want to help?"

"I don't think it does any good to insult his intelligence with cheap tricks. Which does not mean I don't want to help."

Ellen gazed questioningly at Julia. I stepped in front of Higgs.

"He's made up his mind," I said. "Argue, all right. But no tricks."

Julia tugged at my arm. "Let's go," she said. "It's time."

And sullenly, with a glance back at Higgs, I went.

She stayed three strides ahead of me the whole way home, erect as a sentry. As I struggled to keep up with her I could almost see her new image of me, hardening in the forge of her disfavor; I was heartless, a brute, disrespectful of old women.

"I'm sorry," I called out. "I do want to help. Really."

"Really?" Julia said, without turning, without missing a step.

I put everything I had into it. "Really!"

But even as I said it I wanted to take it back. Not, I mean, that I was happy about what now was almost certain to befall Higgs. Yet there was some part of me, I recognized now, that was counting off the hours before Friday noon. I wanted Julia the way she'd been before. Once Higgs was gone—all right, once he was dead, or electro-encephalographically so, or whatever—there could be reverses. My faults would amuse her again.

How could we have been so careless? *Good marriage,* nothing—the Higgses' marriage was pathological, toxic, anyone could see that, and we'd exposed ourselves to it, twelve hours a day, like fools. No wonder we fought. We should have been wrapped in lead foil just to set foot in there. We should have worn welder's masks and taped gauze over our mouths. Ellen—I was warming up now. How much of Higgs's silence could be traced right back to his half-mad wife? What had she been whispering to him in that poison swamp, their bedroom, all these unrecorded years? Maybe Treech hadn't been so wrong with his touched-up photographs. Maybe she had a reason to be so cagy about the meaning of "because."

But now it was almost the end of all that. We'd have it back the way it had been. I was jumpy with good news. Julia was starting to increase the ground between us; I slowed down and gave my unhardy lungs a rest as she receded, without a look back, down the street. No matter. I'd catch her.

The next day—Thursday—we sat, silently, in our customary chairs, out of ideas. The grasshoppers were the loudest I had ever heard them; though that might just have been my nerves. Ellen was crying again, and had been since the morning. Every once in a while she rose and moved to Higgs, leaning on his shoulder, sniffling. Then she would shoot me a furious glare, which I returned in kind. I was still angry about the phony telegram; Ellen's casual imposture of Henderson's voice was an affront to me, and, I was sure, to Higgs as well. Who were we to talk him out of this? It was beneath his dignity, and I wanted badly to apologize. But I had to wait until I had him alone. I got my chance late that afternoon, when Ellen and Julia went upstairs to fill the snack bowl and transact some unspecified business. Higgs sat, quiescent, the checkerboard before him set up for a game; but I was through with checkers. I had a speech to give, and by that time I had worked it out in some detail.

I turned away from Higgs, toward the row of masks and the half-height windows. In front of me was the broad ceramic face of an Asiatic warrior, his nose chipped half away, his once-jeweled helmet stripped by some forgotten vandals. His eyes were rolled upward as if arrested in the throes of violent death, or passion.

The window before me was at ground level, facing away from the cliff; beyond it, a gentle rise obscured most of the world outside. Over the little hill I could see only the roofs of the dormitories, and, off to the left, the skew, patinated figure of Tip Chandler, my old perch. What would the hoary miner, sponsor of learning, thirst-crazed envisioner of the second Athens, have thought of the place his hacked-out veins of gold had built? Even to me, a native, it was strange; that the pursuit of knowledge could have come to this, a young man and an old one in a basement room, both specialists in an ornery language, neither quite willing yet to speak. The warrior mask rolled its flaking eyes at me. Athens, I was certain, was never like this.

With some effort I called my planned remarks back to mind.

"Professor Higgs," I said, "we're all very sorry about what's happening." I felt like I was dictating a letter. "I don't know exactly what conclusion

you've come to about this—I've given it some thought, haven't settled
on anything, but anyway, I know that if you've decided not to reveal
what you've come up with, or haven't, you have your reasons. I won't—
wouldn't—try to change your mind. And I'm sorry about the way
they've been behaving; your wife and Julia, I mean. They mean well. But
they don't understand the other issues here, the academic issues, the—
well, I don't have to explain it to *you.*" I laughed—as I had decided earlier I would laugh—meaning to indicate fellowship, inexpressible shared
experience. "But be assured that I'm behind you on this, and I think
what you're doing is—well, I'm embarrassed, a little, but it's brave; really
brave. And I'll try my best to carry on the way you would want."

There, I'd said it, and discharged my last responsibility. I took a
deep, satisfied breath. And when I turned back into the room Higgs
was staring at me.

Shocked, I stumbled backwards, as if his gaze possessed a compo-
nent of physical force. I realized instantly that everything I had just
said, everything I'd thought since the day before, was a lie; an embarrassing, pretentious lie. The academic issues—what did I care? What
were they, even? Perspective fled me, my cool remove drew away like
scrim. All that mattered was rescuing Higgs, getting him to talk,
excusing him from the Society's therapy. If he didn't speak now, he
never would; they would shock him and shock him until he died—I
knew this.

Higgs's face had taken on an expression of frank interest; his lips
pursed, he cleared his throat. The grasshoppers chirped feverishly.
Anticipating, I thought of Higgs's voice, the few sentences I'd heard
on that decaying reel of tape: *Henderson between the wars . . .*

Then Ellen and Julia came back down the stairs. I spun to warn
them off; but it was too late. At their appearance, Higgs's head had
snapped back to his accustomed position, and his countenance had
once again gone blank. I was dizzy with rage. I moved unsteadily
toward Ellen, my hands clenched, murder in mind.

"Any luck?" Julia said, and at this all my fury slumped inward on itself.

There was nothing to be gained from it. The chance was lost, through nobody's fault, my flush of hope as quickly gone as formed. At least I could spare the women the knowledge that they'd ruined everything.

"Only the usual kind," I said.

"Will you listen to those grasshoppers," Ellen said mildly. "Sounds like that rain is finally coming."

That night I saw McTaggett. He'd called me at home and commanded me in a thick, hoarse voice to meet him at a bar downtown, the Tooth and Nail. It was a single solemn room, done up in velvet and dark wood, like the front parlor of a funeral home. For some reason there were little ceramic dogs everywhere: lined up along the bar, nestled between the dusty stoppered bottles, arrayed in twos and threes atop the drink-ringed tables, frozen in their sundry poses like a circus act surprised by a kitschy Medusa. I had never been there before; the bar was unpopular among the undergraduates. Its clientele tended toward the aging and the broad, bourbon-drinking people, people for whom casual tippling was a distant, gauzy memory. Students found it depressing. McTaggett was the only person under sixty in the place.

He had evidently been there for some time. He sat heavily on a stool, his red-rimmed eyes focused with apparent fascination on the mirror behind the bar, and on the counter to his left was a heap of wadded napkins. As I sat down beside him, he plucked a fresh one from the dispenser on the bar, blew his nose dramatically into it, and added it to the pile. A ceramic dog was perched on a miniature stool in front of him, balancing a ball on its nose. The dog's eyes were fixed in an attitude of painful concentration.

"You took your time getting here," McTaggett said, without taking his eyes off the mirror.

"I live a ways away. I had to take my bike."

The bartender looked my way. She was a bleak, strict-looking woman optimistically lipsticked in a ghostly shade of coral. I ordered a scotch; then, thinking of this afternoon, made it a double. My usual drink was a gin and tonic. But I was embarrassed by the thought of drinking something with fruit on it here.

"So he hasn't said anything," McTaggett said glumly.

"Not yet."

The strict bartender brought me my drink, which I gulped at silently. It was McTaggett who had brought me here; it was his responsibility to say whatever needed to be said.

"Did you know that this school once produced a championship basketball team?"

"I think so," I said. Everyone knew that. It was still on the school's letterhead.

"My senior year. I was on that squad."

"Is that so?"

"Yes," he said, "it is so. Many people don't even remember this today. Times have been better. Things," and here he leaned close to me, as if imparting some confidential cipher, "have changed. Of late."

"It's something," I said helplessly.

"We had a reunion a few years back. All those boys—they're in advertising now. They're claims adjusters. They got married and moved East. I'm the only one left. You know what makes a good basketball team into a championship basketball team?"

His question caught me off guard. I managed an inquisitive noise.

"*Execution,*" he said significantly, and mimed an easy layup. But the way he said it didn't remind me of basketball at all. He had spoken with the relish of a hanging judge.

"Listen," I said, "what are we here to talk about?" I wanted out of the Tooth and Nail. The old men's murmurs, the amber half-light, McTaggett's soft mountain of napkins, the prancing figurines, had begun to unnerve me, like predictions of an unappealing future.

"I'm getting to that," McTaggett said.

"Because I've got to go."

"You haven't finished your drink yet."

"You can have it."

"Let me buy you a sandwich."

"I ate at home."

"You know what?"

"What?" I said, guardedly.

McTaggett folded his hands in his lap and leaned stiffly back on his stool. "He'll talk."

Suddenly I became willing to stay a few moments longer.

"You think?"

"He'll talk," McTaggett said again. He sounded almost sorry; but then, he always sounded sorry. "You know how the cops catch a criminal?"

I wondered if he were changing the subject again.

"Fingerprints?" I guessed.

"It's not fingerprints. And not powder burns either. And not eye-witnesses. The way they get him is that a criminal will always talk about the job. *Always*. He'll tell somebody. It's a law of human nature."

"Is Higgs a criminal?"

"Jesus Christ," McTaggett said. "It's an *analogy.*"

He gestured wildly, in the process striking a sidewise blow to the ceramic dog on the bar. The dog's stool tipped, wobbled, and finally fell; the dog cracked in three pieces, and the ball, freed from its perch, rolled to the edge of the bar and dropped to the floor with a little crash. McTaggett stared dumbly at the scattered shards of dog.

The strict bartender glanced over from the register.

"Put it on my tab with the other ones," McTaggett said.

I stood up. "Now I really do have to go," I said.

McTaggett turned to me, seemingly startled that I was still there.

"I'm glad we had this talk," he said.

"Me too."

"Best to the wife."

I nodded. I could think of no reason to correct him.

Riding home through the gnatty evening, passing in and out of the greenish, fathomy light of the streetlamps, I tried to reflect on what McTaggett had told me. But I found, to my surprise, that I had no more capacity to think about Higgs. The next morning he would speak, or he would not speak; correspondingly he would not be carried off by Treech to the psychiatric hosptital, or he would. It was as simple as that.

So I thought.

That night I slept at my desk again. I dreamed I was a basketball player. More than that: I was a *spectacular* basketball player. I twisted and knifed through the futile coverage of my faceless opponents, sank jumper after unerring jumper. There was a sense that the game was of great importance, a championship, and that not much had been expected of me.

At the same time, I was a sportscaster in a well-appointed broadcast booth high above the action. My color man was Henderson. In my dream he was a man of about thirty.

"How about that young Grapearbor?" I said.

"I'll tell you, Sam," Henderson replied. His voice was honey-smooth and every word was served up neatly as a lozenge. He had no accent. "This plucky youngster has just come off the bench and taken over this game. And I think I can say that everyone is extremely excited about the tremendous performance of the young Grapearbor that we're seeing here tonight."

"Another three for Grapearbor!" I cried, hitting the basket effortlessly from midcourt.

A sumptuous platter of food had appeared in front of Henderson: long, knobby breads, wagon-wheels of cheese, wine bottles, crudité rafts becalmed on dark, still lakes of bean dip, pastry shells and meat salads, stuffed capers, apricots wrapped in strips of bacon, whole smoked fish, tropical fruit. Henderson lifted a dripping veal chop to his mouth and ripped off a chunk with his teeth.

"Well, it all comes down to this, Sam . . . all the practice, all the hype . . . and I've got to tell you, I never thought it would come out quite this way. The ghost of Tip Chandler is living today, Sam, and he is smiling."

Henderson bent down into a vast tureen of soup, and when he came up his face was smeared with it, and gravy from the chop, and other foodstuffs I could not identify. Back in the game now, I launched myself daintily from the top of the key and floated fairylike, untouched, to the basket, where—just as the buzzer sounded—I slammed home the winning field goal with a contemptuous jerk of my wrists. The force of my dunk broke the glass backboard from its moorings; it shattered wonderfully on the hardwood beneath the spot where I still hung from nothing, beaming. The crowd boiled forth from the stands. From the exits and from the seams in the roof there was an angry pinkish glow, the color of sunrise; it was a fire. And the stampeding fans were celebrating victory and fleeing the flames at the same time. Henderson lifted a paper napkin to his lips and drew it deliberately across his face, back and forth, seemingly unaware of the smoke coiling into the booth. The napkin was growing larger; now it was the size of a piece of writing paper, a poster, a bedsheet. Henderson's whole body was hidden behind it. He said something I couldn't make out; and then the smoke rose up to cover everything, the booth, the stands, the elevated scoreboard, the fire too.

When I awoke, the real sunrise beating on the windows, it had occurred to me how Higgs might yet be saved.

CHAPTER 7

THE GRASSHOPPER KING

It was already half-past seven; there was no time to dawdle. I rifled through the papers on my desk, then, not finding what I wanted, I upended my wastebasket, dropped to my hands and knees and dug frantically through the crumpled sheets of rough draft, wax paper squares, the weeks of used tissues—no luck. I turned out the pockets of every pair of pants I owned. Finally it occurred to me to look under the bed, and there, amidst the gum wrappers and the news magazines I'd been meaning, with all sincerity, to get to, was my object: the paper napkin on which Charlie Hascomb had written his phone number.

The napkin was just out of my reach, and I had to shoulder the bed a few inches to get to it. The motion woke Julia up a little.

"What are you doing down there?" she said drowsily, poking her head over the edge of the mattress. Her nightshirt drooped away from her freckly collarbone and I was stopped short for a moment with affection. Then she woke up a little more. I watched her remember what day it was, our macabre schedule, and how angry she was at me.

"Come on, what?"

One more shove and my thumb and forefinger closed on the napkin.

"Don't worry, darling, sweetness," I said, standing, straightening, my heart hurrying as if I'd been injected with a new and potent hormone of resolve. I was bursting with reassurance; but I was still not ready to explain. "Honey," I said.

Julia lay back on her pillow and shut her eyes.

"Romance," she said. "What's this for?"

"We're going to meet an old friend of mine."

"Today?"

"Bear with me," I said. "Go back to sleep." I left the apartment—shutting the door gently, so as not to awaken her any further—and called Charlie from the pay phone on the corner.

It was five rings before he answered, and it took a little while after that for me to impress upon him who I was.

"Sammy," he said. He sounded groggy and a little incredulous. "Of course. What's going on?"

"You told me to call you sometime—remember?"

"Yeah," he said cautiously.

"I need your help with something. It's very important. I wouldn't ask you if we weren't old friends."

"How much do you need?"

He had grown suddenly more alert.

"I don't need any money. I need you to do me a favor."

"Well, good goddamn," he said, evidently relieved, "I guess I'm always good for a favor."

"Fine. Meet me at the corner of Ovid and East Main in fifteen minutes."

"Urr. Can it wait?"

"Actually, no."

"Fifteen minutes," he said. He made it sound like a sum of cash. "ok. But what's so urgent?"

Over the top of the telephone box I could see the scowling Greek sandwich-maker, half-obscured by the reflection of dawn in his plate glass storefront. He maneuvered himself deliberately about the space behind the counter, turning his machines on, dipping below my sightline to indecipherable tasks.

"Let's just say," I told him, "I need you to talk to someone for me."

Charlie arrived ten minutes late, unevenly shaven, wearing a too-small t-shirt with "STONED AGAIN" decaled across the front. The street was empty except for a rangy old man sweeping the sidewalk in front of a jewelry store. A phalanx of low, squarish clouds was marching up from the east side of town.

"This had better be good," Charlie said. "I had to get my father to take care of the store. I'm in very big trouble if a certain parcel comes in before I get back."

"You'll be back before lunch," I told him.

Rising before us, shadowing the streetcorner, was the desultory concrete parallelepiped of the college repository. I led Charlie inside. The security desk was manned by a surly-looking undergraduate, bent ferociously over a paperback. At our appearance, he jerked upward, startled and resentful.

"See some ID?" he said.

I displayed my card. He directed an interrogative grunt at Charlie.

"Dr. Hascomb is with me," I said. "He's a visiting scholar from Tunisia. He's consulting with us on the degradation of storage media."

"Tunisia."

I chastised myself: keep it simple. "Dust storms," I said. "Dry heat. The scirocco. There's no more inhospitable environment for information."

"I'll bet," the undergraduate said without interest, and waved us through. Triumphantly I led Charlie through the low portal into the dim realm of the stacks.

The shelves crowded our shoulders on either side; we proceeded through the corridors of Italian periodicals, botanical drawings, endless minutes of forgotten societies. The floor was wire mesh and beneath us one could see the shelves descending three stories into the earth, if one cared to look. Charlie did; I didn't. I was cultivating an atmosphere of perfect assurance. I'd need it. We stepped into the rickety elevator and I pushed the button for the bottommost floor.

"This isn't exactly how I expected we'd see each other again," Charlie said, as we emerged.

"Chance is a funny trick player," I replied.

We had come out into a vast, cold room, one of whose walls was lined floor to ceiling with wooden drawers, of a flat antique kind that suggested pinned butterflies or Latin-labeled beakers; we used them for lecture tapes. I wheeled the stepladder into position, climbed up almost to the top (above me, through three layers of mesh, I could just make out the surface world) and came down again, huffing, with Higgs's tape. I slid it into the machine, leaned down on PLAY, and beckoned Charlie silent as the familiar recording began. "Henderson between the wars was a figure of solitude and an object, when his solitude was interrupted, of derision and contempt . . ." When the waterlogged screeching began, I shut off the tape.

"Well," Charlie said, "you were right. Your storage medium's degraded."

"Come on," I said impatiently, "can you do him?"

"Do what?"

"Can you *do* him. Higgs. Do his voice."

"Play it again."

I did so; and afterwards Charlie scratched his forehead, leaned back, coughed, and Higgs began to speak. "Henderson between the wars," Charlie said, "was a figure of . . . isolation? An object of scatological skulduggery on the part of his peers, held fast in a perfect balance between his Roman Catholic faith and his carnal appetite for his teenaged relatives . . ."

It was not perfect; but it was very, very good.

"Charlie," I said, "I'm going to make you a star."

He grinned uncomplicatedly. "I always knew," he said.

When we emerged from the stacks, the surly-looking undergraduate turned his eyes up wearily. He had shut his paperback. Strange to think that for him, nothing of any interest was happening that day.

From the look of him, nothing of any interest might *ever* have happened. Camaraderie overtook me. I wanted to warn him that one day, through no fault of his own, he might do something important.

But of course he wouldn't have believed me.

"Looks pretty bad," I told the undergraduate. "This place is an information catastrophe waiting to happen."

"Really?"

"Salaam," said Charlie. We pushed out onto the wakening street.

It must be obvious by now what I was up to. If Higgs would not speak, then Charlie would have to speak for him. But what should he say? I had to keep it brief. The longer the speech I asked Charlie to fabricate, the greater the chance of some betraying error. After a little thought I decided he need say no more than "Red whistle." Having Higgs refer to "Sudetenland, My Mother" would be the most potent endorsement possible of my own work, and I thought it was not too selfish, considering that I was saving Higgs's life, to give myself a boost up in the process.

Ellen had been right about the rain. When Charlie and I came out of the repository, the first huge drops were splattering against the windshields and store windows, and a startling cold wind was toying with the limp flags of the auto dealership. By the time we got to Higgs's house the rain was falling in sheets. Mud boiled up from the cracks in the front walk, expelling earthworms onto the flagstone where they lay pink and dazed, ready for the end.

Ellen and Julia were waiting for us on the stoop, as I'd called ahead and asked them to.

"This is my friend Charlie Hascomb," I said, raising my voice to be heard over the rain.

"Charlie, you remember Julia. Charlie, Mrs. Higgs."

"I'm *wet*," Julia said. "Can we go inside now?"

"Not just yet. I need to explain something first."

"That you can't explain inside?"

"The tape recorders—*the tape recorders.*" I felt a guilty excitement at my adopted air of mystery. I almost wished I could maintain it longer. But, as I've said, there was no time to dawdle. I nodded at Charlie.

"Sammy has a plan," Higgs said. And Ellen gave a little gasp, glanced up at the thundering firmament, and fainted.

Julia moved to catch her, too late. Ellen dropped to her knees and then slumped backwards onto the path. A moment later she came to with the cold rain slapping her face. She glared up at me from the walk. Her dress was striped with mud and a gaping tear ran up one side of it. I saw now that I should have introduced my secret weapon in a less dramatic manner. But no second thoughts—I resolved against them. There would be no time. I helped Ellen to her feet and began to explain what came next.

I had read enough crime novels to know that when it came to a frame-up, every complication was an invitation to mishap. So I'd kept the plan as simple as I could. I would go down to the basement and make a "final plea" for Higgs to speak. Ellen, Julia, and Charlie would follow, all together so as to mask the sound of Charlie's footsteps. Charlie, standing behind Higgs, would say "Red whistle." The four of us would rush up the stairs (together, always together) to call Treech. Finally, I would leave the house on the pretext of purchasing a celebratory bottle of champagne; in that manner, Charlie, too, could leave, without an unexplained opening and shutting of the door.

If all went as planned, there would be no evidence on the tape that anyone but Julia, Ellen, and I had been in the house that morning. It was imperative, I reminded my accomplices, that no one say anything contradicting that impression. If some contingency made it absolutely necessary to mention Charlie, he was to be referred to by his code name.

"What code name?" Charlie asked.

In fact, I hadn't thought of one; but something about the fierceness of the elements, the rain crashing to earth, put me in mind of the quiet moment I'd shared with Ellen, in the Higgses' kitchen. I thought of stillness, yellowness, the smell of something frying.

"Saucepan."

"That's a terrible code name," Ellen said. But Charlie was in favor.

"I'm a saucepan!" he proclaimed. "The secret saucepan! Operation Saucepan!" He drew his face close to mine; no more than six inches of water and wind between us. "This is so much better than being at work," he said.

The four of us went over our respective parts until I was convinced that every possibility of error had been eliminated. We stood at the door, dripping from our sleeves and chins, wearing mad conspiratorial smiles.

"This is great," Julia said. "I mean it. It's workable." She put her hands on my shoulders. "I'm sort of shocked." Her bangs dangled before her eyes like foliage and her nose was starting to run. She kissed me.

"Love is the downfall of all secret agents," Charlie said.

"Shut up, saucepan," I said. We went together into the house, Julia and Ellen first, Charlie and I behind, our shoes squelching quietly on the linoleum, synchronized. Charlie leaned toward me again, as if to whisper some last encouragement in my ear. But I put my finger to my lips. From here on in we were sticking to the script.

I went downstairs to deliver my supposed petition. The basement was crazy with grasshoppers; the whole local population must have been driven from their homes by the rain. They huddled in the corners and nestled among the artifacts, and at any moment dozens of them were in midleap, so that the room seemed held at a low green simmer. This, I thought, was for the best. The chattering of the grasshoppers, along with the steady tattoo of the rain on the windows, could only help obscure our trickery.

I sat down across from Higgs. The checkerboard lay between us, still in a drawn position from the last game Higgs had played with Julia. There was a grasshopper perched on one of his red kings. It was poised so motionlessly that I hadn't seen it for a moment; I had taken it for a part of the checker. It seemed a new kind of man entirely, a grasshopper king, part of some variant game that no one had gotten around to teaching me. The grasshopper faced me, a strangely mottled green, its tiny limbs shoved forward like a supplicant's; but there was something defiant, I thought, in its pose, in the unforgiving set of its thorax. I waved my hands in its direction, trying to shoo it away. But the grasshopper ignored me. It seemed absorbed in a private contemplation.

"Fine, then," I told it. Julia, waiting halfway up the stairs, gave me an anxious look; I was off the plan. I made a little grimace of apology.

"Fine, then, Professor," I said, louder, and slid into my prepared remarks. "We can see you've made your mind up about this. We've tried to persuade you in every way we could that it was in your best interest, and in the best interest of the field, for you to speak; but you've decided otherwise, for reasons of your own. And we—I think I'm speaking for Julia and me, and of course Mrs. Higgs, and your colleagues here at the university—we respect that decision on your part, and on all of our behalf I just want to wish you good luck through whatever lies ahead."

Julia upped her thumbs. Was I good: officious and up-front as a bank president! I felt ready to pull out a railroad watch. But I wasn't through yet. I took a long breath, and then—drawing up from my grottoed interior the memories of a lifetime of frustration, my thousand humblings, all the mistakes I'd made despite the clarity of the right course and the right courses I'd unaccountably veered from, my vanities, my uncharities, my prejudices, which had deformed my field of vision into something like the surface of a sphere (inalterably finite, I mean, but without even any boundary I could beat my fists against) and the concomitant unlikeliness that any of this would ever, in any way that counted, change—I started to cry.

"Oh, God, Professor Higgs, please speak! Don't you know what they're going to do to you? Can't you understand? I'm begging you! Speak, Professor! Please, Professor, speak! Speak! *Speak!*"

I choked off a convincing sob and gave the agreed-upon hand signal to Julia, who relayed it to Ellen at the top of the stairs. Ellen and Charlie came down together, locked in step. Charlie's eyes were clamped shut, and his breaths were deep and measured. He was getting into his part. Ellen led him to his spot, by Higgs's side, and bent him down a bit so his head would be the right distance from the recorders. Crouched over Higgs, Charlie looked like a kibitzer, about to suggest to his companion some arcane maneuver by which he might transmute the abandoned, drawn position into victory. I gave Ellen the second signal; she squeezed Charlie's arm; Charlie opened his eyes.

It was difficult for me, at first, to interpret the sudden tightening of Charlie's features, the drawing back of his brows, the bloodlessness of his face. For a half-second I riffled through possibilities: stage fright? the long-delayed arrival of his moral character? But neither of these adequately explained Charlie's dawning expression, which could only be called horror. His eyes were frozen; I followed their direction downward, over Higgs's shoulder, to the red king and its insect tenant, and then I realized what had happened. *The criminal*—in my mind, the sad, incontestable voice-over—*always makes one mistake: one fatal mistake.* And mine had come to light. I had forgotten about Charlie and his bugs.

Charlie's hands flew to his chest; he jerked his head back and forth wildly, taking in for the first time the cluttered, teeming basement, effervescent with lower life. His jaw fell open.

"Grasshopper," he croaked, and then I was on him, one arm around his windpipe and my other hand over his mouth, but of course I was too late. At least he had spoken in Higgs's voice; he must have been too terrified to drop out of character.

We had to get Charlie out of the house, I thought; then we could work out an explanation, play-act whatever transition was needed, and bring him back down for a sequel. We still had an hour. And just as I thought this, there came from upstairs a peremptory double knock—RAT-tat. Treech had come early.

Panic blossomed, my gorge rose. Charlie turned his eyes to me questioningly. His neck was fish-cold under my arm, and fish-moist

too, with sweat. OK, I thought, OK, OK, OK. I clung to this reassuring
iamb like a scrap of boat and in a moment I had regained my clarity;
redoubled it, in fact. I breathed evenly and with assurance. The house
seemed laid open before me like a blueprint. It was perfectly simple;
here was Treech's path, here Charlie's, two threads strung through the
rooms. All I had to do was make sure they didn't cross.

"Grasshopper," I said. "Yes, Professor, I'm starting to see it . . ."

I indicated the row of half-windows with a motion of my head.
Ellen, catching my meaning, pulled open the one above Higgs's table.
A gush of frigid rain spilled into the room, sending an outburst of
grasshoppers skittering away. The opening looked just tall enough to
let Charlie through. I turned him around to face me, my hand still
covering his mouth, and attempted to convey to him through my
fierce gaze alone that once I let him go, he was not to flee upstairs, nor
to make any other sound, but rather to climb as quietly as possible out
the window, depart on foot, and await further instructions. Then I
released him; and whether because he had gotten my meaning, or
because he was simply attracted to the most immediate means of
escape, he made for the window at once. I headed upstairs to hold off
Treech until order could be restored.

When I opened the front door Treech was huddled under the lintel, drenched despite his huddling. He pushed his way past me and
dripped angrily onto the rug.

"Some people would consider it rude to make a person wait outside on a day like this," Treech said. He was wearing a sad orange rain
hat in the shape of a frustrum, along whose drooping brim rainwater
collected into drops and fell. I guessed Ellen and Julia would need
about forty-five seconds to eradicate the evidence. I started a mental
count: *one-one-thousand, two-one-thousand, three* . . .

"Is it raining?" I asked.

For an answer Treech merely flung his sopping rain hat to the floor.

"Things are a little hectic," I told him. "Understandably."

Treech nudged close to me and maneuvered his face into a version of toughness. "Look," he said. "You know where I stand and I know where you stand. The discussion is over. So let's see him."

"You're an hour early." *Eleven-one-thousand.*

"People in desperate situations change their minds. Sometimes at the very last minute. I'd hate to miss that."

It was a natural opening to tell Treech what had just happened; rather, what we meant him to believe had just happened. But if Treech thought Higgs had already spoken I would never be able to hold him off.

"He's still eating breakfast," I said instead.

"So?"

"I think you'd rather wait for Ellen to clean him up." I had inserted myself between Treech and the stairs.

"I don't mind."

Treech tried to shoulder me aside, but I stood firm. When he feinted left, I moved with him; when he tried to duck under my outstretched arm, I crouched to block him. I guarded the basement door as grimly as if my life savings were behind it—which, in a way, I suppose they were.

"Why don't you wait up here?" I said. "Put your feet up."

"I wouldn't hear of it," he said, and charged straight at me. *Twenty-seven-one-thousand.* His head thunked against the fork of my ribs. I held my ground.

Treech rested his palms on his knees and glared at me.

"I am tired," he said, chuffing like a dying engine, "of being treated like an intruder in the household. I've been proud to call myself an associate and colleague of Professor Higgs for many years and I belong here as much as any of you. Certainly as much as *you.*"

How could I deny that?

With some effort and even a little dignity he pulled himself straight up. "All I want is what you want, Samuel. No more waiting." He turned away from me and took a few steps toward the door. "When I think of what it used to be like . . ." he said. The orange rain hat lay in a crumple at his feet like an awful dog.

"I've heard about it," I said, to keep him talking. He looked pathetic, in his drab, slump-shouldered coat, feeble and somehow sprained. I relaxed.

Quick as a snake he was past me; he kicked me hard in the ankles and I dropped, helpless, to my knees. It had only been thirty-eight seconds.

"No," I said, "wait a minute."

Treech paused at the top of the stairs. Glee was stretched across his face; and then, improbably, terrifyingly, he shrieked at me: *"Your Momma!"* And he started down.

But immediately he was met by Ellen coming up. Her hair was plastered to her face and she seemed on the verge of tears. Treech, off-guard, allowed himself to be backed up to the foyer.

"What happened to your dress?" he asked Ellen. She ignored him.

"The saucepan," she said tightly, "is stuck in the window."

Treech looked back and forth between us, his eyes narrowing. "What?" he said. He shook his head as if trying to dislodge something. "What?"

I tried as best I could not to blanch. "We use it to prop the window open," I explained.

"In this weather?"

"That," I said, "is why we have to take it *out* of the window."

"I can't budge it," Ellen said.

I made a move toward the stairs. "Maybe I should give it a try."

"I'm good with mechanical things," Treech said.

The three of us halted, our attractions and repulsions momentarily summing to nothing. The last shreds of my clarity fluttered away. My stomach felt like something huge and flat had settled there. How could I have thought this would work?

"For goodness' sake," Ellen said, "you're the guest. Sam'll do it. Let me fix you a drink."

"I don't drink."

"You'll have a soda."

Ellen hauled Treech off by one arm. I rushed downstairs to dislodge the saucepan. I would not have much time.

In the basement I found Julia struggling tearfully with my old friend's backside, broader now than I remembered it, broader too than the aperture through which it was necessary, at all costs, that it proceed. Charlie's legs were kicking jerkily, in a loose frog-style, moving independently in wild ellipses; it was a manner of kicking, I thought distractedly, for which I knew the exact Gravinic verb. It wasn't helping. Charlie was stuck fast. I clambered onto Higgs's table, forced Charlie's legs down by main strength, and applied my right shoulder to the task of pushing him through. His shirt had pulled out of his dungarees, and a squared-off ripple of his flesh bulged from the edges of the window, chafed red from his efforts. Silently I cursed, individually and as a class, all the Clappy Burgers, each soggy carton of Happy Special Onion Os that I had watched him joyfully consume. Through the adjacent window I could see him scrabbling for purchase on the lawn outside; but there was no handhold there, only the slippery wet grass.

Without some leverage I was lost. Through labored pantomime I conveyed to Julia that she should pass up to me one of the Paiute bison spears that lay bundled under the sign of North America. The flint tip had long since been appropriated by some enterprising collector, and the shaft, as I had hoped, was thin enough to wedge between the top of the windowframe and Charlie, fitting neatly into the groove that nature had provided him. Hoping Charlie had enough sense, or was already sufficiently uncomfortable, not to yell, I leaned down on the free end of the spear with all my weight. I was rewarded with a gratifying bit of give. Upstairs, voices were raising: Treech and Ellen having at each other. I pushed down on the spear again and again, timing each thrust to coincide with the rebound of the last. My face and chest broke out in sweat and the muscles of my arms burned each time I let the spear up. I was making progress; but not enough. Treech was at the stairs.

191

"I've had enough of this," he said, his needle-sharp voice perfectly clear even over the grasshoppers' chattering, even over the rain, even over the blurry tone of exertion sounding in my ears. "I will not be shanghaied around. I will not be obstructed." And now came his footsteps, ominous and wet.

"Wait," Julia shouted desperately, "I'm not dressed!" But Treech would not be dissuaded, now, certainly not by modesty. He was halfway down. His arrow-shaped shadow slunk along the basement floor. I readied myself, aching, for a final push; and as I did so, a grasshopper, stirred by some unguessable impulse, heaved itself out of the drenched mess, rose and fell in a perfect, inevitable parabola whose intercept was the exposed stripe of Charlie's back. When it touched him—just as I threw myself down on the spear with the meager remainder of my strength— he kicked violently outward and caught me squarely on the side of the head. I stumbled back, remembering just too late that I was standing on a table, but before I went down I saw Charlie's legs vanishing out the window, into the storm. I landed with a crash against the sarcophagus. The mummified Arab, as if startled out of sleep, tipped forward from his case and fell. His chin caught the edge of the table and his head snapped neatly off, rolled in diminishing circles in front of Higgs, and came to rest sitting jauntily on one leathery ear; and this was the first thing Treech saw when, a moment later, he burst madly into the basement. His eyes widened. Quickly he surveyed the room: the head, and the rain pounding on the head, which was pounding also on Higgs's table, and on placid Higgs, from the open window; Julia, weeping and fully clothed; the absence of a saucepan or breakfast; and myself, slumped against the empty coffin, bleeding into one eye, still clutching the pointless Paiute spear, the decapitated Arab sprawled across me like an exhausted lover. Treech covered the distance between us instantaneously, seemingly on wheels. He leaned down; his bewildered, furious face drew kissing-close to mine.

"I demand an explanation," he said. "Some explanation is required." Reflected in his glasses, hardly distorted, I could see my own face. To my joyous surprise, I saw that my features had of their own accord formed themselves, at last, into the knowing, sidelong smile of Gregory Corso.

Then Treech's face seemed to waver away from me, doubling and quadrupling as it went. I thought I might have a touch of concussion.

"Grasshopper," I told him, weak and triumphant. "He said 'Grasshopper.'"

And the room grew red, and subsequently black.

Three weeks and some hours later I sat at a lengthy and impeccably set table on a marble stage, a melting gin and tonic—my sixth—in front of me, a cooling plate of roast beef and mixed greens at my left hand, untouched. I hadn't had a bite all day; but my stomach felt as if I'd been scarfing down chili by the quart, chocolate syrup, cold sticks of butter.

The first thing the Henderson Society had done—once I'd roused enough to feed Treech our story, once he'd played the tapes back, once he'd managed to stammer his astonishing news into Ellen's dusty telephone—was declare a banquet. Nearly five hundred members and former members had shown up, filing between the cherub-choked pilasters of the convention center, née Temple of Reason, the same bookless library that had hosted the champion Prospectors thirty years before. The scholars were spread out before and beneath me like an allegorical painting of scholarship. Their voices bouncing off the marble were titanic. I thought I might be sick. The dining part of the evening was coming to a close. From every part of the hall I could hear the soft, final impact of forks coming to rest, tines down, on plates; and fit, smiling waitresses in smart vests had materialized to clear the plates away. In a few minutes it would be time for the speech. The speech was to be given by me. And I had no idea what I was going to say.

All week I had wrestled with the problem of how to suitably commemorate my hoax before the very people it was intended to delude.

I had assured myself as the days passed that the solution would come to me, in a dream or a daytime visitation; but the clouds had stayed shut, and I'd woken up each morning as clueless as the night before, and here it was, almost time. If inspiration arrived now it would have to get straight to the point.

With me on the proscenium were the surviving principals of the Higgs affair. Ellen was there, along with Higgs himself, sitting at the table's head. Rosso and McTaggett sat side by side across from me; Dean Moresby, wheelchair-bound now, was at the foot of the table, the point farthest from his daughter. There was dour Slotkin, my predecessor, and to his left, seated in order of their service, *his* predecessors, whose names I had immediately and willfully forgotten after the initial round of introductions. The president of the Society was there, flanked by Treech and Mayor Meadows. Next to Treech sat Cheryl Hister, middle-aged and sallowed, with her husband beside her and a grim toddler clamped in her lap. Once again they'd made her wear her Happy Clappy's uniform; sallowed too, it bound her across the breasts and belly like a post-surgical dressing. Even Karl-Heinz Sethius had made it. The Society had flown him in, and now he sat on Higgs's other side, a tiny bright-eyed lawn statue of a man, talking vigorously to his correspondent, whether in English or German I couldn't tell, either not noticing or not minding Higgs's failure to respond.

Julia was at my left, observing the proceedings with a sharp, unsettling eye.

"But these are the same people who were ready to kidnap him," she'd said the night before. "It just seems weird to be their guest of honor."

"But what can I do? Protest? Make myself absent? It would look funny. Which is exactly what we have to avoid."

"I know that," she said. "I'm just saying."

In the end she'd come along willingly, had even displayed a little enthusiasm at the outset; but that had drained as the room filled. She remarked sourly on my series of gin and tonics and snubbed the scholars to whom I grandly introduced her—ever more grandly as the series of gin and tonics proceeded. Finally, recognizing that the night, for her, was past salvaging, I asked her simply not to say anything that would jeopardize my new standing among the Hendersonists.

"Then I won't say anything at all," she'd responded.

Despite what I'd told Julia, I was not very worried about arousing suspicion. The scholars had swallowed our deception without a hint of skepticism; they had practically lined up to be fleeced. All the precautions I'd taken against exposure seemed foolish now. The scholars, handed what they'd awaited for so long, were in no mood to ask questions. Instead, they had thrown themselves fully into the project of deciphering Higgs's revelation. Already some had approached me with lines of Henderson's where insects appeared, asking almost demurely for my opinion.

All the same, I was desperately afraid of making a poor impression. In spite of all that had happened, these were my colleagues now.

Rosso got up to introduce me, and there went whatever calm I had. A dribble of sweat nagged at the collar of my hastily rented tuxedo. Rosso was lauding my unflagging devotion to the field, my academic courage . . . what was "academic courage"? Hardly listening, I didn't catch it. I was trying to compose my speech, or at least some innocuous opening from which I could spin off five minutes of nothingness—but all I could think of was *ladies and dupes, ladies and dupes, ladies and dupes* . . .

Then the introduction was over, and I found myself standing. I remarked the smoothness of my rise from my chair, and the great distance that now separated me from the half-drained gin and tonic I had left on the table—my seventh. I was more drunk than I had realized. With my head high and my mind empty of all thought and with the tag I'd forgotten to take out of the tuxedo pants rubbing a now-raw spot on the small of my back, I made my way to the lectern.

"Ladies and gentlemen," I said, my voice thundering from the P.A., queer and timbreless. "Scholars, friends, members of the Society, my soon-to-be colleagues and collaborators!"

I stopped to let that sink in. I was thinking of Higgs at Trieste—the audience reshaped itself into that long-ago crowd. There they were, sooty and bombed-out, innocent, rapt, and their various tongues all silenced in expectation. What would Higgs have said in my place? I felt that with a word—if I knew the right one—I could strike some resonant linguistic frequency, set the columns shivering on their plinths; the walls would bend outward in a soft plié, and the ceiling would come down to meet us. But I had no idea what that word could be.

I realized with a start that I had been silent for some time.

"Let me conclude," I began, "with a joke, from which I think all of us, as academics, have much to learn. It seems there were these two racehorses.

"One night, the two horses were discussing their ambitions.

"The first racehorse said, 'Listen. This business is all-or-nothing. Every race ought to be like life or death. Someday you break your leg and bam, that's it. If you were good enough your name lives on after you.'

"The second racehorse snorted and replied, 'If that's the way you want it, fine. Me, I take it easy. I may never be famous but I'll live long enough to retire. I'll carry little kids around on trail rides. Peace and quiet, my friend, peace and quiet; that's the goal in life.'

"The two horses argued far into the night, each putting forth persuasive arguments for his position, neither gaining any clear advantage. Just before dawn a dog sidled into the stable.

"'You two make me laugh,' the dog said contemptuously. 'For your information, I just came from the house, and I heard both of you are being put down in the morning for glue.'

"The first racehorse turned to his companion, overcome with surprise. 'My God!' he said. 'A talking dog!'"

The scholars chuckled doubtfully.

"I think we can agree that all of us here tonight are talking dogs," I said. "Albeit some of us talk more than others."

JORDAN ELLENBERG

And with that, having nothing more to say, I sat heavily down. I was dismayed to find that someone had taken my drink away. Rosso stood and beckoned up the crowd; they popped up from their chairs, clapping lustily and whistling, and over the loudspeakers came the recording of Higgs's appropriated voice, spliced into a loop: "Grasshopper. Grasshopper. Grasshopper. Grasshopper." The words, repeated over the applause and the taped drumming of rain, sounded martial, like a coded plea for reinforcements from a plane lost in a hostile zone. I imagined Higgs strapped into a cockpit, plunging toward the wine-dark fields of occupied France, murmuring into his crackly radio: "Grasshopper. Grasshopper. Grasshopper," as if his life depended on it, all the way down.

"That was disgraceful," Ellen whispered in my right ear. Somehow she had spirited herself into the chair next to mine. I realized that she was even drunker than I was. She smelled like a rum cake.

"I'm sorry," I said. "I should have prepared something." At the time there had seemed to be a reason for my feeble joke. No amount of effort could recover it now. I was exhausted and aware again of my uncomfortable tuxedo.

"No," she said. "No, no, no, *no.*" She jerked her hands about in despair of getting her point across. "It was just what Stanley wanted."

We both looked down the table to where Higgs sat. He was eating rolls from the wicker basket on the table, chewing methodically as his phony pronouncement rolled through the hall like a call to action, like ventriloquism. Beside him, Sethius had turned his attention to Mayor Meadows. He was chattering contentedly—it was definitely German—and the mayor was nodding, or nodding off. His lucid hours, I'd heard, came between breakfast and lunch, if they came at all, which (I'd heard too) was now at best a fifty-fifty bet. He had never faced a serious opponent.

Mayor Meadows propped his chin up on his fist.

"Come again?" he said amiably. And Sethius was off again, in his stutter-step German, and the mayor started up nodding, and I saw that his elbow was planted in his bread pudding; and this sight was so unutterably sad that I almost began to weep. I wished Julia would say something. I lifted one hand to my temple.

Ellen slapped it away. "Don't you be sad," she said.

I muttered some kind of denial.

"We won," she said. "You saved him."

Well, maybe I had. I looked at Higgs again; wasn't he a little different? Still silent, sure, his eyes still fixed forward like a plebe's, yet different, I told myself, some tension in his posture gone; but I could have been imagining this, and it would have been natural for me to do so.

And things were different for *me*, anyway; that much was clear. My job was finished, and so was my time with Higgs. Oh, I could go back to the house, back down to the basement—but I would only be a guest now. My life before Higgs had diminished, in my estimation, to a dreary prologue; and here I was already in the epilogue, not ready yet, I thought, to sum up what I'd learned. But Ellen was right. We'd won, and it was over. I allowed this fact to buoy me up to a wistful gladness. Happy now, I felt no less like weeping. But then, I was very drunk, and like all drunk people I was looking for an excuse to cry.

But I didn't cry, because now the scholars were coming toward me in a wave, clambering onto the stage, approaching me with hands outstretched. All of them had veiny old man's hands—even the women. As they neared me I could hear their noises of congratulation, thrillingly subservient. I was expected to shake every one of those pale hands. Above me, the lights were booming out, row by row.

"Julia," I whispered, "keep me company. This is the part I hate."

She turned slowly, like a turret, to face me. She looked incredulous and a little perplexed.

"You love it," she said. And I had to admit that she was right.

I saw Higgs one more time after that. It was two weeks after the banquet; I had spent the interval in congress with the visiting scholars, one at a time, twenty minutes each, nine to five. Each professor, I learned, had his own theory about Henderson, which he held tight to his chest like a helpless chick, guarding it from the cruelties of the world and enveloping it in warm assurances, feeding it the occasional regurgitated worm of his researches. And each was certain that from my "recollections" he could glean some once-and-for-all advantage for his cherished hypothesis; his chick would fledge, would own the air, while the others grew skinny, pinkened, and finally died open-beaked, half-buried in the bottom of the nest.

"Are you absolutely certain Dr. Higgs didn't mention lactation?" one scholar would say; or another, "Did anything in Professor Higgs's body language suggest Henderson's resigned acceptance of phenomenology?"

"Grasshopper," I told them all, pleasantly, finally. "All he said was 'Grasshopper.'" Then I sent them off, with a handshake that surprised them, even, at first, me, with its hammy state-senator firmness. At the door the outgoing scholar met the incoming one, the former trying to conceal his disappointment, the latter his scorn. And me? I was hiding a grin, a doozy, the kind they paint on clowns. I *liked* disappointing them. And I liked the puppyish expectance on their faces as they angled open my door; and I liked the sun-struck little office the department had supplied me, and I liked the secretary outside, perched on her ergonomic chair, blank-faced as a seal on a rock. *From now on,* I told myself, and I didn't have to finish the thought; didn't, in fact, have time to, because the next disappointment was already arranging himself in the seat across from me, already with his hands squirming in his hair, beginning to set out the foundations of what he'd come for.

Finally the last interview—with a genial Zimbabwean who wanted nothing more from me than some inkling that Higgs was aware, as anyone serious must be, of Henderson's lifelong preoccupation with the redistribution of mineral rights—came to its crestfallen close. The other scholars had dispersed to their institutions with their downy

theories and I was free to go. I passed out of the building into the driz-
zling, gouachy afternoon. The breeze smelled of distant barbecue and
dust. I affected a jaunty hands-in-pockets step, imagining myself an
absurd musical hero, peeked at by girls in windows. My thoughts
wandered: the epinumerative case and its dual, possible triple function, all dependent on what was being overcounted and to what end;
a woman passing by me with shopping bags, her mysterious frosted
lipstick and fruitcake scent; then some words, just for sound, erudite,
flagrant, derelict; and the handsome cash prize the Henderson Society
had voted me, which would serve admirably in lieu of a new job to
pay my rent; and could you barbecue in the rain or would it have to
be inside? And another woman, in a marble-gray suit with heroic
shoulders, and the position that would soon be offered me at
Chandler State, which I would accept, and Julia. I stopped at a florists'
and bought a spray of orchids the color of sunset. Carrying the flowers
only reinforced my feeling that a song was about to start. Somehow
the sun came out without the rain ceasing.

When I came into the apartment Julia was asleep, her head hidden
under the covers as always. I stood in the doorway a while and
watched the rise and fall of her chest beneath the blankets, the simple
almost-periodic motion squeezing out the rest of my thoughts the way
breaking waves can, or turn signals not quite in phase. I could think
of no good reason to wake her. So I slid the orchids into a soda bottle with some water and set the bottle on the floor by the bed. Then
I opened my briefcase and took out a sheaf of British diplomatic communications on which I was hoping to discern Henderson's stealthy
mark. I was happy to return at last to my work.

Julia's fingers appeared at the edge of the blanket; she pulled the
covers away from her face. Her bangs were tamped flat across her eyes
and one cheek was red, where it had rested on her hand.

"I'm awake," she said.

"Sorry," I said. I sat down at my desk. "Go back to sleep, I'll be quiet."

"You didn't wake me."

I lowered my eyes to the top document on the stack, a welter of code words and abbreviations, and parts blacked out; each page, I could see, would take me hours. But now that our race to save Higgs was over, hours seemed like nothing, like billion-mark notes, like solar energy. What did I have but time?

From behind me, Julia said, "Can we move back to New York?"

"Yeah, OK," I said. "Pack your things."

"I'm serious."

I swung my chair around so it faced her. She'd propped her neck up on the pillows and pulled the covers halfway back over her face, so just her eyes showed—a soldier peering over the edge of a trench.

"You hate New York," I said.

"Maybe I just needed some time away from it."

"So let's discuss it. I'll have choices. What we can do at the end of the year."

"Can't we just move back now?"

"That doesn't really make sense."

"I know," she said; whether despairingly, mischievously, or out of sheer perplexity I couldn't tell. Her voice was perfectly featureless. But then she started to cry. *Really* cry; it was a minute before she could even speak. She mopped her face with the hem of the blanket.

"What if I had a job there?" she said. "A really, really good job?"

"Then of course we'd discuss it."

"What if I were in love with another man and he lived here and I didn't want to be around him anymore for your sake?"

Sudden fearful sickness, like smelling mercaptan. "Are you?"

Her shoulders slumped and she let her eyes slide shut. *"No,"* she said. "That's not the point. I just want to know what you'd do."

"What brought this on? Can I ask?"

"Nothing."

"There has to be something."

"No," she said. "There doesn't. There doesn't have to be anything."

She'd stopped crying. The corners of her eyes were a dull, punched red.

"I don't really know what we're talking about," I said.

"I don't either. But let's go. I'm sick of it here. I don't want to live—" she lifted an arm out from under the covers and gestured in a circle, "in this, and be Mrs. Assistant Professor of Gravinic Language and Literature."

"OK," I said, "OK. We don't have to do it that way."

"Sometimes I think I liked it better when you hated everyone," Julia said.

I had that same pinched, benighted feeling I did at the end of a checkers game: all those possibilities leading to failure, one route out. Higgs had made it seem so easy. I sat down at the corner of the bed and we stared at each other silently while I considered the problem of what might save me—or at least what might not doom me.

But instead I found myself thinking of an afternoon years before, not long after Julia and I had met. We'd been sitting on Tip Chandler's statue, on an eerily hot day in November, and each time someone walked by us, Julia had cried out, "Damn, Sam!" I couldn't remember now how it had started. Each broken reverie, every startled pigeony neck-jerk, was a star turn, was the funniest thing ever, and I was bent over with laughter; my stomach hurt, I was sweaty and my nose was starting to run. We were a monstrous nuisance, but at the same time I had never felt closer to the perchless, nicknameless, vendettaless masses who passed beneath me every day. In my mind our victims made allowances for us, smiled envious inward smiles, wrote off our bad behavior to the exuberance of—here, I'll say it—love. As they hurried off I read congratulations in their scowls: *Well, good, Sammy,* they were thinking—with something like civic pride. *It's about time.* "Damn, Sam!" Julia bellowed after them. The next day I'd woken up with sunburn banded across my ears and cheeks like a blush.

Julia drew her other arm out from the blankets and touched my hand.

"I'm OK," she said. "I'm sorry. Work."

I knew it was wrong to accept. But I could think of nothing else to do, nothing else I had, at the moment, to say. So I returned to my desk, sat, arranged my pens and papers in the customary way; and only when everything else was in order did I notice the absence of a familiar weight in my lap. I had left my copy of Kaufmann at Higgs's house.

I came over to the side of the bed. Julia had shut her eyes again, and her free arm was thrown over her face as if in answer to a blinding flash.

"Julia."

"No," she said, "it's OK."

"I have to go to the house. Do you want to come?"

"Uh uh."

"We won't be there long. It's brisk out. You love brisk."

I meant to invest my voice with aren't-we-glad-it's-all-over, an unanswerable cheer, but instead I just sounded tired and shrill, like the director of a failing cruise, like a camp counselor—grotesque, grotesque.

"Or we can go later," I offered.

"No," she said, "just go now."

"That's fine too."

I stepped backwards and in so doing kicked over the bottle I'd left by the bed. It cracked neatly along the neck and water began burbling onto the floor.

"What was that?" Julia said.

I pulled the dripping orchids from the glass.

"I brought you flowers."

She peered over the edge of the bed at the mess I'd made.

"OK," she said, with a little smile—was it a smile?—"I'll sweep it up. And you still should go."

"Are you throwing me out?" I said. I rested one hand on her cheek and kissed her, tasting her warm bed-breath and the salt of tears.

"Go to work," she said, sweetly, like an invalid. "I release you."

"You got it," I told her. "I'm gone."

Before I'd gotten halfway up the street my relief had rolled over and exposed its underside of miserable regret. I had read about, or maybe only seen on television, couples who thrived in the clinch, and I wished it were that way for me, but not so: I just felt old, muddle-hearted, made for solitude. Was I supposed to have stayed? Yes, surely, and it wasn't too late to turn back. But I kept walking as I played out the things I could have said, could still say. I could tell her how I'd almost killed Higgs. That was a thrilling thought for me: honesty, purgation. But I had learned to mistrust my impulses in that direction. In my life so far I'd seldom failed to reveal what I saw as the truth—I'd spoken my heart on delicate subjects, the flaws in people's characters, their misapprehensions. What had it gotten me? A name as a straight shooter? Consultation on delicate matters? No, nothing but trouble and a tired philosophy-class uncertainty about what honesty was, anyway, and how one might come by it, and how, when the time came, to use it. I walked on, stoop-shouldered, with the bleak certainty of having committed an inalterable wrong sitting heavily inside me like a sudden cold stomach full of food. I should have stayed. She wanted me to stay. This contemplation occupied the whole of my trip through the drizzly afternoon, which by now was not brisk after all, but ponderous, the rain slack and unpleasantly warm, the sort of rainy day which no amount of saving for can rescue.

When I got to the Higgses' house I found the front walk blocked by a university maintenance truck, two of its tires sunk into the damp lawn. Uniformed men were proceeding in steady ant-like columns from the front door to the rear of the truck, carrying bulky boxes. One man emerged from the house struggling with a tall, squarish item hidden by a blue tarpaulin. When the wind lifted the tarpaulin's corner I saw that he was carrying out one of the Society's tape recorders. I pushed past him and into the house, through the empty foyer, into the kitchen where Ellen was.

She was sitting Indian-style on the floor, with her whole china service laid out in front of her like a dinner party for phantoms. She picked up a plate and laid it carefully in a wooden packing crate by her side. Behind her the cupboards were thrown open and nothing was left inside. The drapes were gone.

"Your book is on the table in the basement," Ellen said.

"My book," I said. "Right. Would you mind telling me what's going on?"

"We're moving out today," Ellen replied, lifting a plate up into the gray daylight, peering at its underside for cracks. "My brother-in-law in Tampa's just died and my sister needs someone to stay with her."

"So you're just taking off. Leaving the house behind."

Ellen shrugged. "It's not ours. I'm sure the college can use it for something."

"I'd think you would have let people know you were going."

"Like who?"

Like me, I meant, of course; but really, what claim did I have? I was speechless. Yet I couldn't say, now that it had come to this, that I was entirely surprised. Over the past thirteen years the house had settled into a perfect, silent fixity, with only the Society's continuing vigil as reminder that Higgs had ever spoken at all; like a vibrating string resolving into stillness and the memory of a tone. Now the silence was broken, and it hardly mattered that it wasn't Higgs who had broken it. I thought I understood Ellen's position. For her to continue in her routine, as if nothing had changed, as if the world (or our little twig of the world) were still waiting breathlessly outside for her husband's secret knowledge, would be a kind of comedy she had no stomach for.

Ellen's expression relaxed a bit. She seemed to recognize that she'd bested me. "Stanley and I hate good-byes," she explained. "It's better to keep these things quiet and peaceful."

"Is it all right if I say good-bye to you anyway?"

"Do what you have to."

"Good-bye, Mrs. Higgs." I stuck out my hand and she, all business, shook it.

"On the table in the basement," she said.

The basement was stripped bare. The cast-off museum was gone—everything returned, I supposed, to the anthropologists, or cached in cool, locked rooms along the nether corridors of the repository. No sign of it remained but a sequence of mask-shaped regions on the wall where the paint was not as spiderwebbed as elsewhere, and the taped-up names of the continents, written on notebook paper in Julia's neat hand. There was only one tape recorder left.

Higgs's corner was conspicuous in having been left alone. My chair was still there, across from him, and there was Kaufmann on the table, and beside it, the checkerboard, the pieces set around the perimeter in neat stacks of three and four like the columns of a ruined temple.

"One last game?" I said. Admittedly, it was a sentimental impulse. But despite what Ellen had said about good-byes, I suspected Higgs had a little sentimentality in him. Certainly he knew how to put a drama together, which was almost the same. I sat down and began to array the red checkers into alternating rows. After a moment, Higgs did the same with the black.

"I'm sorry Julia's not here," I said. "It's probably my fault."

Higgs responded only by making his first move, and starting up the murmur in his throat. I found myself believing, for no reason except that it seemed appropriate, that I would beat him this time. It would be the natural close to a certain kind of story: Higgs, the old maestro whose purpose, after sundry trials, is finally concluded in the very person of me, the aw-shucks protégé, and so forth. It implied the endless circle of learning and teaching, children and adults, kill the father, scatter his parts . . . And indeed, I was playing him close.

"A rare performance for Grapearbor," I said. "The young man holding his own."

I jumped a black checker, evening us at four men apiece.

"She says she wants to move back to New York. I mean, we could— I just need a little more time here, I'm involved here now. Did I tell you I'm writing a paper with McTaggett? Higgs trying to sneak up the left file there, but Grapearbor's having none of it . . . Shouldn't I just marry her? Why should I possibly not? But I keep hesistating . . ."

One of the workmen came downstairs. He hesitated on the last step as he saw me.

"Didn't mean to break in on you," the workman said. "I'll just be a second."

"Don't worry about it," I told him, though in fact I was annoyed at the intrusion. My next few moves, I was certain, would be crucial ones.

The workman jerked the cord of the last tape recorder from the wall with the solemn carelessness of a nurse disconnecting a feed tube. He wound the wire into a tight bundle and tied off the plug end with a sudden square knot. Then he draped a tarpaulin over the recorder, and, grunting, lifted the package until he could get his knee under it.

"Last one," he said brightly, and took it up the stairs. I was relieved he hadn't asked me to help.

When I turned back to the board I saw an opportunity that I had somehow missed before, by which I could take command of the central squares, by which I could transform the whole landscape of the board. My men were a convoy, rolling inexorably toward Higgs's king line. His were trapped in culverts, screaming for their mothers.

"I asked her to come here with me," I said, "but she wouldn't. Should I have insisted? Or what? Or do you think I should have stayed?"

Triumphantly I set my checker down; and just as I took my hand away I saw my error. I had overlooked an obvious, shattering response. Higgs did not miss it. I made my only legal answer. His next move would be one that, in all our afternoons of play, I had never seen before: a quadruple jump. I hadn't won.

The noise in Higgs's throat stopped. I grew hot, must have been, of all things, blushing, imagining his disappointment. It was a mistake not even Ellen—not even *Treech*—would have made.

"Go ahead," I said. "It's my fault. Do what you have to."

But Higgs did not make the move. He stared down at the board, his face overtaken with what looked like fierce, sad calculation—it took me a moment to understand this, so strange was it to see him display any expression at all. The position on the board seemed to remind him of something long unavailable.

"My advice," Higgs said, "is to be careful of hasty marriage."

Then he picked up his king and removed the rest of my men.

"My game," said Higgs.

Ten years passed.

PART
THREE

"*Once a certain degree of insight has been
reached,*" *said Wylie, "all men speak, when
speak they must, the same tripe.*"

—Samuel Beckett

CHAPTER 8

HISTORY

Now that the porter is gone, now that I've pressed three corrugated dollars into his grizzled hand (an old tattoo at the join of palm and wrist, a bleary peace sign); now that I've followed him, my single bag on *my* shoulder despite his entreaties, up the deep-pile eggplant-colored staircase to my room; now that I've walked stiff-lipped and chest-out past the loitering young toughs on the sidewalk into the hotel I've chosen; now that I've found the hotel, pinned shoulder to shoulder between two of the lacy, balconied apartment houses that loom like burly old ladies above the park; now that I've paid the cabdriver, now that I've hailed him at the airport, now that my plane has flopped to the runway with an impact that dashed my hoarded peanuts everywhere—now, that is, that I've arrived in New York; now that I've left Chandler City—I feel a little sick. I have to sit down on the bed, here in this indistinct room composed of earth tones, a wallpaper of muted stripes like geologic eras, a globe lamp, the requisite fixtures. I get up, kick my bag into the closet, shut the doors, and sit back down. What am I doing here?

No, wait. I'm not up to that yet. It's Sunday, January 7, 1996, about half-past eleven. Through my license-plate-sized window I can see the entrance to the restaurant across the street, and the beginning of the line where couples are waiting for brunch. I put my head against the wall to the window's right, bringing an outdoor table into view. A man and a woman are eating omelettes out of rustic iron pans. They're holding hands; the sleeves of their cable sweaters join and form a tube across the table. The sunlight is so even and precise that I can see the ice cubes in their glasses, and their faces are all contrast, Rushmore-like. I could read their lips if I knew how. I pull a chair up to the window and stand on it so I can look down at my own side of the street. The toughs are still there, huddled in clawed-up olive drab windbreakers, with logos sewn on, and exhortations drawn in marker: FIGHT! and CONNECT! and NO FEAR, and what must be people's names in a flouncy graffiti. Every one of them has hair chopped short as a recruit's. From overhead I can't tell if they're talking, but I suspect they're not. They're saying everything they need to just by standing there.

What am I doing here? I'll try to explain.

I came home from Higgs's house so twisted up with joy that it was all I could do not to launch myself into the air with each step; and if we're to be completely honest (when if not now?) I stopped a few times and did exactly that—picture it! Myself, lank and a little rank, in my pale green interviewing shirt and matching tie, lifting off like a salmon from the mud-streaked sidewalk, flailing at the sky with one fist—*yes!* It was cool out now, at long last, but by the time I got home I'd sweated through my shirt. I stood exhausted at the door, clasping my hands one in the other, trying all the bodhi tricks I knew to rein my heartbeat in. Failing, I went inside.

"I'm so sorry," Julia said. *"Look* at you. Sit down."

She took me smartly by the shoulders and placed me on the side of the bed. My orchids sat in a new pot at my feet, with an odd-looking garnish that I saw after a moment was a ring of chocolate bars embedded in the soil. Julia pulled up a Three Musketeers, my favorite, unwrapped it partway, handed it to me.

"Did you get your book?"

"Mm hmm," I said. My mouth felt like a jammed machine, choked solid with sweet nougat and gratitude. Julia sat down beside me and felt my forehead.

"Look at you," she said again. "You're spectral. I think you're poised on the shimmying shaking line between life and death."

"Nn nn," I replied. I sucked the nougat off my teeth and swallowed hard. "Not so. I have news."

"Me first," she said. "I have an announcement. I'm going to learn Gravinic. Which I know sounds weird so don't stop me and which I know will be hard. But my advisor wants me to have a foreign language, and think about it—I'll have some kind of sympathy with what you do, with what you're doing—I got my own copy of Kaufmann, look—OK?"

"Are you serious?"

"Look at me."

I did; she was. There was no twist to her lip, no telltale furrowing above one eye. Her features were in perfect balance, smooth and without strain. Stern, her hair pulled back in a tight barrette, she looked like a photograph, an old one, a daguerrotype entitled "Her Faith in Him."

"That's so crazy it just might work," I said. Love rumbled in my ears, socked me in the gut, memories zig-zagged past my defenses and smote me, stupid little ones—waiting in line at the supermarket, a heartbreaking glance backwards and downwards at me as she stepped off an escalator into a cascade of glare (the airport? a mall?) kisses without number, sleeping on her typewriter in a pool of dingy light with her fingers cross-laced over the Appalachian curve of her neck, saying my name, saying the word "wow", a long way ahead of me on a street, sleeping again but in bed, then waking—I saw what I would have to do. I'd tell her everything, what I'd done and what Higgs had finally said, tell her and no one else. I'd told lies, yes, and failed to bring up certain truths, but in the end it had come out all right; and now this new secret, this last one, would bind us together forever.

But something held me back. It was Higgs. He must have felt something like this for Ellen, when they met, or not long after; he too must have swooned, must have thought he could reduce all the conundrums and unsatisfiable demands of the world to just one question: yes or no. Ellen had said yes. And Higgs—I knew now—had never stopped regretting it. I turned away from Julia and let my eyes rest on the wall, its supple, ancient stains like shadows from a fixed sun. What I proposed was irreversible. And if word got out . . . I could already hear the scholars, the whispers across the continents: how convenient for Higgs to talk again, just after the recorders were gone, wouldn't you think once would be enough? Worse than that: with two revelations to choose from, some would prefer the second, and among those maybe some ambitious enough to play the "grasshopper" tape a little more closely, perhaps side by side with Higgs's lecture, with an expert present; or might they find just a trace of an unexplained, unexplainable shout, toward the end of the reel, just before the window frame crashed down?

"Your news," Julia said.

I needed time. With time, things would settle in their places. I'd sweat out all these fervent endocrines and be able to make some sense.

"The Higgses are moving out," I said.

"Actually," Julia said, "I knew that. I meant to tell you. Ellen told me at the banquet."

To my surprise I couldn't summon up the slightest resentment.

"Let's never fight again," I said impulsively.

There was her smile again, the cocked corner of her lip. "Well, *sometimes,*" she said. "With love and fellow-feeling."

"With love and fellow-feeling," I repeated.

I would have agreed to anything. I just wanted it to be over: that day, this story. I plucked a Kit Kat from the pot, peeled back the foil and took a bite, half-expecting a mouthful of ashes. But no—it tasted like chocolate. I dropped backwards onto the bed and thought of the moving truck that must even now be carrying the Higgses out of town; implausibly I imagined the back door swinging open, and Ellen and Higgs sitting there in twin armchairs among the crates, imperturbable now and from now on, watching Chandler City shrink away.

I took another bite, and as I crunched down into the wafer like a layer of soil I felt something like relief, except pleasureless. Or like despair, but not so sad.

Gravinic didn't last. At first Julia went at it with her usual forthright industriousness, and we'd pass whole evenings in harmony and study with the words for "moon", say, spread out on dozens of flashcards on the bed. But before long she tired of the rococo conjugations and fine semantic shadings that so captivated me, and of my coaching, which sounded like carping to her; eventually it sounded like that to me, too.

I didn't tell Julia what Higgs had said. I thought about it, yes, as I'd planned to, and on several occasions resolved to come out with it that hour, that day, but each time my urge to unburden myself was weaker, while my reservations retained their full force. And before long I saw that my decision to keep my secret was just as irreversible as the other would have been. If I told her now, I'd have to explain why I'd waited so long; and the fact was, I didn't think I could. I found myself spending more hours than necessary in my little office. There was something at once inspiring and soothing about my secretary, with her headset phone that never rang and her still, enciphered face. She had a loose-leaf binder full of crosswords and she worked them all day long. When I came home, long after sundown, Julia and I fought—fought without a trace of fellow-feeling, and finally, though I can't say when this moment came, without love either. So we never married.

Am I rushing this? There isn't much to linger on. Our fights were the usual ones: petty domestic contentions, followed by hot silence, occasional half-hearted attempts at talking it over. In the end she always forgave me, and after a while I began illogically to resent her lenience. Once she'd been so ready to correct me—why not now? Couldn't she tell I was hiding something? Didn't she know I'd have to own up if she forced me? I thought she must be building up a case against me. Each little dispute was a new article, filed away with her damning commentary penciled in.

The day she left she'd reveal it to me entire, its unanswerable bulk all the good-bye and consolation I deserved.

But when she packed her things and went, it was without a hint of confrontation. With her hand on the knob I blurted out: "Don't you want to tell me something?"

"Like what?" she said. Through the window I could see the taxi with her boxes piled in front of it, and the driver sitting on the hood, hands in pockets—he'd seen this sort of thing before.

"Like what an asshole I've been. Like everything I've done wrong ever."

I watched her search for a rejoinder. Then she relaxed. She opened the door.

"No," she said.

So: Julia and I never married, or, I should say, I never married, and Julia married someone else, a gentlemanly professor named Simeon, to whose fifty-word advertisement in the hopeful back pages of the *Lantern-Bugle* ("EXPECTATIONS REASONABLE, NO GAMES") she had, kind as always, responded.

I met Simeon just once, at the engagement party. He had tired eyes and his puffy, contourless surface made no suggestion of internal architecture beneath; I thought cutting him open might reveal a perfect cross-section of undifferentiated vegetable stuff, like cooked potato. I prowled the perimeter of the room and watched him with a naturalist's eye, swearing I'd see in him what she did, even if it took all night. Julia left his side to tend to something, and his knuckles flew immediately to his lips. He seemed on the verge of a stammered retraction. I took this chance to approach him.

"Hey," I said. I gulped fraternally at my drink. "No hard feelings. I'm happy for you both."

I was being sincere; but my reassurance seemed to make him even more uncomfortable. He chewed at his knuckle furiously. Deep potato currents, I sensed, were flowing where all was ordinarily placid.

"I hear you're a chemist," I said.

"That's right—a polymer man."

I had nothing to add to that.

"It must be really interesting," I tried.

"Well, it is," he said, sounding hurt.

"I meant, of course it is."

"Yes," he said.

I see I'm making him sound worse than he was. In fact he presented a certain genial and soft-edged charm. I supposed he was gentle, handy, even-tempered, susceptible to a romantic impulse now and then—he'd said as much in his ad. (I'd trudged through the microfiched old newspapers for days until I'd found it.) She could have done much worse; here, of course, I was thinking of myself.

Simeon and I stood there nodding at each other and exchanging weak, sporadic smiles until Julia arrived, accompanied by my parents. She'd moved in with them after all; she slept in my old bedroom now, beneath where Gregory Corso still smiled and awaited his first ecstatic forkful of wax beans. For a second, standing there in my bunched-up sprung-collared tuxedo (the same one, I was wretchedly certain, I'd rented for the Henderson Society banquet) with my parents and Julia fanned out before me and the band playing "Memories," I felt as if some incautious step had dropped me into an alternate history; that Mesozoic butterfly had flapped its wings one extra time, with all that that entailed, and I was the groom, not him, and millions of people had never been born . . . Then I met Julia's eyes and saw in their uncomplicated amity that time was still on track. My father shuffled his feet like an unquiet child.

"Getting acquainted?" my mother said brightly. She had one hand on Julia's arm. My mother had taken to her so quickly and with such force that she let Julia suggest changes to her recipes, a privilege never before granted, and already the de-wheatgermed hamburgers and the BLT with bacon and lettuce standing in for breaded lentils were beginning to draw new faces to our door.

"Like gangbusters," I said. Simeon nodded gravely.

"Simeon's in chemistry," she said.

"He was just telling me."

"When the two of them met, he was holding his diploma out."

"What?" Simeon said. "I don't think so."

"You're sure you weren't holding your diploma out?"

"I'm sure."

"I thought you were."

"It's in storage."

My mother encompassed us all in a conspiratorial glance. "The reason I thought you were is because there was chemistry between you."

Julia's eyes flicked across mine, then came to rest on Simeon's. She took a step closer to him—bodies in motion, I thought, imagining everything schematic and viewed from above.

"You get it?" my mother said. "Then there would have been *chemistry* . . . between you!"

"That's good," Simeon said, while I burned, with embarrassment, with envy. My mother beamed. "That's very good," he said.

Simeon was offered a job at a company in New Jersey that, Julia wrote me in her first letter from there, "buys up unsafe products and makes them into plastic—asbestos, lead paint, old car batteries now, and, if Simeon's team comes through, DDT . . ." Julia started teaching art in a private girls' school. She writes me once a month or so—the achingly perfect, no-nonsense declinations of her script like an affectionate chastening. Her letters are made up of good wishes, earnest advice, and virtuosic simulations of interest in the departmental politicking that fills my drab, occasional replies. It's hard to tell one letter from another, except by the things she includes: recipes clipped from the "Bachelor's Banquet" in her town paper, photos of her tiny, scrubbed children, cartoons about professors, magazine articles she suspects will interest or vex me. All these things I read and throw away. The letters themselves I keep, though I never look at them.

At the end of every letter she asks me when I'm coming for a visit. Each time I put her off. I tell her I'm afraid I'd never come back.

Once I asked her if she missed Chandler City.

"I don't know if that's the way to put it," she wrote in reply. "I miss *you*, Sammy. I suppose I miss a few of my teachers. I think of Ellen sometimes—I do miss her. But I certainly don't miss Chandler City, as a *city*, if that's what you mean. I guess it seemed to me the sort of place you could either *be* from, and then leave, or just stop there for some amount of time. I can't picture it as someplace to end up."

And indeed, no one did; no one but me. Rosso retired to Georgia eight years ago, at his doctor's behest. Slotkin teaches at Yale. Dean Moresby lived just two years after I saw him at the banquet; Karl-Heinz Sethius is dead too. Treech is in New York City, rewarded for his successes with an executive post in the Henderson Society. And McTaggett went to Kyoto, the first American Gravinicist, I'm told, in the Far East.

Charlie stayed in town a while longer. As it turned out, the certain parcel *had* arrived on his father's watch, and consequently he too found himself out of a job at the end of my scheme. Feeling responsible, I persuaded my parents to take him on as a waiter. To everyone's surprise, he was a tremendous success. It happened like this: one night, bored, contemptuous, sick to death of the smell of couscous, he began to hurry the night along by waiting tables in character. And just like that, stardom—within weeks the whole city had heard of his uncanny skills. He specialized in tough guys: Reagan, Nicholson, Elliot Gould. "People feel bad about being served these days," Charlie told me. "Deep down they want a waiter who won't take their crap." We had lines out the door. Holistic awareness on the rise, according to my mother. She told anyone who'd listen: it was the satori-quake we'd all been waiting for, and the first shock was here, right here in Chandler City. But as soon as there was money enough my parents franchised the restaurant and moved back to New York. Happy Clappy's is a Grape Arbor now. Charlie left soon afterwards, eloping with an enamored customer to

Philadelphia, where he used his acquired knowledge of the vegetable trade to open a produce market, which, he gives me unsurprisingly to understand, is also a head shop.

Ellen came back to Chandler City when her father checked into the hospital for what no one pretended was anything but the last time. I met her there, out in a bright hall lined with ficus trees and the brass-etched names of the donors. She looked different. I wanted to say younger, but it wasn't quite that. The haze in her blue eyes was gone. She seemed a participant in the physical world in a way she had not before; I remarked her shadow, the shape her weight made on the vinyl cushion of the bench.

"How is he?" I said.

"Well, dying. You can see him if you want."

"I saw him yesterday."

This wasn't true. I hadn't visited the Dean, and had no plans to. I didn't have anything to say to him and I was afraid that in his gummy blindness he would mistake me for someone who did.

"I wondered if you would come," I told her.

"Why?"

"I didn't think you were going to forgive him."

"I haven't forgiven him."

"But you're here."

Ellen nodded.

"I thought you were never going to speak to him again."

"Nothing's final," Ellen said. "Not things like that."

"I guess not," I said. Glumness settled on me, more than could be accounted for by the headachy tube lights and the frost-cool nurses clicking through their rounds, from one exhausted package of malfunction to the next.

"And Professor Higgs?" I said.

"He's well."

"Still playing checkers?"

"With my sister. I mostly play mah-jongg now."

I raised my eyebrows.

"It's true. And I pick up trash at the park with a stick, too, and go to lectures about gardening. I'm being an old lady—why not? Tampa's filled with us."

"So you like Florida."

"We both do."

I leaned forward. "He told you that?"

"I just know," Ellen said. "All right?"

"All right. I got it."

"I was sorry to hear about Julia."

"How did you know?"

My question seemed to take her by surprise. "She wrote me."

"So she told you the whole story."

"Yes," Ellen said.

"We probably have pretty different perspectives on it."

"It's always that way."

Two stout doctors came squabbling by us. Ellen and I watched them until they turned the corner. I wondered if someone had just died.

"There are other women," Ellen said.

"Yes, I've heard that."

"But really," she said, and a little urgency entered her voice. "You should think about that."

After a little while she looked down at her watch. "Visiting hour's starting," she said. "Are you sure you wouldn't like to come in with me? I don't mind."

"I'm sure."

"Then I suppose I'll see you . . ."

"Whenever," I said. "Under happier circumstances."

"Yes," Ellen agreed. "That sounds nice."

But six months later she was dead. Something in Florida—its thwarted swampiness, or all those old ladies—had released her constitution's long-suppressed complaints. One day, as she folded miniature hot dogs into jackets of dough for her afternoon's company, something in her lungs lay down gently and relaxed. The mah-jongg club found her kneeling at the counter with her head against the formica. She had died so quietly and gracefully that no one in the living room had heard a thing.

I didn't find out about this until three years afterwards, when one Charlotte Amanezar, a student nurse at a retirement complex in Clearwater, wrote to tell me that Higgs, too, was dead. Ellen (remembering my feelings on good-byes?) had listed me as after-next-of-kin.

The retirement complex was called Sylvan Woods. Ellen's sister had sent him there. His considerable pension paid for it all: a room of his own, swimming lessons, new-American high-fiber cooking by a two-star chef, and Miss Amanezar, his private attendant. I learned all this from the brochure she sent me, which had Higgs on the front cover. He was sitting in a sturdy-looking chair, angled three-quarters to the camera, in his usual attitude of distant calculation, as if he were momentarily to deliver an accounting of the costs and benefits of spending one's twilight years at Sylvan Woods instead of some other, cheaper place of repose. One could imagine which way the sum would go.

Miss Amanezar thought I'd like to know that Higgs had been a model patient, popular among the staff and clientele. (Why not? He would have listened politely to people's war stories, their dimly recollected oat-sowage. He would never have sent his food back.) His funeral, a simple service, had been chock with mourners. "And I too," she wrote, "will be sorry not to have him with us anymore; though I hope you will comfort yourself as I do that he has been taken to a better place."

I looked at the brochure again. It was hard to imagine a better place.

The cause of Higgs's death was recorded as "respiratory failure"— the coroner's shrug. Miss Amanezar assured me that his passing had been painless and that, to the last, Higgs had been in perfect health. "It was just as if God had reached inside him and switched him off. Just like that."

And me? I stayed in Chandler City, stayed alive. On occasion this thought occurred to me, banal and agreeable: *I have done well for myself.* The department granted me my doctorate the day my Sethius paper was accepted. A month later they offered me a permanent position.

Of course, they were not the first to do so; I had offers stacked on my bookshelves from every Gravinic department in the country, and most of those elsewhere. They'd sent me glossy campus albums, photos of my office-to-be, and the *letters*—committee chairs, distinguished men, fawning and wheedling like eunuchs. They were just the kind of letters Higgs used to get. And like Higgs, I decided to stay home. For maximum effect I kept my motive obscure; but in fact it was perfectly simple. I was happy where I was. I still lived in the L-shaped apartment, almost unsqualid now that I had it to myself. There seemed no reason, apart from the sentimental one, to move out. The ordinary thing, I understand, is to see the lost loved one in every corner, to move out (alternately drink, act, play football) in order to leave the accusing spirits behind, so that one might at last forget. But there was not a trace of Julia in the apartment. Even at the moment she'd left there hadn't been; even, I thought now, for some time before that. So why move? It was bad enough that other people did.

I took McTaggett's place, teaching the rudiments of Gravinic syntax for the first few weeks of each semester, and returning to my own investigations once the last of my students slunk bemusedly away. Even when Rosso left us, grinning and coughing, and I was named department chair, I continued to teach—still harboring some hope, I suppose, of finding a successor. So far I have been disappointed.

My deception was never uncovered. I came almost to believe in it myself, so implausible was the alternative version, my audacious, half-cocked secret-agentry, its unreasonable success. Even the most credulous, the dullest, zittiest, movie-hooked teen would have to shake his head: "Never happen." But it had happened. And within months the silt of time and study had closed over my hoax and it was good as proved, good as if witnessed by angels. After a year: not a Gravinicist of any note but was willing to hold forth on how obvious it should have been to everyone what Higgs would say—and how, in certain of the Gravinicist's own papers, it must be said by somebody, one could make out glimmerings of the revelation to come; one could, that is, so long as one was willing to read fairly, and not with an eye toward denying the insights of others, in the interest, presumably, of one's own rather far-fetched claim to primacy . . . And back and forth, and so on.

I held myself out of this wrangling, and once I was certain I would not be found out, I ceased even to read the claims and counterclaims. My interests lay elsewhere. I was bent on realizing my Jugendtraum, the new history of Europe—though before long it became clear that this ambition, dizzy, avaricious as it was, had been too small. It was the whole world we were after now. My colleagues and I placed copies of *Poems Against the Enemies* with Lin Biao on the Long March, and with an aide-de-camp to Abdel Nasser, of mysterious provenance, whose advice to his commander on the eve of the Six-Day War— "Strike now, and their limbs are pulped, their penises lie as dry sticks for the chickens to peck apart; wait, and ichor runs from our own ankles, and defeat, the black washerwoman, claims her husband"— differed only in its relative cordiality from the speech of the Minister of Ants in Henderson's "Feces: for Thisbe." And more, and more, until there was not a two-bit revolution anywhere, no civil war, no organized slaying of any kind that had no Henderson in it.

And no one cared but us. I couldn't blame them, the real historians. We had our methods, and they had theirs: hundreds of them. So it was capital behind everything? You could make a case for that. Or the concentration of poor old agrarian man in the cities and the towns, or the coming dust-up of the races, or whatever was fashionable these days—you'll forgive me, I hope, if I can't take these "revisions" too seriously. Year by year they supplant one another—what is it, *genetics* now?—while we Hendersonists stay fixed on course.

They're not bad, all these theories I read about: they make sense, they fit with what we know, they have constituencies we can only marvel at, and if they have no proof, well, neither do we. Remove Henderson and the world might be unrecognizable; but then again it might be exactly the same. It's circumstantial, what we do. In this way all historians are alike. We're right, and all the others wrong—that's the only difference. Each year it seems a smaller one.

My life settled into a spare, periodic state. I woke each morning at quarter to seven, drank two tumblerfuls of orange juice and ate a carton of yogurt; then listened to the day's news on the radio—Ellen's legacy, that habit—while I brushed my teeth and shaved, and was ready to leave at thirty-five past. I returned home at five-fifteen and ordered a pizza for dinner. (Even the Greek and his egg salad had left town.) After that I would work for five more hours, arrange my papers for the next day, shower, floss, and fall asleep without incident. My dreams were reassuringly conventional, tending toward boundless vistas, gliding, conversations in which I was not immediately involved. I often saw columns of figures and dates.

It seemed to me I had achieved a modest sort of pinnacle: a perfectly unmarked, unremarkable existence. My world was a closed system of which I had an absolute understanding. I knew what went where and what served what purpose. Higgs had been right about marriage: you couldn't be too careful. Another person, however closely aligned to my own temperament, would inevitably have introduced perturbations into my routine—noise, one could say, in the signal— and I had begun to value quiet above all else. I had accumulated a great store of it. A girl came by twice each week, once to pick up my laundry, again to bring it back along with the meager groceries I needed: soap, skim milk, toilet tissue, rat traps. The girl was seventeen or so, heavy-chested and sullen, but not dull; she learned quickly not to speak to me, and that one knock was enough. I changed faculty meetings from weekly to monthly, then eliminated them altogether. No one complained. When I did have to talk to someone—my typist, my undergraduates—I grew furious at the slow approximateness of speech.

I often thought of Higgs as I ate my nightly pizza. There were still those who speculated about his silence; but that was not what I was doing. I knew the truth now. There was really, in the end, no alternative to silence—so I told myself, with a certain tired satisfaction, as I lifted my oiled, grainy fingers one by one to my mouth. Each of my fingertips was stained a cheery, burned-looking red. There was nothing to say. There was just nothing to say. I supposed I had turned out much like the other professors after all—their nervous habits just beginning to make themselves known in me like a familiar syndrome—and while it was not the life I had planned for myself, it was, in its way, a rich one; and I had chosen it.

My serenity was disturbed only once: that was the day I received Miss Amanezar's letter. I had always casually imagined that Higgs and I would see each other again, would compare notes in the safety of reminiscence, like high-school reunion guests confessing their erstwhile crushes and their never-punished pranks. As ludicrous as this fantasy was, I found I felt a little remorse at seeing it finally torn down. When I was finished reading I slipped the letter into the drawer where I kept my personal correspondence (that is, my mail from Julia) and put it from my mind. Before me on the desk was a stack of Belgian deeds of trust, with which I meant to demonstrate that a certain acquaintance of Henderson's had, in the early 1950s, been in a position to influence administrative policies as regarded the Congo. But I couldn't concentrate. I was beset by thoughts of Higgs, of the farce we'd played out, of Julia and Ellen; then I found myself wholly occupied by the task of *not* thinking of these things. The Flemish street names broke up, recombined, a dancing grid of diphthongs; hopeless. I took out the letter and read it again. *A better place . . .*

I decided—and I shouldn't have to say how momentous this was—to go out for a walk.

I was not surprised to find myself heading for the campus, and, once on the campus, toward the cliff. I came to the site of Higgs's house. It was already two years since it had been demolished—but I'll say more about that later. Now there was a gigantic cubical absence where the house had been. It was to be the foundation for the Moresby Research Center. At the bottom of the pit, a few distant workers were hacking dispiritedly at objects I could not make out in the hazy dimness of the afternoon. The red, scrubby hole looked like an outsized grave, like the graves the Russians were digging for Soviet statues. I'd heard about it on the radio: they had to lower them in with cranes, the hewn-out commissars and their deputies, wet-cheeked like ikons, but with vodka, from the bottles the crowds tossed at their clumsy granite heads. The onlookers lined the hole like the edge of a parade, shivering, cheering each smashed bottle, as the cold gusts of freedom whipped their threadbare coats around. But for Higgs, I thought gloomily, there'd been no one—no one but Miss Amanezar and whatever docile patients she'd conducted to the Pinellas County burying ground. I burned on his behalf at the placid, cotton-mouthed devotions she must have seen him off with. There was nothing he would have hated more—he the insister on precision, the enemy of every empty word—than to be subject, in his last aboveground moments, to the exhausted and puerile shaggy-dog jokes Miss Amanezar called prayers; and poor Higgs's boxed-up corpse, in every last case the painful, obvious punchline. Nobody deserved that. Not even the living.

Beside me on a broad picket sign was an artist's depiction of the Moresby Center as it would look when finished. The building was a windowed taper standing on the cliffside, matter-of-fact as a stalagmite, surrounded by impressionistic renderings of trees, cars, and students. Beneath the drawing was a list of the departments that had won a coveted space: chemistry would be housed there, and agricultural science, Spanish, creative writing, and drama, some branches of history. Anthropology, of course. I thought there was something a little belligerent about the building, its solitary height. To me it looked like the college, fed up at last, lifting a middle finger to the plain.

I turned away from the yellow safety rope. I felt skittish, inclined to bolt; but I was not yet ready to go home. Whatever impulse had brought me there wasn't satisfied. I walked away from the cliff, toward the forest path, and in a few minutes I had arrived at the statue of Tip Chandler. To my surprise—how long *had* it been?—the founder stood upright. The patina was scrubbed off, too, and he was circled with a waist-high fence. I supposed they didn't want people sitting on him now. On a stone at my feet a bronze plaque was inset: "HE LOOKED AT THE DESERT AND SAW ATHENS." I looked at Chandler. In his new posture he had lost the embarrassed dignity I had always liked him best for. Now he seemed serious, a believer, a little scary to be close to—much as he must have been in life.

Next I went to the classroom in Gunnery Hall where I had stumbled on McTaggett's class. The door was locked, and pressing my face against the grilled rectangle of glass I saw that the room had been converted for storage. It was row after row of prefab shelving now. Cardboard cartons, overflowing with printout, were heaped in the aisles. I abandoned campus and headed into town. The Tooth and Nail was still there, but inside it was unrecognizable. There were stucco partitions everywhere, and the lighting was pure white and sourceless, as in an art museum. At one end of the bar a group of wide-shouldered young men in business dress were arguing talmudically about the rules of Canadian football, as the Canadians tussled and disported on the big screen above them. Near the entrance, thin-faced girls stood in a circle, sucking at mixed drinks, planning something. I backed out.

My last stop was the coffee shop I had used to frequent with McTaggett, and where I had met Charlie again. I was hardly surprised to find it replaced by a Grape Arbor franchise. I bought a cup of coffee and sat down at the counter. Here it is, I thought: ordinary life. I gave my neighbors a covert once-over, assigning to each a set of circumstances. The natty gentleman at the far end of the counter I felt to be a salesman of luxury cars; the woman at his side was a traveling executive who'd share his room tonight; then there was a hard-hat; a defrocked priest; a pair of angry youths; a folksinger; and next to me, communing defeatedly with a cruller, a hobo. None of them knew a word of Gravinic. If, through some absurd mischance, they were to hear it spoken, they would not even recognize it as a language; it would be just gibberish, even the boundaries between words impossible to make out, a hash of phonemes, babble, baby-talk. Higgs was dead. And it seemed to me that his death had propelled me into a subtly revised version of the world, one in which his long silence had never been broken; or perhaps there had never been a silence at all, or even a Higgs. Why else would everything connected to my secret be excised? I wondered whether my apartment was still there. A mad suspicion gripped me that an atlas, in this new world, would not even show the Gravine. In its place there would only be the careful stippling of landform, or a legend indicating scale.

"Are you drinking that?" the hobo asked me. "It's gonna get cold."

I met his eyes, startled; and as I did I was struck full on by a vision of his solitary life, knocking hopefully at the back doors of farmhouses, huddled under straw in the corner of a freight car, pursuing something unguessable back and forth, east and west along the rails. He used what he needed and answered to nobody. He was my double! I felt like taking him by the shoulders, bursting into tears, calling him brother; but even in my agitated state I knew I was incapable of making such a scene.

Instead I leaned toward him and said, "I *understand* you"—trying to inject into that phrase as much as I could of my desperate comradeship.

The hobo nodded, tranquil. He placed his hand nearer my cup.

"You're not the first person to tell me that," he said.

I left the hobo my coffee and waded out into the crowded, twilit avenue. People pushed by me, muttering darkly; car horns went off. Across the street a man dressed as a steer was handing out coupons for a steakhouse. It was a far cry from Athens. But then, I thought, where was Athens now? These days I supposed they had municipal buses there, and pickpockets and flower shops and a bickering local government like any other city. The shrines to philosophy and art had all been broken up and carted off, stone by stone, to air-conditioned museums and the vast backyards of the wealthy. Time had worn the statues down to noseless anonymity. Maybe it was inevitable that it should happen that way.

The traffic carried me toward home, and when I arrived at the old warehouse I found that my apartment was still there, the same as I had left it. My pizza box still rested open on the table; next to it sat Miss Amanezar's letter, and the promotional brochure. I put them back in the drawer. The Belgian deeds awaited me at my desk. I let the familiarity of my surroundings rise up and over me like a warm pool; my terrifying glimpse of the world outside my circumscription began to recede; and as the sun slipped gasping below the line of buildings, I sat down again to work.

Four years later, a pair of London policemen, responding to complaints from a small convoy of collection agencies, hacked down the door to a Fleet Street flat and found a body that had been dead for a long time. The putrefaction was so far advanced that one of the constables had to rush from the room, eyes smarting, to throw up. When the stronger-stomached one, left to carry out the official procedures by himself, tried to turn the corpse's face up, the jaw sloughed off and a vile, lumpy fluid gushed over his hand. He didn't have time to run; he just crouched in the corner and coughed his breakfast out.

The apartment, aside from its occupant, was perfectly empty. There was no furniture but the bed and a low table, no books, no toiletries— no sign, that is, that the man who lived there had done anything in decades but eat and sleep. On the center of the table sat the empty envelope in which Higgs had sent his letter, forty years before.

"The deceased appears not to have been tampered with," the policeman wrote in his report. "No identifying marks. No evidence of foul play."

Downstairs, the other constable wiped his lips. A grandmotherly Indian had let him use her sink.

"But why on earth didn't you report the odor?" he asked her.

"The odor?"

"The odor of the . . . deceased. From upstairs. Didn't you find it suspicious?"

"Not a bit," the woman said.

"How can that be?"

She shook her head, frowned with what looked to be infinite patience; for the stupid world, its stubbornness.

"It's smelled like that for thirty years."

So Henderson was dead, and as if that weren't bad enough my telephone kept ringing. The calls started in the morning, and kept up through the following day, and the next; first people calling to see if I knew, then to make sure that I knew, then, assuming that I knew, asking what I was going to do about it. *Do* about it? I tried to be polite, though I hardly remembered how. The appropriate formulas came to my lips only slowly, and emerged with the inflections all flattened out and wrong, as if I'd memorized them syllable by syllable. By the time I went home I was exhausted to trembling.

On the third day, when the hubbub had largely died down (it was just the outliers now, lonely one-man Gravinics departments in Singapore and Perth refusing to accept they'd been the last to know), my most recent secretary came into my office to tell me that someone was waiting outside.

"He'll have to make an appointment," I said. "That's the system."

The system was that when people called for appointments, my secretary put them off—repeatedly, if necessary. In this way I avoided seeing almost everyone.

"I know," she said. "But he's come from Japan."

"McTaggett?" I said hopefully. She shook her head. "His name is Kosugi," she said.

"Oh," I said, suddenly without the will or vigor to resist. "Send him in. Thank you, Denise."

My secretary lingered a little longer in the doorway. I looked down uncomfortably. Oh, God, I thought, wasn't her name Denise?

"I just wanted to say I was sorry about Henderson."

She cast her eyes down at her headset mike. For the first time I noticed that she was not pretty.

"OK," I said.

She slipped out the door and in a moment was replaced by Koiichi Kosugi. It had been many years since I'd seen him. He was treeish and stern, wide through the shoulders, and his business suit was of a deep, expensive blue. Kosugi had spent the last decade throwing himself into ludicrous business ventures from which he had emerged, time after time, unruined; all the while adding to his collection of Hendersonia, now the largest in the world. Henderson's littering citation was in his hands, and several rare first drafts—rare because Henderson so seldom wrote second drafts.

"Mr. Kosugi," I said resignedly. "What can I do for you?"

He wheeled away from me so that the great tailored drape of his suit billowed at me like a map of the open sea.

"The Immortal Henderson!" he boomed.

"Died," I said. "I know."

"Is the name of the conference you're having. Starting December sixteenth. The ninety-fifth birthday."

"Would-have-been birthday."

"Don't stop me. I'm paying, so no difficulty with that. You just need to notify everyone. And arrange for the hall. Are we settled?"

"This is sudden. Even if we do agree to go ahead."

"Let me worry about that."

"Then can I ask—"

He turned to face me. "OK. Ask."

"Why?"

He put his hands deep, deep in the pockets of his blue, blue suit.

"I found something," he said.

The morning the conference was to begin, a morning out of which wet snow dropped limply to the red, chopped earth of the campus, I was met on my way to Gunnery Hall by a local television crew. Their leader was a small-boned and purposeful blonde whose face, as I approached, resolved into a mask of professional interest. I recognized her, though I never watched television. She was always riding in parades.

"Professor Grapearbor," she said, squarely in my way. "Got a minute for the six o'clock news?"

"One minute," I said.

She made a curt, unreadable signal to the cameraman, who was slouching behind me on the path, chewing gum. He trudged over to his camera, which was covered with a tarp to keep the snow off. A red light lit.

"That's right, Tom," said the reporter. "And it's all right here in Chandler City, where eggheads and experts from here to Tokyo have gathered to pay tribute to one of literature's all-time greats. I'm here with Chandler State's own Professor Samuel Grapearbor, a Henderson authority. Professor, would you describe this conference as a civic coup for Chandler City?"

"No comment," I said.

She looked at me oddly.

"I mean yes."

"According to experts," she went on, "Henderson, who died this year in London at the age of ninety-four, has left us a long-lasting legacy. Professor, how is it that his poems are still relevant to us today?"

That they'd been relevant even at their writing was news to me. I wondered what experts she'd consulted. I searched for some response that would not make me seem a fraud, or a hopeless rube.

The cameraman made an impatient circle with his hand, catching my eye. He pointed at the camera lens: look here. I obeyed. I had read somewhere that in order to appear relaxed on television one was supposed to imagine the faces of the viewers across the glass, to make a sort of conversation out of it. Try as I might, I couldn't do it: couldn't make up arbitrary faces. And I needed a backdrop—where would people *be,* at six o'clock? In living rooms? Kitchens? The Tooth and Nail, maybe, watching the big screen? Were they together or alone? Decent or in-? Were they even paying attention? Or were they occupied in something else while they waited for the weather to come on? How was I supposed to make all these decisions? It was ordinary life again, that enduring and intractable mystery. I didn't think I was getting any more relaxed.

"Professor?" the reporter said. "Relevance? We can edit this out."

"I don't know," I told her. "Luck, I guess."

"Well, we all need that, don't we?" she said brightly. But annoyance had crept into her voice and I felt I knew her a little better.

"I'm afraid I'm running late," I said. This was a lie. I scooted around her and set off down the path. She followed me. So I put my head down and hurried away like a perpetrator. The cameras lumbered along behind us.

"Any truth to the rumors that playboy multimillionaire Koiichi Kosugi will be unveiling a previously unknown Henderson work today?" She was matching my pace easily.

"No comment," I said, over my shoulder.

"Do you yourself know what's on the agenda?"

"I don't know any more than you do."

This was true.

"One more thing," she said. "Some of our viewers will remember you as the person present when the late Stanley Higgs broke his thirteen-year silence. Do you think Professor Higgs would be proud of this weekend's activities here at CSU?"

I sped up again, half-jogging now, my feet slipping alarmingly on the slushy path. Finally I was outdistancing the crew. It was the cameras that held them back. "No," I said breathlessly, "comment."

The session was scheduled for one o'clock, but at twelve-fifteen, when I arrived, the hall was already half-full. I proceeded to my seat on the stage. Beneath me, the Henderson scholars filed in. In their neat progression down the rows of seats, in their scarves and flapped fur hats and Gore-Tex parkas buttoned over their noses and mouths, they looked like perplexed schoolchildren, called in on a day when class should by all rights have been canceled by the storm. But looking closer I saw that they couldn't be mistaken for children at all: they were soft around the eyes, grayed and diminished. They looked, that is, like I felt. The shuffling, muttering sound of old men rose off them. I would not have been surprised at that moment to look down and see my own hands spotted and trembling, grooved with age.

One by one the conferees settled into their empty seats and began tugging at their outerwear. The run-off from the piles of hats and coats made channels down each row to the soggy, mud-stamped carpet of the aisle.

At the dot of one, Kosugi bounded onto the stage. I had thought his other suit was expensive; but this one was so black, so rich, that sitting behind him I felt I was looking through a rent into intergalactic space.

"I'm very pleased to introduce today's keynote speaker," Kosugi said. He produced a massive grin. The scholars leaned forward.

"Because it's me!"

Kosugi held up a gray sheaf of papers.

"I am holding in my hand," he said, "something of great interest to all of you—something I've obtained through no small effort and expense."

Not true, I knew. The manuscript had come to him in the mail, with a San Francisco postmark and no return address. All the money and time he'd spent had been in search of his mysterious benefactor. He'd come up with nothing.

Kosugi laid the papers on the rostrum. He adjusted his astonishing suit.

"Little Bug's Son," he began.

Everyone knows the story of foolish Little Bug and his four wives, but most modern people have forgotten the important events that took place afterwards.

Just weeks after the evil widow's feast, even before all of Little Bug's gnawed bones had been boiled down for soup, the wicked daughter, Clarissa, began to suspect for private reasons that all was not right. Before long it was obvious to everyone that Clarissa was with child by her late husband.

"Kill it, mother! You must kill it at once!" cried Clarissa, upon realizing the frightful truth.

"Silence!" the evil widow commanded. "Let me think. Possibly this misfortune may be turned to our advantage."

Indeed, the widow reasoned, the issue of her daughter's brief marriage might well be a stroke of good luck. While Little Bug had indeed been delicious, she did not much like having to take up her share of the chores again. With a grandson, she might be released from work for the rest of her days.

So Little Bug's son was born, and grew quickly into a stout boy, who, having inherited his father's suggestibility, uncomplainingly took over the chores from his evil grandmother, his wicked mother, and his two cruel uncles. The evil widow gave him the name You Boy, after the family's manner of addressing him. Thanks to Clarissa's blood, You Boy was a little cleverer than Little Bug had been, and so he was able to take over the cooking and the tax figures as well as the menial tasks of the farm. The evil widow and her family had never been happier.

Meanwhile, not far away, a surprise had come to light. A district surveyor, chancing upon the abandoned farm of Little Bug's grandmothers and grandfathers, had discovered a gigantic cache of silver coins, which the grandparents, in their wisdom, had amassed over their lifetimes. With the coins was a will, naming Little Bug as the rightful inheritor of the treasure.

Soon, news of the great trove and the missing grandson reached the ears of the traveling salesman, who recognized at once that the heir must be the very man he had once advised as to the selection of a wife. He set off that same day for the evil widow's farm to bring Little Bug the news of his good fortune.

The evil widow invited the traveling salesman in for tea, thinking only to beat him senseless and take his walking-bag. But when she heard the story of Little Bug's treasure, she realized that much greater gains were within her grasp.

"Alas!" she cried, hiding her delight. "I do know the poor boy you speak of—he was my son-in-law! But, woe to us, he passed on not a day after he married my darling Clarissa."

And she collapsed in tears.

Now the salesman, in his line of work, had developed a fine talent for distinguishing truth from falsehood; and although he did not trust the evil widow a bit, he sensed that what she had told him was not a lie.

"Then Clarissa is heir to the fortune," the salesman said reluctantly. "Let us go to the city, where I will bear witness that I saw Little Bug on your farm."

So they made ready to leave; but just then, You Boy, who, thanks to Clarissa's blood, was a little cleverer than Little Bug had been, and who had all along been hiding in the wood cabinet, burst out into the room, filled with fury at the way the widow had tried to cheat him. He took up a fireplace poker and with one well-aimed swing knocked his grandmother's head from her shoulders. The widow's children rushed in at this noise; and the traveling salesman, having instantly perceived the true nature of the situation, drew his sword and ran Clarissa through the belly. Then You Boy and the traveling salesman chased down the two cruel sons, who had fled over the rise, and beat them to death with their fists.

Afterwards, the two of them used the treasure to make themselves great lords. The salesman, who had brought the news of the inheritance to You Boy, became known as Speaker; and You Boy, who had concealed himself in silence, took the name Listener; these were the two first kings who founded the country of the Gravine. As for the evil widow and her two cruel sons and her wicked daughter, Clarissa, King Speaker and King Listener ate their flesh in a stew, then scattered their bones in every direction. Wherever one of the bones fell, another country sprang up, in which the people's speech was confounded with lies and half-truths and words that could not be understood at all; and this is how the other parts of the world came to be.

Late in the afternoon, after the day's program had ended, after the scholars had dispersed to their medium-priced hotels, there came a quiet rapping on my office door.

"Denise?"

There was no answer. I felt quite sure now that I had misrecalled her name.

"Come in," I said wearily.

It was not my secretary. In my doorway stood a tremendously old man, filthy, heaped with snow, hunched so sharply that his face was level with the knob. He looked as if he had been exposed to an experimental shrinking ray, still years away from readiness, which had acted more efficiently on his soft tissues than on his stubborn tall man's skeleton. His skin was wrapped tight as parchment around the bones of his arms and hands; his ears were minuscule; his nose had retreated into his skull, leaving as reminder only a pair of labored, gasping openings above the trembling line of his mouth. He listed to one side, and his legs were bent under him—as if varying rates of contraction were beginning to pull him into an entirely new shape. His hair was gone. A dull, directionless hate embered in his eyes. I recognized him.

"Henderson," I said.

He made no motion to correct me.

"But they found you—"

Henderson rolled his lips back and extended one yellowed finger at his mouth. It took me a moment to see what he meant. The gold crown. If it had been Henderson in the apartment they'd have found it in the wreckage of his head.

Then who was the corpse? Some derelict, I supposed. It was easy to imagine Henderson dragging the body upstairs in a tied-off sack, feet first, with the dead man's head banging on each step. As decrepit as he was he seemed wound around some undiminished strength. Possibly he'd killed the man himself.

Possibly, I thought, he was here to kill me.

I composed myself, rose from my chair.

"It's an honor to have you here," I told him, in Gravinic, and extended my hand. By my choice of words and inflectional endings I had conveyed not only the sentiment above, but our difference in age and status, our previous unacquaintance, and the fact that the appositive predicate ("to have you here") denoted an event for which I had waited for quite some time.

Henderson looked down at my hand as if it contained a tawdry, offensive gift.

"This is America. It is English. Bloody."

His voice, escaping from that shrunken mouth, was little more than a whistle. His accent was atrocious.

"Walking us," he said fiercely. He raised his hands to indicate outside.

I stepped around my desk. "I'll show you the sights. Good idea. You've come all this way."

Before we left I went to the closet and got out an oversized sweatshirt I never wore.

"Here," I told him. "It gets cold at night."

His thin polyester Oxford was soaked through with snow. He squinted down at the sweatshirt in his hands, then jerked it over his head. Stenciled across the sweatshirt was the legend, "PROPERTY OF CHANDLER STATE ATHLETIC DEPARTMENT—XXL." He looked like someone's hideous idea for a mascot.

Outside the daytime was beginning to give way. The sun was an unpublicized presence behind the city skyline; the moon, gibbous, exposed itself intermittently between the clouds. At the horizon, where it was a little clearer, I could see the rising winter stars: Procyon, Sirius, and so on. Henderson was walking with me across the frozen ground. He held his arms in front of him as we went. I guessed his eyesight was going, or his sense of balance. He looked ready at any moment to drop to all fours.

So far I'd been too surprised to be surprised—now it started to leak in, the unlikeliness of this, measurable in magnitudes I only knew the names of: milliards, googols. Something was required of me.

"I never dreamed I'd really get to meet you," I said.

Henderson made a noise like this: "Hyeagh!"

"You're the most important poet of the century."

"Becch!" He spat a little crater in the snow.

We came to the Moresby Center. There the ground sloped down as we approached the cliff. Henderson lost his footing once in the slush and grabbed my arm to keep from falling, with a grip as strong and consistent as a blood pressure cuff. The next day I'd find five bruises in a perfect ring around my elbow.

I was wearing a heavy coat and a wool cap that pulled down over my ears, but my nose was running, and my eyes hurt from the cold. Henderson seemed unaffected by the weather—though his hands and face were bare. And our walk hadn't winded him a bit. When we stopped the snow began accumulating on top of his bald head. I felt foolish for having given him the sweatshirt. For a moment it seemed eerily plausible that Henderson really was immortal; that he would just go on getting older, his skin stretching tighter over the concave places, his voice ever higher, ever quieter. He would construct a new seclusion and this time he would be careful to be unreachable by mail.

Before us the Center jutted from the red earth like a nail through the back of a hand.

"This is where Professor Higgs's house used to be," I told him.

"It is a bastard," Henderson said softly. He meant Higgs.

"Maybe it is," I said, not sure who I meant, or what. But my answer seemed to please him. He nodded.

I thought I knew then what Henderson had come for. He wanted to know the truth about Higgs: the only person who had gotten to him. And I was the only person who had gotten to Higgs. So it fell to me to tell him.

So I told him; so I told him everything. I had no idea what he might already know. I told Henderson about Higgs's rise to academic prominence, his single-handed popularization of Henderson's work, the basketball championship, the dentist's letter, the one-sentence seminar, the order of baked potato, and Higgs's subsequent retreat into silence. I proceeded to my own unpromising beginnings, getting along quickly to my accidental introduction to McTaggett and the Gravinic language, and my rapid conversion into an apprentice Gravinicist; then I moved to the outset of my employment. I described in detail the strange appointments of the Higgses' basement, my initial antipathy toward Ellen and the manner in which it abated, once Julia joined the scene; the visits of Dr. Treech; Ellen's provocative views about marriage; and our checker-playing habits. All this he listened to attentively, bringing close to me his tiny ear. I recounted my argument with Julia and the arrival of the Sethius letter, whose contents I paraphrased; then I came to the notice from the Society, the threat therein, the doctored photographs and the purchased judge, my inadvertent culpability, and our fevered, doomed efforts to convince Higgs to speak. At last I came to my scheme, my enlistment of Charlie Hascomb, my meticulous planning followed by my seemingly fatal omission; the nevertheless successful outcome; and finally, Higgs's actual last words.

"After he beat me," I told Henderson, "he said 'My game.' And that was the last time I ever saw him."

I was dizzy and out of breath; I had hardly stopped talking in the half-hour since I'd begun the story. But I was also something close to overjoyed. My secret, now that I was unburdened of it, seemed laughable and puny—*that* was what I'd been carrying around so long? I thought of a picture I'd seen in a textbook, the month I'd been pre-med: a tumor in a bottle, snipped out of someone's lung, just a moist, gray, unimposing clump, harmless now that it was on its own. Henderson had released me, just as I, maybe, had released Higgs; and now, like Higgs, I could do what I pleased. I could leave if I wanted, and never come back. History I could abandon to Henderson and the leaders of men, his unwitting stooges—no one would know the difference.

The windows of the Center were still mostly lit. The offices were stacked in alternating rows like cells in a stalk. Behind each rectangle of light there was a chemist, a dramatist, a creative writer, an anthropologist, or something else. Our Babel, I thought, this welter of disciplines, our own bituminous tower. Something had gone wrong; the confounding of the tongues had proceeded on schedule but the victims had failed to scatter, as intended, across the span of the earth. So the tower had been completed. At the building's base, bulldozers trundled across the clay like slow beetles, moving piles of earth from one spot to another, to undiscernable purposes. There were annexes in store: more Centers built to this one's plan, more people's names to be honored and preserved.

I imagined the world advanced a hundred years. I was dead, my name forgotten; this was the central comforting fact. The city was all towers, bristling at the sky like a dusty bed of spikes. Tip Chandler had torn himself loose again. Now he was face down in the clay. Names filed past me, a catalogue. Julia was dead, my parents too. Ellen was long dead. Charlie, McTaggett, Slotkin, Treech: dead, dead, dead, dead. Higgs was dead.

But for now I was not dead, only dead-to-be; there was just the one tower; it was almost unequivocally nighttime. Down on the plain, the cities were blinking on. Henderson let my arm go. Everything preternatural about the moment had fled, leaving me an ordinary exhaustion, and a pained relief like the slumping down after a long run. Behind me, in town, people were fixing dinner, watching me on the six o'clock news.

"Well?" I asked Henderson. "Seen enough?"

I still thought he might reveal something to me; there was so much that was still shaded; but of course it would not have been

Henderson's way to explain everything. Or anything. He had what he'd come for.

"Then let's go," I said.

And he was gone; he sped away from me on his spindly legs, skipping over the snow like a waterbug, faster, I found, than I could follow. I saw my sweatshirt disappear over the rise.

The next morning I bought my ticket to New York.

It's amazing: the way this denatured, anonymous room (my off-white sepulchre) has in five days' time become manifestly my own, and all it took was this stack of two-hundred-some sheets of hotel letterhead stacked on the chilly formica of the desk. My finished pages I keep at my left hand—sound familiar? And at my right, the shrinking pile of blank paper. When the pile runs out I call the porter. I've run out five times so far. Each time I tell him how much more I'll need, and each time he arrives with the same forty pages.

"Sorry, sir," he says. "House policy."

It's no such thing. Each time he comes up here he gets a dollar. Good business—I applaud him. He'll go far.

The last time he came up he asked me what I was writing.

"A letter," I said.

The porter looked doubtfully at my accumulated work.

"To an old girlfriend. She doesn't know I'm here."

He broke out in a low, wide grin. "Hey, man, I hear you. Tell her good."

I gave him two dollars.

But this isn't my letter to Julia, not yet. I'm putting that off. There's that story about Woodrow Wilson: his secretary comes into his office and says, Mr. President, they want you to give a one-hour speech on the state of the economy, how long do you need? And Wilson says, give me a month. The next day the secretary comes back and says, now they say they want a two-hour speech, and Wilson says, I can have it in a week. And the next day the secretary comes back in and says, big surprise, now they want three hours, and Wilson gets up and says, where are they? I'm ready now.

So this is my three-hour speech.

This morning, Thursday, I stepped out for breakfast (in this city, I find to my delight, egg salad can be had at six-thirty in the morning, and at every corner; I chose to patronize a genial, frizzy-haired Cambodian who called me "Captain" and could have been cousin to my Greek) and, on my return, found the young toughs back in front of my hotel. They were all wearing schoolbags now. It seemed they were waiting for the bus. I looked at them for a little too long; one of them, a blond boy, caught my gaze. He seemed to be the leader.

"Hey, mister," he said.

"Yes?"

The whole group of them dissolved in laughter, all but the one who'd spoken. "Nothing," he said. "Just being sociable."

"You're all in school?" I said.

The blond boy had a little death's head bauble stuck in his left ear. "Yeah."

"Where?"

"Rockley," he said. Someone said *"Suckley."* Another one: *"Dickley."*

"What's your favorite subject?"

"Are you serious?"

"Sure."

"School's a crock," the blond boy said. (*"Crockley,"* someone whispered.)

I raised my eyebrows.

"It's not *reality,*" he explained. "You know what I mean? Reality's about taking risks. Going to extremes."

"He's extreme," another boy said. No—it was a girl. Her olive T-shirt had a little red star on the chest. "He's a merciless skater."

"I have been close to death many times," the blond said proudly.

"Geometry, especially, that sucks," said the red-star girl.

"I took French for two years," a fat boy put in, "and all I learned how to say was *bawn jore.*" The girl gave him five.

"So are you selling or what?" the leader asked me.

Their surliness, so careful, so new; I wanted to gather them all to my arms, rummage through their untouslable brush cuts. Youth was just as I remembered!

"I'm afraid not," I told him. "Actually, I just moved here."

At this, a burst of good humor, razzing from the rear.

"That is *wack,*" he said. "Why?"

"I'm starting a restaurant."

It was the first thing that had come to mind; but really, I thought, why not? Cooking was the only real job I had ever had. My family name, even now, might be an asset. Kids like this would work for me; maybe these very kids. I anointed them one by one. Blond boy: you will be my fry cook. Red-star girl: prep, salad, soup. Fatso: security.

The bus rumbled up at the curb; not a bus at all, I saw, but a well-appointed Japanese minivan with a stopsign-flap attached. It must have been a good school.

"Peace out," the blond boy advised me, and raised a fist.

"No fear," I said.

I'm almost out of paper again. I call the porter and ask for a ream to be sent up. He arrives seconds later with forty pages.

"You know what you should tell her?"

It occurs to me that he would make a perfect maître d'.

"What?"

He sets the paper down at my right. I hand him a dollar.

"Tell her you've changed."

"Now come on," I say, "that's too easy."

"But the point is, don't say how. Then whatever she really wants out of you, that's what she'll think it is."

"You don't know Julia. She takes convincing."

"I don't have to know her. This always works."

"Besides," I say, "I really *have* changed."

The porter stops in the doorway. "Hey, man," he says. "You're getting the hang of it." Then he clattered down the stairs.

But I have, but I have, but I have. Perhaps I can even say how. I lived with my secret, all those years, as with a wife—as Higgs, I thought now, must have lived with his silence, and Tip Chandler with his vision of a second Athens rising from the scrub. Now my secret's out. I should never have kept it in the first place. Was *that* what Higgs had meant?

I don't know. I won't ever, now; I've set both feet down in the new world, the Higgsless and Hendersonless world, where everybody else lives—merciless skaters, restauranteurs, mere mortals. There has to be something to it or it would not be so phenomenally popular.

I'd like to try explaining all this to the porter, but I don't expect I'll see him again. I won't need more paper than I have. And if I've rushed over these last parts, I'm sorry; it's just that I've been feeling, these past few hours, about ready to put this aside and write to Julia. I think I won't have much to say, not until I see her. There are just a few things:

I miss you.

Regards to Simeon.

I look forward to meeting the children.

I thought it might be nice, after all, to see New York.

But I promised I would tell what happened to Higgs's house.

After Dean Moresby died it was agreed that a new building should be erected in his honor; and while a show was made of considering other sites, it was clear from the start that his memorial would go up on the ground of his daughter's house. No one was using it now anyway. No one really wanted it. And the view, it was murmured: think of the view.

McTaggett and I arranged a small ceremony for the day before the demolition. It was February. We shivered, walking up the flagstone path: I, McTaggett, the Mayor, Rosso, some more professors, some cousins of the Dean's. McTaggett unlocked the stout front door and we followed him down to the basement. Higgs's table and chairs were still there, but everything else was gone. The concrete floor was so cold I could feel it through my shoes. I could not say I was sorry that the house was going down.

"Sam?" McTaggett said. "A few words?"

I had prepared a short address: our debt to the deceased, the importance of commemoration, some relevant aphorisms I'd dug up. The speech was folded up in my coat pocket. I couldn't bring myself to take it out.

"I think in a case like this it may be better for each of us to remember Dean Moresby in our own way," I said. Nods all around.

"Then it's your show, Mayor Meadows," McTaggett said.

Rosso handed a bulky circular saw to the Mayor, who immediately bent almost double beneath its weight. I plugged it in. We were going to take a square of concrete from the floor, to be used as the ceremonial cornerstone of the new building. In my notes I'd had something like this: "As progress must stand on a foundation of history . . ." It was an awful speech.

"Are you sure you're all right?" McTaggett said. Wordlessly, the Mayor pulled the trigger and the saw roared on. He grinned—his false teeth as smooth, as perfectly aligned as typewriter keys. He lowered the saw to the floor. The diamond-tipped blade bit into the concrete with a high, intolerable keen and a spray of choking dust. I covered my eyes with my hands. The blade sank into the floor: a quarter-gone, then half. Then it stopped.

"There's something—" the Mayor shouted.

That loose sick feeling struck me, that one I thought I'd never have again: *one fatal mistake.*

"Pull it out," I said, but not loud enough, or quickly enough, and in fact I'd probably only just started saying it when the water burst from the pierced main and was on us. The blast knocked me to the wall, then whipped me in somersaults across the floor. I could hear it thrumming on the ceiling like gargantuan applause. I was trying to find something to hold onto, or a place where I could breathe. A hand grasped my neck, another the front of my face—Mayor Meadows? He was torn away before I could tell. The pressure of the water made concentric circles behind my clenched-shut eyelids, black and red, then yellow—my breath was going.

But then I was outside, in a tremendous current, and in a moment I hit something solid: a pole. I wrapped my arms around it and clung there as the water beat against me.

I had washed up at the suicide fence. I was holding onto the emergency phone. I pulled myself to my feet, dragged one hand across my face, and looked back toward the house. Water jetted from both basement windows. That was the way I'd come. The water rushing past me was ankle-high and filled with sticks: Higgs's table.

Inside, the water was still rising. I watched the froth rise up above the first-floor windows; then those windows exploded outward too. On the left side of the house, close to the ground, the siding was beginning to crimp and bulge like a botulistic can. I locked my wrists and ankles around the pole. After that it was all very fast; the house peeled open, water smashed me, pulled my hair, tugged one of my shoes off and over the cliff. But I held to the pole. When I could see again, the house was cross-sectioned, like a doll's house. In the center the water gushed upward from the broken main to a point a little higher than the roof. I could see the others now; they were on the campus side of the house, collecting themselves. Everyone else must have made it up the stairs. They hadn't seen me yet.

The last wave had knocked the telephone receiver off its cradle. It was already ringing. I picked it up; someone at the hotline, I supposed, could connect me to whatever municipal power one notified at a time like this. A woman answered.

"Crisis Hotline, tell us about it."

Her voice was breathy and without nuance. A leaf of aluminum bigger than me was caught in the suicide fence. As I watched, the water tipped it up and over the edge. It tumbled down the cliff with a sound like—no—like no sound I'd heard before. All over town, showers were drooping, faucets dwindling out. For the moment we were living in a desert again.

Could I really explain?

"Crisis Hotline, *tell* us about it."

She sounded perplexed. Who did she think I was—a fool in love? A fat and lonely shut-in? A teen bullied into it? A holder of exhausted credit cards? There were so many paths that led to the phone; so many crises already solved and recorded in their spiral notebooks. I was sure my own story was like nothing to be found there. I knew I should say something; but I couldn't imagine how to begin.

"Sir? Or Ma'am? Can you tell us where you are? Is someone threatening you? If you can make a sound safely, please make it once for yes and twice for no. Sir? If you can stay on the line another minute or so we can trace the call and we'll have police there. Ma'am? Can you tell us where you are?"

A man came on the line.

"If you're saying something, we can't hear you. Please bring your mouth closer to the receiver if you can safely do so. If you can't safely make a sound, just stay on the line and we'll find you."

The woman: "Larry . . ."

"It's OK. It's probably just a prank call."

Was I supposed to hear that? Beyond the fence, to the east, the sun was an innocuous white spot on a sky as blue and blank as pool water.

Behind me, a shout; the others had seen me. Here came their footsteps now, squelching in the mud.

"Are you still there?" the man said. I hung up the phone.

RECENT FICTION FROM COFFEE HOUSE PRESS

MINIATURES
A NOVEL BY NORAH LABINER

BINGO UNDER THE CRUCIFIX
A NOVEL BY LAURIE FOOS

THE WHITE PALAZZO
A NOVEL BY ELLEN COONEY

THE LAKESTOWN REBELLION
A NOVEL BY KRISTIN LATTANY

MY LOVE, MY LOVE
A NOVEL BY ROSA GUY

THE MERMAID THAT CAME BETWEEN THEM
A NOVEL BY CAROL ANN SIMA

LITTLE CASINO
A NOVEL BY GILBERT SORRENTINO

SOME OF HER FRIENDS THAT YEAR
STORIES BY MAXINE CHERNOFF

THE IMPOSSIBLY
A NOVEL BY LAIRD HUNT

CLUB REVELATION
A NOVEL BY ALLAN APPEL

THE COTILLION
A NOVEL BY JOHN OLIVER KILLENS

THE COMPLEXITIES OF INTIMACY
STORIES BY MARY CAPONEGRO

Good books are brewing at coffeehousepress.org

FUNDER ACKNOWLEDGMENTS

Coffee House Press is an independent nonprofit literary publisher. Our books are made possible through the generous support of grants and gifts from many foundations, corporate giving programs, individuals, and through state and federal support. Coffee House Press also receives support from the Minnesota State Arts Board, through an appropriation by the Minnesota State Legislature, through an appropriation by the Minnesota State Legislature and a grant from the National Endowment for the Arts; and from grants from the Elmer and Eleanor Andersen Foundation; the Beim Foundation; Buuck Family Foundation; the Bush Foundation; the Butler Family Foundation; Lerner Family Foundation; the McKnight Foundation; the law firm of Schwegman, Lundberg, Woessner & Kluth, P.A.; St. Paul Companies; Target, Marshall Field's, and Mervyn's with support from the Target Foundation; James R. Thorpe Foundation; The Walker Foundation; Wells Fargo Foundation Minnesota; West Group; the Woessner Freeman Foundation; and many individual donors.

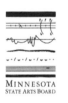

MINNESOTA
STATE ARTS BOARD

To you and our many readers across the country,
we send our thanks for your continuing support.

Good books are brewing at coffeehousepress.org